Lovers

&

Comrades

ROBERT BLAIR OSBORN

Lovers & Comrades

Robert Blair Osborn

To Ivy,
A fellow historian
and researcher.

Sincerely,
Bob *March 2, 2017*

I Street Press
Sacramento, California

Library of Congress Control Number: 2016937206

Osborn, Robert Blair

ISBN 9781530963089

This book is dedicated to Clay, whose life ended too soon.

Table of Contents

Foreword

To write this book, I relied upon personal accounts, official testimony, oral history, biographies, and monographs. While the main characters of the story are fictional, they are based on real people. Any misrepresentation or omission of historical events is mine alone.

"Lovers & Comrades" draws upon several periods in the twentieth century. The story jumps around in time and refers to period-specific events, people and items. I have provided a list of characters, a timeline, and a glossary to help the reader in this regard. Highlighted words appear in the glossary at the end of the book.

Also, a few words about romanization. The Wade-Giles system of romanization was used widely before 1949. For historical reasons, I still use Wade-Giles for Chinese words that appear in settings before 1949. I use the other major system of romanization, Pinyin, for words that appear in settings after 1949. The major exception is "Ai-ling," which in Pinyin is written, "Ailing."

List of Characters

Lisa - Hong Kong born Chinese American. In the present day, she works in the pharmaceutical industry and travels frequently to China and Japan.

Quentin - retired foreign service officer paralyzed by a major stroke. Fired by the State Department in 1951 for aiding a Communist government. Former lover of Ai-ling and Marisa.

Ai-ling - interpreter for Mao Zedong and the Chinese Communist Party during the War. In 1949, she escapes to Taiwan with the Nationalists. Quentin's former lover.

Professor Mathieson - Professor Emeritus of modern Chinese history at U.C. Berkeley, and Quentin's former boss.

Marisa - former secretary of Quentin's at Hancock Oil and Gas in Rio de Janeiro. Later becomes an executive at Chevron in California.

Tak - second generation Japanese American, retired professor of Chinese history at Sacramento State, former officer in Army Intelligence. Served with Quentin in Taoyuan, China.

Matsuda - former Japanese prisoner of war in Taoyuan. Later, becomes well-known labor organizer and AIDS activist in Japan. Reputed father of Ai-ling's son.

Nationalists (also, "K.M.T.," or "Kuomintang") - until 1979, the only Chinese government recognized officially by the United States before, during, and after World War II. The Nationalists were led by Chiang Kai-shek.

Communists (also, "C.C.P.," or "Chinese Communist Party") - fought against the Nationalists for control of China, and ultimately succeeded in 1949. Led by Chairman Mao Tse-tung.

Timeline

1909 - John Quentin Liege ("Quentin") is born in Peking (Beijing), China. He is the fifth of five boys.

1932 - Britka and Quentin meet at U.C. Berkeley.

1936 - Britka and Quentin marry in Berkeley after graduating. They move to Shanghai. Quentin gets a job at an import export company.

1937 - Quentin is hired by the State Department. He and Britka move to Peking.

1939-1945 - Quentin and Britka move to Chungking. Quentin begins work at the American Embassy.

1944 - Quentin is assigned to PAX Mission in Taoyuan. Britka is evacuated from Chungking. She ends up in San Francisco.

1945 - Quentin is recalled to Washington, D.C. Before he leaves, he meets Ai-ling one last time in Shanghai. She is pregnant.

1951 - Loyalty Research Board investigates Quentin's dealings with the Chinese Communists. State Department fires him.

1956-58 - Quentin and Britka move to Rio de Janeiro. Quentin gets a job working for an American oil company. He has an affair with his secretary.

1958 - Back in the U.S., Quentin gets a job at U.C. Berkeley.

Mid-1980s - Quentin retires from U.C. Berkeley.

February 1989 - Britka dies.

May 1989 - Ai-ling reappears after a 44-year absence to see Quentin again.

June 1989 - Quentin suffers a stroke that leaves him unable to move or talk. In Beijing, thousands of protesters die as the People's Liberation Army retakes Tiananmen Square.

October 1989 - Quentin dies at St. Matthews Senior Care in Albany, California.

Lao Du

Until 1979, my father hated Mao Zedong. He had been a card-carrying member of the Chinese Communist Party in his youth back in China, but a series of events changed that. When I was in high school, we were living in Oakland, California. My father told me one night, after my mother and sister had gone to bed, that my mother had a miscarriage back in China. He called it "Blue baby sickness." It was what happened when pregnant mothers didn't get enough protein. The history books referred to that period as the Great Famine, and it continued for another couple years. Left with nothing to eat but tree bark and insects, half my father's village died of hunger.

My father left his village and was caught by the authorities. He was sentenced to work in a labor reeducation camp forty miles away. That was where he met my mother. They got married, and my father told her how he had found a shortwave radio and was secretly listening to the **Voice of America**.

That was how my father learned English. He heard about Kennedy winning the presidency and Wilma Rudolph winning three gold medals at the Summer Olympic Games in Rome. He knew that life outside China was very different, and that Chinese news, which was controlled by the Communist Party, was full of lies.

My parents decided to run away together. They hid under seats in a bus leaving town and bribed their way onto a boat going to Macau. From there, they went to Hong Kong and found an apartment in the New Territories.

My parents became anticommunist. When I was four, we emigrated to the U.S., and my sister and I went to Saturday school in Oakland Chinatown, where we learned Mandarin Chinese.

Prominently displayed over the front of the classroom, behind the teacher's podium, was an oversized portrait of **Chiang Kai-shek**, President of the Republic of China. The school forced us to sing the Chinese Nationalist anthem before class began. My sister complied, but I refused and got expelled at age six. My father felt a deep sense of shame.

By 1979, however, my father changed his mind about Communist China. **Deng Xiaoping** visited the U.S., and President Carter established diplomatic ties with the People's Republic. My father started taking flights every year through Hong Kong, back to China, to visit relatives.

My mother, however, never went back to China.

My own feelings were complicated. Growing up in the United States during the Cold War, I knew there were two Chinas: "Red China" (The People's Republic of China) and "Free China" (The Republic of China). Red China was opening up to the West, and I was inclined to think more favorably about my parents' relatives back on the mainland. Unfortunately, a series of events changed that.

In the fall of 1987, I went to the People's Republic of China to study intensive Mandarin at **Beijing** University. There, I saw firsthand the seeds of discontent that fueled the Tiananmen protests a year and a half later. There were handwritten posters pasted to the sides of buildings with the names of Communist Party officials accused of giving plum government jobs to their relatives. Meanwhile, Beijing University graduates were being assigned crappy jobs in remote provinces like Gansu or Anhui.

Chinese students at Beijing University lived six to a room and had hot water every other day. There was zero privacy, so they sneaked off to the campus lake and hid behind the bushes to make love. The dances were policed by school officials and were thoroughly depressing.

Meanwhile, just outside the school walls, ordinary people were starting bicycle repair shops, selling magazines, cigarettes and food. Some even went high-tech and started selling computers. In the downtown area, you could exchange American dollars for Chinese renminbi with gray market clothing dealers at double the official exchange rate.

It was widely known that bicycle repairmen were making four to five times what university professors made, and many students started questioning the value of a college education, especially when all the good jobs were going to the sons and daughters of Communist Party officials. Student groups formed and began protesting in front of the Communist Party headquarters, but the police shut them down.

After I returned to Berkeley in the summer of 1988, the fervor in Beijing seemed to die. Beijing summers are very hot and sticky. Evening temperatures drop only slightly. I thought maybe the extreme weather doused the revolutionary fire, but I was wrong.

The next spring, students protested again, only this time it was more political. **Hu Yaobang**, the more empathetic of the two chosen successors to Deng Xiaoping, died, and the students demanded a reassessment of his political record. They also raised the same grievances about nepotism and economic inequality. Deng Xiaoping had initiated economic reforms that threatened the traditional "iron rice bowl" of guaranteed employment, but he avoided any political reforms. More and more groups joined the student protests, and the political situation in Tiananmen Square quickly got out of hand.

On June 4, the **People's Liberation Army** went into Tiananmen Square and opened fire on thousands of protesters. The day after, a long convoy of tanks started down the main thoroughfare next to Tiananmen Square. A solitary figure walked out into the middle of the street and stood in the path of the oncoming tanks. The image is seared in my mind from watching it on television. The man wore a white, button-down shirt and black pants, and he held two plastic bags in his hand. The lead tank stopped and then pivoted to the left to go around the man, but he

3

shuffled sideways to stay directly in front of the tank. Then, he climbed onto the front of the tank and started pleading with the tank driver.

Tiananmen was for me what the **J.F.K.** assassination was for my parents' generation, and Tank Man's defiance, bravery, and charity resonated with me.

Twenty-six years later, Beijing is almost unrecognizable, except for Tiananmen Square and the buildings surrounding it. Few Chinese will openly talk about what happened, or how many people died. If you visit China and do a web search from your hotel room, or from any computer, you won't find anything about Tank Man or the student protests, because the government blocks it.

Much has changed since 1989. I'm married, I have two kids in private school, I make two car payments, and I live in a house with a market value that is less than what my husband and I paid. I'm a very practical person, but as I get older, the passage of time reminds me that life is short: friends move away, relatives die, history fades.

The one thing that still bothers me whenever I think back to that time is what happened while I was working as a student intern at a retirement home in Albany, California.

I had just graduated from U.C. Berkeley, and I got a paid internship at St. Matthews Senior Care, which was located just north of Berkeley. Most of the residents at St. Matthews were either comatose or delusional, and had to be medicated regularly. St. Matthews was where senior citizens went to die.

I was living in a studio apartment in Lake Merritt in Oakland with another Chinese American girl who was in her last year at Berkeley. She spent most of her time studying at cafes with her organic chemistry study group. They drank mochas and talked about valence bonds.

I had no aspirations to go into health care. I landed the job at St. Matthews through a friend of my mother's, who owned a chain of Cantonese-style take out restaurants, and had recently bought St. Matthews as a place to stash his ninety-five year old mother.

My job was to clean bed pans, pick up laundry, and do whatever else the nurses asked me to do. Grunt work was reserved for people like me, because it was cheaper than paying nurse union wages.

I worked four days a week. I had twenty-five residents to look after during my four-hour shift. On good days, the rooms smelled like Pine Sol; on bad days, they smelled like urine.

There were eight nurses on the day shift. Three were Filipino. They did most of the work. The other five non-Filipino nurses showed up for work and did very little. If the weather was good, the nurses wheeled residents out to the garden so they could get some sunshine. If it was raining, the nurses wheeled the residents into the movie room and popped in a VHS tape of "My Three Sons" or "Mayberry RFD." The nurses, meanwhile, were hooked on "Jeopardy" and "The Price Is Right."

I had been at St. Matthews only two weeks when Mr. Liege arrived.

An ambulance brought him from Alta Monte Hospital. One of the Filipino nurses said that Mr. Liege had suffered a stroke and had recently emerged from a coma. A doctor came by on the second day and said that Mr. Liege was paralyzed everywhere but his eyes. He couldn't speak or move.

The doctor introduced himself as "Dr. Merkel." He said it was too early to say how much damage had been done to Mr. Liege's brain, but his outlook wasn't good.

"Some patients experience partial recovery," Dr. Merkel said. "They find ways to communicate. The hardest thing about this is his brain could be working just fine, but he's trapped. His body can't interact with the world around him. If he is going to recover, the speed of the recovery will be a strong indicator for his medium to long-term survival."

According to the chart, his full name was "John Quentin Liege." He was seventy-nine years old. He was born in Beijing, China, on July 2, 1909. His wife was deceased. No next of kin.

Mr. Liege had a breathing tube taped to the bottom of his throat and feeding tube coming out of his mouth. He was unable to swallow. A catheter drained his urine. A bedpan was sandwiched between his legs. A nurse showed me how to adjust the pillows around him every hour or so to keep him from getting bedsores.

---

*I am at the air base in **Chungking** writing a letter to Britka. Then, I am climbing into a twin engine **C-47**, strapping on an oxygen mask. The pilot says, "Hang on, it's raining; there's no telling how windy it is up there." We take off due east, for the Himalayas. Then, we bank north, toward **Sian**. Many planes have crashed here. Some are shot down by Japs; others catch fire from the engines overheating. The ground beneath us is littered with frozen bodies, ammo crates, and **C-rations**.*

8-23-44 (Wed) Chungking

Taoyuan has a reputation for fresh, edible produce. Apparently, it is the only place in China where they do not use human waste for fertilizer. In Chungking, we've been fortunate to have fresh tomatoes and raw cabbage flown in weekly from Taoyuan.

We took off from an airstrip several miles outside of Chungking. Once we were airborne, we banked north, heading in the direction of Sian. We passed over shiny green farmlands and small houses that eventually gave way to black and white jagged mountains and steep gorges. We climbed higher, and I could see the immense Himalayas to the west. It reminded me of the hair-raising trip over the **Hump** the day before.

I wore ear protection to drown out the head-splitting drone of the engines. After an hour or so, I fell asleep on a box of toilet paper. When I woke up, I looked at my watch and over three and a half hours had gone by since takeoff. I looked out the window and the ground had changed to dull gray and brown. We were following a small valley, and I saw a pagoda on top of a hill surrounded by small caves.

The plane started descending and we touched down at 15:25 on a tiny airstrip next to the cemetery. As we were finishing our taxi, the right landing gear dropped suddenly. There was a horrible sound from the right engine as it came to a halt.

"We hit a ditch," the pilot yelled from the cockpit. I looked out from the small window behind the cockpit: impossible to see anything. The whole plane pitched now slightly to the right.

"We're not getting out of here anytime soon," the co-pilot said as he pulled off his headset. He worked his way past me down to the back of the plane and turned the handle to open the cargo door. He dropped the step ladder.

I stood up, leaned against the fuselage and walked over to the open door. Sure enough, the right engine's propeller was buried one foot deep in the ground.

The flight engineer went down first and I followed. We walked over to the propeller buried in the dirt. The air smelled dry and sandy.

In the distance, I saw two camels and an ox-cart coming in our direction. There were three peasants walking with them.

The pilot came down the stairs.

"I'll be a horse's ass," he said. "I've landed here five times and this has never happened."

"We'll have to radio for parts," the flight engineer said.

"Maybe not. Let's see if we can dig it out," the pilot said.

The co-pilot joined us under the right wing. "We might have thrown a master rod, possibly a bearing."

"Well, first order of business is to get us out of that ditch," the pilot said as he turned his attention to the greeting party coming our way. "We'll have to see if we can get some coolies to help us."

The peasants stopped ten feet from us.

"*Hwanying, hwanying,*" said one of them with toothless grin. He wore a green cap and faded, button down coat and loose fitting pants.

The peasants took my duffel bag and loaded it onto the saddle of one of the camels. They put the pilot and co-pilot's bags on the other camel.

The landing strip was on a hill, and the ride down was bumpy with potholes and protruding pieces of granite on the road to town. I saw a group of people in the distance gathered around someone standing on a box talking to them. Further away, peasants with hats and scarves covering their heads were bent over in fields harvesting rice.

When the oxcart arrived in the town, a small group emerged from one of the cave-based dwellings built into the side of the hill. Two young ladies in their twenties stepped out in front. The one on the left was wearing round spectacles and had her hair pulled back in pigtails.

"*Hwanying,*" she said, "Welcome!"

The other had shoulder-length hair held back with barrettes.

"*Wo shih sun aimei,*" the one in pigtails said, "I'm Sun Ai-mei."

"*Wo shih sun ailing,*" the other one said, "My name is Sun Ai-ling."

I introduced myself. They looked like sisters. I asked them, and the one in pigtails said they were not related to each other.

A week after Mr. Liege arrived, he had a visitor. She was Chinese and looked to be in her late sixties. She had dyed, brown hair permed in short curls and wore bifocals with plastic brown frames. Her handbag had the Chinese character for "peace" embroidered on it.

I asked her how she knew Mr. Liege, and she said they were old friends. She spoke English with an accent that reminded me of my Auntie Lim from Hong Kong, who lived alone in a one bedroom walkup and served tea in imitation Wedgwood China.

I told her my name was Lisa.

She asked if I was Chinese.

"Yes, Chinese American," I said.

She asked my Chinese name.

I told her it meant, "Little deer." I told her how my parents came to California from China.

"It's nice to meet you," she said. She reached out her hand out to shake mine. "My name is Zhang. Zhang Ai-ling."

She put down her handbag and came around to face Mr. Liege. She looked in his eyes.

"You know, we had tea together just the other week," she said to me while looking at him. "His wife, Britka, passed away last year. I recently moved back to the States from Taiwan and paid him a visit. He showed me an album from his recent trip to Brazil. He said it had been over thirty years since he had lived there. We agreed to meet again the following week. When I did come by, there was no answer at the door. I went around back and tried the pantry door, which was open. I went inside and found him on the kitchen floor, still breathing. I called 911 and stayed with him until the ambulance came."

"The doctor said it's possible he suffered memory loss," I said.

She turned her gaze back to Mr. Liege and looked into his eyes. "*Lao du, ni jide ma?*" she said in Mandarin, *Do you remember?*

Mr. Liege stared at her, his eyes blinking naturally. There was no movement around his cheeks or mouth.

She opened her handbag and pulled out a wrinkled black and white photograph with a group of men kneeling side by side a young woman in calf-length pants and short pigtails standing in the middle. In the background was a cave entrance.

"Is that you?" I asked her.

"*Shi de*" she said, nodding her head.

She held it up to Mr. Liege so he could see it.

Of course I remember that photograph, Ai-ling. It's from Taoyuan. You still have that smile of yours. Cheeks still rosy like a red delicious apple.

I moved in closer to see if Mr. Liege reacted in any way to her. His eyes darted to the television on the wall. CNN was showing a wrap-up of the events in China in the weeks since Tiananmen. They included the clip of Tank Man standing in front of the convoy.

A man is standing in the center of Chang'An Avenue, holding up his arm. He's holding a plastic bag and swinging it over his head. He's standing in front of a long line of army tanks. The tanks can't get past him. I am there with him, standing before tanks.

"Turn it off!" she yelled at me. "He doesn't need to see that."

Surprised by her outburst, I grabbed the remote control and pressed the "off" button, and the screen went dark. I returned to Mr. Liege's bedside. I asked her if Mr. Liege was in the photograph.

She pointed to a tall, skinny man with a crew cut standing in the back.

"That's him," she said.

His face had a pained look, whereas the other men were smiling.

I asked her where the picture was taken.

"Taoyuan, 1945," she said.

I knew that Taoyuan had been the Communist Party's base of operations during World War II. It was incredibly remote, thousands of miles from the coast, in a high desert plateau region where few people lived. The U.S. Army sent a team of American military observers to Taoyuan to observe the **Communists** and help them recover downed American pilots.

"Were you there?" I asked.

"Yes," she said, and she pointed to the young woman in the picture. "He was a political advisor for the State Department. I was one of Mao's interpreters."

There's the old Chinese myth about the fisherman who ventured up a stream and came upon a blossoming peach grove. He followed the trees up to the water source and came upon a cave next to a high cliff. He thought he could see light through the cave, so he got out of his boat and climbed inside. The cave became very narrow, but eventually the fisherman made it to the opening. He came out of the cave to find a beautiful village with cottages arranged neatly in a row. Men, women and children were happily working in the fields and were surprised to see the fisherman. They invited him to their homes and slaughtered a chicken in his honor. They gave him wine and asked him about his home. When he asked them the same questions, he learned that the ancestors of people in the village had all fled from wars over a thousand years before. Since that time, they had lost all contact with the outside world.

Eventually, the fisherman had to return home, but before he did, the villagers made him promise to not tell anyone else about their whereabouts. Of course, once the fisherman returned home, he told people about the village. He even left markers so that he would be able to find the place again. Nevertheless, when he took a group back to the peach grove, the markers weren't in order, and the group got lost. After that, nobody tried to find the hidden village.

The other men here are all **G.I.s** (26 total) and are all part of "PAX Team" and led by Chinese-speaking Colonel Hathaway. Colonel comes from farm in Goleta, California. Like me, Colonel Hathaway was born in China to missionary parents, but he returned to California for high school.

Our first dinner was a real "to do." **Chou En-lai** and other leaders treated us to fabulous welcoming ceremony in meeting hall. After the meal, General **Chu Teh** kicked off the dancing in the *yan-ke* style common to northern **Shensi** and bounded about like a drunk Russian Cossack and then everyone joined in. Chinese ladies from local language schools danced with us and wanted to practice their English.

Taoyuan is about as remote as you can get. Take a globe, spin it slowly westward from the shores of San Francisco, across the Pacific, past Japanese island of Kyushu, over to China. Spin a little more, slowly this time, inland across the same latitude, and stop in the center of China. You find an area called "Shensi." From there, inch up little northward and right between the confluence of two rivers coming down from Huan Mountain lies the village of Taoyuan.

The town's name, *"Tao,"* meaning "peach," and *"yuan"* meaning "river source," comes from the ancient poem by Tao Yuanming about a fisherman who stumbled by accident upon utopia. The people in the poem fled from war during the Qin Dynasty, around 220 B.C., and since that time had lost all contact with the outside world. That certainly is not the case here. There's radio contact all over China from here.

Nearly all the buildings in town were destroyed by Japanese bombers a few years ago. So, to make due, the Communists built caves into the sides of mountains and moved there. Everyone lives in them.

I asked Ai-ling how she and Mr. Liege met.

"Lao Du came to Taoyuan..." she began.

"I'm sorry....Why do you call him *Lao Du*?" I asked.

"Lao Du -- it is his Chinese name. I don't know how he got it. '*Lao*,' as you know, means 'old,' and '*du*,' means 'capital.' I think he got it when he was a schoolboy in **Peking**. Lao Du and I met in August of 1944. He came with a group of U.S. Army officers. It was called the "PAX Mission.""

"Was Mr. Liege in the Army?"

"He was assigned to the Army by the U.S. Embassy, so technically, no. When he came to Taoyuan, he had separated from Britka. She had been evacuated from Chungking because of the air raids."

August 23, 1944

Dear Portia,

I'm sorry for not writing sooner. On the eve of my departure from Chungking, I suddenly realized I hadn't written in almost a year. Quentin and I have split up. He is off on a new adventure to the Chinese hinterland. I am being evacuated.

As you know, we moved to Chungking in the early spring of '39, after Quentin was offered a position here with the embassy. Chungking is the quintessential "Plan B" sort of capital. The Chinese refer to it as one of the three "furnaces," because in summertime you can boil an iceberg. You thought Charlotte, N. Car. was bad. The air sucks energy out of your skin's pores, and, if it ain't violent hot (summer), it's bone-broke cold (winter). I can't think of any place that has fewer days of sunshine. Seattle, which

I've read is the rain capital of America, can't compare. The only silver lining is that the cloudy skies and fog keep the Japs away.

The locals here are loony. Not a week after the Japs bombed Pearl Harbor, the Chinese went bananas, shooting off fireworks and making toasts to each other. We're on the same side as the Chinese, which was why I was confused. My driver explained that they were celebrating the fact that we Americans were going to enter the war. The Japs had been bombing this city with impunity. The Chinese are convinced that this is their moment. The Americans were going to take care of everything!

So much for wishful thinking. Delusional is more like it.

I don't think I can stand another summer of air raids. Last summer was the worst. Sirens daily. Bombers came in waves of five, ten, sometimes twenty planes, with long periods of quiet in between. The unpredictability made it impossible to leave the shelters. I brought books and magazines with me, but words just passed across my eyes. Quentin used a shelter near the embassy. He said that he brought his typewriter and files with him. I wonder how much work he got done?

My life here is through. I married Quentin knowing that life here was going to be hard. Exotic location, new experiences -- those were draws for sure.

Peking was the best. The Great Wall, the Forbidden City, the Summer Palace. **Yunnan**, on the other hand, was a distant second, but even there we were able to travel and see the giant Buddha at **Le-shan** and the caves at **Hsi-shuang Ba-na**. Then, we come to this hellhole.

Exhibit one: the *Good Housekeeping* bunch at the American Club. Like mercury poisoning, I reached my lifetime limit of tennis court gossip -- whose husband was sleeping with his secretary, et cetera. I don't give a damn. If you're unhappy, take matters into your own hands, is what I say. Complaining about it doesn't fix it.

14

I've learned to counteract the drudgery with little things. Putting sweet jasmine flowers in my morning tea, or watching the mist rise off the Yangtze. However, these are just short-lived mind excursions. I practice French with the bartender at the brasserie near the French embassy. With **de Gaulle** in exile in London, the French here are stateless.

Do you remember how we used to speak French to each other because there weren't any French people to be found for a hundred miles?

Quentin used to be around more, and that made life somewhat bearable. In Peking, he came home around five in the afternoon from a full day of language classes, and we drank white wine in the courtyard of the little four cornered house. It wasn't fancy wine, it was whatever we could coax out of the Belgian military attaché who lived next door. Occasionally he came upon real champagne. That was always a treat.

Back then, we really talked to each other. We talked about Amelia Earhart, the Oklahoma dust storm, and the **W.P.A**.

Now, it's "Hi" and jump into the sack. You know the routine.

I would write more, but I think I need to get some sleep. I have something very important to tell you, but it will have to wait.

Yours,
Britka

Ai-ling looked at her wristwatch. She closed her purse and stood up. "I must go now. I look forward to chatting with you again," she said.

Mr. Liege was dozing now.

"Maybe you could come over for tea," she said. "I have more pictures from Taoyuan to show you."

She opened up her purse and pulled out a business card. "Call me tomorrow and we can set something up." She handed me the card. "Don't hesitate to call me sooner if Lao Du's condition changes in any way." She smiled at me in a sort of wince and said goodbye.

The next day, Dr. Merkel came in with a stack of plastic cards, each with a letter on it. He placed the cards on a table next to the bed. An assistant came in rolling a cart holding a Commodore Amiga computer.

"Mr. Liege, I don't know if you can understand me," Dr. Merkel said. "You have suffered a stroke. From the tests we've run, it appears that there has been extensive damage to your sympathetic nervous system. This means that your body's organs are functioning normally, but you can't feel or move anything. Some patients in your condition are able to partially recover to where they are able to eat food through their mouth. Some are even able to communicate. It takes time. The brain has to heal first. I want to see if you are able to communicate with me with your eyes. First, will you try to move your eyes up and down?"

Mr. Liege's eyes blinked, but there was no movement.

"Okay, it might be kind of hard, so let's try again. Please move your eyes up and down for me."

Again, no movement. Only blinking.

"Okay. Let's try something different. We're going to try a blinking exercise, okay?

One blink means "YES," and two blinks means "NO." Do you understand me?"

Mr. Liege stared at Dr. Merkel. His eyes blinked, and blinked again. It was impossible to tell if he blinked intentionally or if his eyes were just blinking because they had to.

Dr. Merkel told me that recovery of horizontal eye movement within the first four weeks of trauma was a good sign. After that, speech and swallowing sometimes followed. Some patients even regained partial limb movement.

"I brought along a device that works through a computer that lets you write words using your finger and a touchpad," Dr.

Merkel said to Mr. Liege. He motioned for the assistant to roll the computer terminal over next to Mr. Liege's bed. Next to the terminal was a modem with rubber cups for the receiver.

He asked the assistant to set it up.

The assistant plugged in the power cord and pressed the "on" button. While the computer booted up, he walked over to the telephone in the room and uncoiled the cord connecting it to the wall. He put the phone down next to the modem.

The screen had a blinking cursor. The assistant began typing on the keyboard.

"I don't expect you to be able to do this today," Dr. Merkel said, "but I wanted to show it to you. It may be something you will be able to use in the future."

Dr. Merkel left the room, leaving only the assistant and me.

The assistant lifted the telephone handset out of the cradle and pressed it into the modem cups. He went back to the keyboard and typed in a telephone number. That triggered the sound of a telephone dialing, followed by a long beep, then the sound of white noise.

Just then, Mr. Liege's eyes started blinking wildly and his heart rate jumped to a hundred forty beats per minute. An alarm emitted from the monitor.

"What's going on?" I asked in alarm.

"Hold on," the assistant yelled. He went over to the wall and hit the emergency button. "Wait here while I get Dr. Merkel," he said, and he ran out of the room.

A nurse appeared immediately. "What happened?" she said. She looked at the heart rate monitor and then looked at Mr. Liege's eyes.

It was an eerie feeling, like he was possessed by a demon.

"I'll get Dr. Merkel," the nurse said. She ran out of the room.

Dr. Merkel came in about thirty-seconds later. He leaned out of the door and yelled, "Get me 10 milligrams of diazepam!" He went over to Mr. Liege's side and held open Mr. Liege's left eyelid. Then, he opened his mouth and looked at his tongue.

A nurse came in again carrying a tray with a syringe and a small vial. She handed it to Dr. Merkel. He inserted the needle into the wax seal of the vial and filled the bulb of the syringe. Next, he opened the intravenous port connected to Mr. Liege's left arm and inserted the syringe. He pressed the plunger all the way down. He removed the syringe and closed the port.

The heart rate monitor continued beeping for several minutes, but the frequency of Mr. Liege's blinking started to slow down.

"What happened?" Dr. Merkel asked the assistant.

"I initiated the modem connection to the mainframe, and the patient went into seizure."

8-24-44 (Thu) 11:55

The lunch gong rings at 12:05 every afternoon, rain or shine (though, thankfully no rain here yet). My roommate is a lanky radio technician from US Army Signal Corps. Harlan T. Burle, but he goes by "Burly." The Chinese call him "*bu li*," which could mean either "ineffective," or, "not bad," depending on the Chinese characters used in his Chinese name. Burly is a former pole-vaulter from Tacoma, Washington.

Helping Burly set up new radio equipment in adobe-made hut near our cave. Had a little trouble getting 2-stroke SSP-12 generator to start up, but changed spark plug and now it chugs along nicely. Diesel scheduled to come weekly with air shipment from **Kunming**. The dust outside is heavy. Need to cover generator with heavy cotton blanket when it is not running.

Setting up two radio sets to communicate with Chungking. First is large unit that sits on table made of two wood planks over barrels. This unit only sends and receives Morse Code. Second unit is smaller and lighter and sends and receives voice.

Word from Chungking on replacement parts for C-47 is some time "next week."

Taoyuan very strategic location for weather reporting. Weather in China flows west to the ocean, so weather out here is good predictor for US Naval Command in Pacific. I am installing psychrometer on thatched roof over radio hut right now to monitor humidity.

Transmission to Chungking is supposed to happen daily. Burly said his transmissions have been picked up as far away as Fort Ord in Monterey, California. I imagine the Japanese can pick it up as well, which is why every message has to be encoded manually.

I file weekly political reports that go to the U.S. Embassy in Chungking. From there, they go to the China Desk back in Washington. A copy is sent to General Joseph **Stilwell**, commander of U.S. forces in China. I wrote my first report by hand and then typed it out on a Smith and Wesson portable with carbon paper underneath. I am keeping the carbons in a shoebox under the mirror.

Our cave is fifteen feet deep, eight feet wide. It is walled off with a wood frame on the outside and thin paper over the window openings. The door to the outside has no lock, which is a concern. The wind blows sand and dust in through a small opening in the paper screen. I keep the window open always with the help of a small rock to let fresh air in. Every morning, we need to sweep the dust off the brick floor. We have one of the few rooms outfitted with a Chinese bed (*k'ang*). Other Americans here are less fortunate and sleep on planks thrown over two sawhorses.

Burly warned me that the *k'ang* is heated with charcoal and produces carbon dioxide. You can get asphyxiation if you are not careful.

The *k'ang* takes up most of the wall to the right of the door. K'ang is a platform (had same in Chungking) with woven straw on top of a hard, adobe base. There is a small opening near the base where we put coal to heat it and keep us from freezing to death.

There is no running water. We have to get water from a well, or down at the river. Local villagers wash their clothing in the river and dump their sewage in it, so I try to avoid the river.

To the north of town sits Chinese Communist Party ("C.C.P.") headquarters, also housed in caves.

Over the next few weeks, Mr. Liege had no visitors. I settled into a routine of changing his bedpan, checking the saline level of his IV, and helping the nurses give him a sponge bath.

I tried to speak to him in Chinese. I don't know if he understood me, but I figured that something was better than nothing.

July 2 came, and one of the Filipino nurses brought in chocolate mousse cake from Chez Panisse. Mr. Liege couldn't eat, so we ate for him.

"*Sheng-ri kuai-le*," I said to him, *Happy Birthday*!

"How does it feel to be eighty?" I asked him.

"I know, it's not easy," the Filipino nurse said. "My mum is turning ninety-five, and she has all sorts of health problems. When I'm not here working, I'm back at home caring for her, making empanadas, which the doctor told me not to do, but she's ninety-five, so what does it matter?"

For his birthday, we decided to give him a haircut, because his bangs were falling in front of his eyes. The nurse cut his bangs with safety scissors. She tried to cut straight across, but when she was done, the line was uneven.

"Oh well," she said. "At least you don't have to worry about it getting in the way now."

"What about his fingernails?" I said.

"A manicure? Sure."

I went to my purse and pulled out a pair of nail clippers.

Mr. Liege's fingers on his left hand were slightly swollen. His nails looked gray and yellowish. I finished clipping that side and pulled back the sheet and looked at his right hand. His pinky looked like it had been broken and hadn't healed properly.

"Look at this," I said to the nurse.

"What is it?" she said, and she came over next to me.

"See his pinky finger? It doesn't look normal."

"No, it doesn't."

August 24, 1944

Dear Portia,

I left off telling you about the air raids. Quentin was out of town. It was a few months after we moved to Chungking. The air raid siren went off, and I slept through it. Sleep was impossible on the bed, so I slept on a rollout pad on the floor with a mosquito net draped over my nightgown. I pointed both electric fans downward to blow directly on me.

When the driver woke me up, I got out of bed and threw on a long coat from the foyer. He led me downstairs, out the main door, down to street level. He took my hand and brought me to a cave dug out of the side of a hill. Inside the cave, it was pitch dark and deathly silent, but I sensed there were many people there. The air in the cave smelled like sulphur. As the bombs hit, I felt my legs shake. I tried to ask my driver how long it would last, but he put his hand over my mouth. The driver hissed at me in **Pidgin**, "No talkee."

The "all clear" siren sounded three hours later, and someone lit a vegetable oil lamp. As the wick's flame grew, I saw hundreds of faces -- all Chinese, all scared. The shelters had to be shared with the whole neighborhood.

We emerged from candlelight into daylight. Smoke was rising from bombed out parts of the road all the way back to the diplomatic quarter. I didn't worry too much about Quentin, because the American embassy is not situated in the diplomatic quarter. Besides, he was off in Luoyang doing research on the famine.

The one upside is the locals have gotten savvy to the Japs and have developed an early warning system. The Japs usually send a reconnaissance plane first before the bombers arrive. The reconnaissance plane reports back on the weather conditions. Whenever we hear the faint sound of a plane buzzing around high overhead, we know that an attack is likely in the next few hours. The Chinese have set up watchers near the air base in **Hangchow**, and when a Jap bomber squadron takes off, the watchers radio ahead to let us know they're coming.

A few days ago, the first clear sky day this year, I stood at the entrance of my house on the stairs outside and watched as twenty-four aircraft approached the city from the South. The air raid sirens had been blaring for three or four minutes already when they passed overhead. I looked up and could see the distinct Jap markings on the belly of the fuselage. Then came the deafening whistling of bombs dropping and exploding on impact. I ran down the stairs and to the shelter. I emerged an hour later, and the air was thick with dust from pulverized brick. I could see all the way down to the end of the road where a large government billboard next to the public bathhouse listed **Dr. Sun** Yat-sen's Three Moral Principles: Nationalism, Democracy, and Livelihood of the People. The Japs probably spared that as a joke. Lofty ideals in a sea of destruction.

I heard later that the Japs made direct hits on the British, Russian, and French embassies. The foreigners who had their apartments and homes destroyed are now sleeping on the floor of the Chungking Club. The tiny American embassy, because of its location on the other side of the **Yangtze**, has so far been spared.

Worse than the bombs are the fires. The bombs destroy the water supply to many of the buildings, and the river is too far down the hill to fill up a fire truck. The only thing left to do to keep the fire from spreading is to make fire breaks by tearing down the thin bamboo and plaster homes with an axe. There are many Chinese families who have been rendered homeless. The **Kuomintang** government doesn't seem to care much about them, so they're left to beg on the street.

Now, I am kicking myself, because I see that I have still not managed to tell you what I set out to do in my previous letter. Time is running out. Please accept my apologies.

Most Sincerely,

Britka

A week or so after Mr. Liege's birthday, I called a professor of mine from Berkeley, Lars Mathieson, who taught modern Chinese history. I asked if he might know anything about Mr. Liege. He came by the next day wearing a button-down shirt, tie and tweed blazer.

"I got the call from my secretary. I'm sorry I couldn't be here sooner," he said. "It so happens that Quentin and I go way back. He came to work for me after he returned from Brazil."

"Brazil?" I asked.

Professor Mathieson smiled. "Yes, Brazil. After China went Communist in 'Forty-nine, many China experts were accused of being Communists or Communist sympathizers. Like them, Quentin was fired by the State Department. He sued the Secretary of State, and in the midst of that battle, got an offer from an oil company to do audits down in Brazil. They sent him and his wife, Britka, to Rio de Janeiro for a few years."

"Was he a Communist?" I asked.

"No. Things were blown out of proportion. Quentin's case had something to do with radios being misplaced or stolen. The State Department blacklisted him. He couldn't get a job anywhere. He eventually won the lawsuit and was reinstated. He collected back pay, used that to pay off the lawyers, and retired with full pension. That's when he came to work for me."

"What did he do for you?"

"Quentin's knowledge of China was -- *is* -- unparalleled. Back when I was getting my Ph.D, I used to read his dispatches from China. He traveled by foot to famine-stricken areas and reported on food shortages and corruption. When he came to Berkeley, he helped me build the Chinese Studies collection at the Library."

"Did Mr. Liege meet Mao Zedong in Taoyuan?"

"Yes, he saw Mao Zedong, Zhou Enlai, Zhu De -- all the top leadership. No other American had that level of access. I suppose the impression was that he was partial to the Communists, but that wasn't the case."

I told Professor Mathieson about Ai-ling and the photograph.

"Ai-ling?" he said. "Sun Ai-ling?"

"She said her last name was 'Zhang.'"

"Hmm. It must be the same person. Perhaps she got married and is using her husband's family name. In any case, Sun Ai-ling taught first year Chinese here at Berkeley around the same time that Quentin was there.

---

*Ai-ling. The last time I saw her was in Shanghai. It was a late afternoon in August. The air was thick and dull with a sense of impending violence. Coolies were loading trucks in the alleys. Their shirts were soaked through. We met at the Willow Pattern Tea House. Old bird keepers were playing mahjong next to us and bantering in Shanghainese. She was wearing a periwinkle **ch'i p'ao** with brocaded collar. She had a small handbag in her lap with the* *character for "peace" embroidered on the side. She said it held her passport. Until that point I had never seen her dressed in anything but the plain, cotton peasant uniforms of Taoyuan. If the K.M.T. had found her, they would have had her shot for treason.*

"When you go home, you must forget about this," she said.

She told me she was pregnant and that neither of us could return to Taoyuan.

She said I wasn't the father.

I asked her who it was.

She said it was Matsuda.

I didn't believe her.

By September, the military crackdown in Tiananmen had fallen off the headlines. Events in Poland, with the election of the first noncommunist prime minister, and in South Africa, with the largest antiapartheid protest since martial law, had taken over the front pages of the New York Times. Nevertheless, Amnesty International claimed that the Chinese government was secretly executing student leaders from the protest and jailing thousands who had participated. Beijing denied it. One of those executed could have been Tank Man.

Ai-ling

Ai-ling left a message at the St. Matthews front desk on a Saturday. I was off that day, so I returned her call on Monday. We agreed to meet at her place for tea later that week. She lived a few blocks up from Cedar Avenue in Berkeley in a high peaked, colonial revival-style home with peeling paint. The driveway was empty when I arrived.

I walked up the stairs and tried to press the doorbell button, but it was pushed in too far and didn't work. I knocked on the door and waited. I knocked again.

"*Ah, Xiao Lu, ni lai le,*" I heard from behind me. "Sorry I am late," she said in English. She was carrying a shopping bag from Andronico's, which she opened and started searching through. She was wearing a Hawaiian print shirt with lavender flowers and knee-length Capri pants. She pulled out her purse from the shopping bag and opened it.

She extracted a large, square key. "Ah! Here it is," she said, and she held it up. She inserted the key into the door and jiggled it a little. She grasped the glass door handle and turned the knob. The door gave way and creaked open.

"*Jin lai,*" she said, motioning me inside. She put her purse on a small table next to the door. The house smelled like the pages of a used book. She turned on the light switch to the living room, which had dormer windows looking out onto Walnut Avenue. Next to the windows was a lone, white fabric, three-seater couch with plastic wrapping on it.

"*Qing zuo,*" she said. She closed the door and walked into the living room and motioned me to sit down.

I sat on the plastic covered couch and looked around. The walls were plaster and devoid of any decor. The chandelier in the living room had three lightbulbs. One was out.

27

I asked her how long she had lived there.

"The place is a shambles, isn't it? I am so busy these days. I simply have no time to keep it up," she said with a chuckle. "What kind of tea would you like?" she said. "Pu-er, Jasmine, Tie Kuanyin, Oolong?"

"I'll have Pu-er," I said.

"Good," she said. "Pu-er it is then." She turned and went into the kitchen.

If you've never had Pu-er, it is reddish brown and smells faintly of sweat socks.

I asked her to tell me more about Mr. Liege.

Ai-ling was standing in front of the stove and tying an apron around her waist.

"As I was telling you back at St. Matthews," she said, "we met in Taoyuan. I was working there as an interpreter."

"How old were you?"

"I was nineteen. I had been trained in Peking, and I was just getting started. My father had studied in Paris during the 1920s. He knew Deng Xiaoping and Zhou Enlai. They studied there as well. My father taught me French and English from an early age."

Deng Xiaoping was responsible for the bloodshed in Tiananmen several months earlier.

"Were your parents with you in Taoyuan?"

"No, they were living in Tianjin, but they were killed in a train explosion."

"That's terrible," I said.

"They were returning from Peking. It wasn't clear if their train was shelled by the Japanese, or if someone had been carrying explosive materials on board."

"How old were you when it happened?"

"It was the year before I left for Taoyuan."

"Were you close to them?"

"My father, mostly. He had wanted a boy. He treated me to all the things a boy would have. My mother cut my hair short. My father taught me how to repair automobile tires."

8-25-44 (Fri) 16:20

Afternoon tea is poured with boiling water from rusting, iron kettle into a dirty ceramic mug. Precious pinch of curled, dry black "real" Oolong tea leaves swirl to the top and gradually expand into long, worm-like strands that slowly sink to bottom after about five minutes. What passes for Oolong here is like weak grass that has to be sucked and squeezed till there is nothing left. The tea shop in the neighboring village will sell me real Oolong for a small fortune.

A few *liang* (a *liang* is roughly 50 milligrams) cost me two bottles of India ink. Ink is also hard to come by, and I get mine through Army requisition in **Ramgarh** by way of Kunming (southern China, near the Burmese border), courtesy of Uncle Sam's weekly airlift. Too bad Army does not deal in Oolong tea.

Cigarettes work like money too, but I refuse to part with my Country Gentleman tobacco and papers.

I am unable to see myself stuck at a desk job back Stateside, taking the ferry every day to San Francisco with the other three-piece suited corpses pushing paper for a paycheck.

Ai-ling came back into the living room carrying a tray with a teapot, two cups, and some small treats.

"It's a little cold in here, isn't it?" she said. "Let me turn on the heat." She stood up and walked over to the foyer. She squinted at the thermostat. She went over to her purse and pulled out her reading glasses. She walked back to the thermostat and adjusted the dial. Suddenly, a deep rumble came from the floor register in the living room.

"Tell me about yourself," she said as she walked back into the room and returned to the couch.

I told her about how my father died when I was a Freshman in high school and that I had an older sister who was studying to be an optometrist.

"Your mother must be very proud of you both," Ai-ling said.

I didn't tell her about my mother. "I had a hard time in school," I said.

Ai-ling made a sour face.

"Do you like moon cakes?" she asked. "I bought some at the Chinese supermarket."

"I love moon cakes," I said. I asked her why she moved back to Berkeley.

"I really love It here," she said. "The activities, the bookstores."

"Did you know Mr. Liege's wife?"

"No, not really," she said.

August 25, 1944

Dearest Portia,

I am so sorry for cutting you off like that with my last letter. I simply had to get some sleep. Now, I can finally tell you what I meant to tell you about two letters ago.

His name was "Gaspar." He has been gone almost a year now.

There is so much I need to tell you in this short time before my sedan chair arrives to take me out of here for the last time.

It was last summer, during the worst of it, that I did something very stupid: I left the shelter in the middle of an air raid and walked to the French brasserie on Tibet Street. I went up to the bar to see if anyone was there. The place was deserted. I walked around the bar and found an open pack of Gitanes and a pack of matches. I hadn't smoked since the time you and I stole Mr. Fellowes' pack of Kents from his desk after lunch recess. The acrid smoke burned in the back of my throat. The jolt of nicotine made me feel alive. I started thinking of creative ways to kill myself.

Suddenly, the bartender popped up from behind the bar and asked me what I wanted to drink. He scared me so much I fell off the stool. He came around and helped me back up. I told him I forgot my purse, and he said not to worry. He said that during air raids, everything was on the house. I ordered an espresso and an anisette. I told him about my dark thoughts. I told him I had left the shelter in the middle of the air raid. He said that was risky but not at all a sure bet. His suggestion was a single gunshot in the mouth. I haven't forgotten that.

We talked all through the bombing, and when it stopped, I ordered another espresso, a buttered baguette, and a hard boiled egg. At that point, a bearded man in his thirties sat down next to me. He wore a blue striped seersucker suit and a silk blue pocket square.

He asked me about my breakfast. I said that the protein kept me from gnawing off the door handle and the anisette calmed my nerves.

"Typical French breakfast," he said. He ordered the same. I remember laughing like I hadn't laughed in a long time. Maybe it was the absurdity of the situation.

He said that humor is the antidote to depression and that, of course, Pernod helps too. He held up his glass, and we toasted to suicide.

He said he was the commercial attaché at the French embassy. I asked him which French government he represented -- Vichy or

Resistance? He said there was only one French government, and that was the one he represented. Then, he handed me the silk pocket square from his coat. "Here," he said, "you have bread crumbs on the side of your mouth."

I remember blushing. I looked like a wreck. My hair was a jumbled mess held under a dusty scarf.

He said something to the effect of, "Times like these call for brave measures." I hadn't picked up on the nuance, but as I look back, he was making a pass. Quentin was on the road so often that I was living alone at the time. I invited Gaspar over for tea the next day, and before I knew it we were in bed together making love.

We made love the next night, right through another air raid. An oil painting we have of the Champs Élysées that used to hang from the moulding in the dining room came crashing down to the floor when a bomb hit the house next door. I almost didn't notice.

I never felt so alive. The next morning, I paid off the household help and told them to not come back. I fired them. The cook, who was a converted Christian, crossed herself and said a prayer. The driver yelled at me in Chinese -- none of which I understood, but I gather it wasn't flattering. The housemaid said nothing and just packed up her stuff.

I managed to see Gaspar a few nights a week. We spent our time at his house. When Quentin returned from a trip, it was without warning. Each time, he would appear in the foyer, a stinking, hairy mess. I refused to so much as kiss him until he bathed, shaved, and clipped his fingernails. Then, it would be off to the bedroom. We had sex, and it was very difficult for me. I had to close my eyes and try to imagine I was with Gaspar, but that was impossible. Quentin is like a machine in bed. He goes full bore. When he's finished, he passes out like a drunken sailor. I feel like I'm here to serve him, like a whore. This went on for two years, with Gaspar and me skulking around late night Chungking like forbidden lovers.

Finally, I had had enough of the hi-jinx. I decided to divorce Quentin and run off with Gaspar to Geneva.

By this time, the Italians and the Germans had quit Chungking and moved their embassies back to Nanking, which the Japanese Imperial forces claimed was the true capital of China. In any case, one night, Gaspar failed to show up at the appointed time. The monsieur at the brasserie said he had been arrested by the German Stasi and sent to a prisoner camp outside Shanghai. I found out later that Gaspar had dual German and French citizenship, and that he was Jewish.

"Enough about me. Tell me about yourself," Ai-ling said. "Where are your parents from?"

I told her my family's story, how my parents had escaped from China during the famine that followed the **Great Leap Forward** campaign, and how they had found menial jobs in Hong Kong, and how my sister and I were born in Kowloon. I told her that my sister and I had attended Chinese school on Saturdays.

"Which one?" She asked.

"Zhongshan Normal School," I said. I didn't tell her I got expelled.

Ai-ling's eyes lit up. "Zhongshan? That's Taiwanese. Do you have any relatives in Taiwan?"

I told her I didn't.

"You know, my brother escaped to Taiwan in 1949 with Chiang Kai-shek and the **Nationalists**."

"Your brother?"

"Well, he was my half-brother. He was a pilot. He trained with the **Flying Tigers** during World War II."

"Is he still there?"

"No. He died a while ago. His plane was shot down. I was living in Datong when it happened."

I said I didn't know where that was.

"Datong is an industrial city in the northern part of China, close to Inner Mongolia. The winters are freezing cold there. I was assigned to work in a brick factory. I worked in accounting."

"So, you were in China while your half-brother was in Taiwan?" I asked.

"Yes, back then, there was no contact at all with Taiwan. No letters, no telephone calls. The only news we got was from the Xinhua News Agency, which was pure Communist propaganda. I was eating breakfast in the cafeteria. I heard on the radio that a U-2 plane had gone down in the South China Sea.

"Over the next week, news reports said it had taken off from a military airport in Taiwan. The pilot was found dead. His ejection seat had malfunctioned. The pilot was Chinese. The patch on his flight suit had a black cat emblem. That was the insignia of the Republic of China's U-2 squadron. Then, several weeks later, news of the pilot's name came out. "Chang Tu-hsia," was his name. I later found out that he had been part of a small group of pilots from Taiwan trained by the U.S. to fly the U-2."

"I'm so sorry," I said.

Ai-ling glanced down at the teapot. "*Aiya*," she said, "I totally forgot about the tea." She placed both hands on the teapot. "I am afraid I will have to make another pot," she said.

"No, please," I said, "it's fine."

"I fear that the tea will be too strong."

"It's okay. I like strong tea."

She poured tea into the two cups. She placed my cup on a small saucer and handed it to me. "Please, have a moon cake," she said.

I took one and bit into it. The crust was soft, and the black bean paste was still a little warm. "Delicious," I said.

"A friend of mine makes them. She runs a bakery in Oakland Chinatown. I am thinking of opening a tea shop next door to her."

Ai-ling put down her tea and picked up a moon cake. She took a bite. "Mmm," she said. "I am sorry, but I did not eat any lunch today."

8-26-44 (Sat). 10:00

I'm sitting in the mess hall watching five beleaguered workers tossing heads of white cabbage onto the back of a three-wheel bicycle (a few spokes are missing). The workers have the splotchy, ruddy cheeks of Northern Chinese. Hearty and able to work through dead of winter and still hum a tune. Their cotton *chungshan* uniforms threadbare around elbows. Truly the heart and soul of the "New China" right here in the flesh.

The Chinese spoken in Taoyuan village has all sorts of regional variations. Locals speak Shensi dialect, while Communist Party members come from all over China. Some accents are so different that people are left communicating with sticks, scratching out Chinese characters in dirt.

Breakfast this a.m. was with whole PAX Team over a Chinese meal of rice porridge, preserved radish, and steamed buns. Colonel Hathaway talked about the mission, how our being here gave the U.S. Government and President Roosevelt a rare opportunity to negotiate a truce between the Communists and Nationalists. I felt like odd man out being from the State Department instead of the Army. The Colonel said that not everyone knew about Taoyuan history, so he had me brief them on how Communists ended up here.

I said that the Chinese Communist Party began in Shanghai in 1920 and spread throughout the large cities. At this stage, Mao Zedong was leader of the Communists, while Chiang Kai-shek (Chiang), was leader of the Nationalists. The Communists and Nationalists fought off and on until 1934 when Chiang began a systematic campaign to destroy all Communist base camps in the Chinese countryside. This led the Communists on their famous **"Long March,"** which was an 8,000 mile retreat from Chiangsi all the way up to the steppes plateau in China's northwest. Less than ten percent of the Long Marchers survived the journey.

The Japanese occupation of China began with the **Marco Polo Bridge Incident** in Peking in July 1937, and Japanese troops began to take over the coastal cities after that. Shanghai was overtaken three months later, and Nanking two months after Shanghai. Japan said it was trying to create a "Greater East Asia Co-Prosperity Sphere," but everyone knew that was just a front for colonization.

With the Communists now mostly in the North and the Nationalists blockading supplies to Taoyuan, my estimate is that roughly four hundred thousand Nationalist troops are being used. That means four hundred thousand Nationalist troops and roughly ninety-thousand Communists fighting each other instead of both of them fighting the Japanese.

The average peasant is now paying sixty percent of his crop in taxes and kickbacks to Nationalist government bureaucrats and warlords. This leaves little to survive on, especially during droughts. Starvation is killing tens of thousands of peasants every year. Meanwhile, back in Chungking, the Nationalists are cooking the books and hiding facts. The people back in Washington only read what comes to them through Chiang and his cabal. The Nationalists are stockpiling Lend Lease jeeps and guns instead of using them to fight the Japanese.

The Communists control a large amount of territory in northwest, while the Japanese control the coastal cities. The Communists have underground operations in Jap-occupied territory with regular radio contact. We get daily updates on Jap troop movements. The Communists also smuggle out downed American pilots from Jap-controlled areas.

Ai-ling covered her mouth while she ate the moon cake and continued. "After my brother died, I stayed at the brick factory for another year. Mao's Red Guards came to the factory. They were just kids," she said, "but they behaved like animals. They hit our plant supervisor with sticks. They made all of us kneel on the ground. They pushed our faces into the ground with their feet."

I told her I had read stories about the Cultural Revolution. Middle and high school students were encouraged by Mao to "storm the headquarters" and take over factories, train stations, and newspapers.

Ai-ling took a sip of tea. "They followed me back to my home," she said. "They broke into my apartment and burned my books."

"What kind of books did you have?"

"Several in English. 'Lady Chatterly's Lover,' 'A Doll's House.' Some Hemingway. They took everything and burned it in the street. They made me wear a pointed cap. They paraded me through the city."

"Could you run away?"

"There was nowhere to go. My sister was living in Shanghai, but she was gravely ill. Tuberculosis. She had a son, who was at university in Peking.

"Is he still alive?"

"Yes, he lives in Dalian. He works for a local television station."

"Do you keep in touch with him?"

"Off and on," she said.

Ai-ling took another bite of the moon cake. She stared out the windows to the street. Fog was rolling in from the Bay, and the sky was becoming dark.

"Do you live by yourself?" Ai-ling asked.

I told her I had a roommate. She was in her last year at Cal. We had met through the Asian sorority. When she wasn't studying **"P-chem"** or **"O-chem,"** she was reading the bible. On Sundays, she went church in Oakland.

In high school, I wore black eye shadow and listened to Joy Division and Killing Joke and hung out with the "mod" crowd in the smoking section of the quad during lunch. I was the only one among them taking Advanced Placement classes. For some reason, my hatred of conformity didn't spill over into my studies. I blame my father for that.

I was accepted to Smith College, my first choice, but my family couldn't afford it. So, I went to Berkeley. My freshman year, I made the on-campus housing lottery, and I got stuck with a short blonde from Encinitas who woke up at four every morning to put on her makeup before running down the stairs to a van outside that whisked her off to the Oakland estuary, where she was a coxswain for the men's crew team.

Freshman year I reconnected with the Chinese American community. Sproul Plaza had tables set up for various clubs and student associations. I was careful to avoid both the Chinese Student Association (Taiwan, Nationalist) and Chinese Student Union (Mainland China, Communist) groups because I didn't want to get caught up in their politics.

I couldn't read or write Chinese. I spoke **Toisan**, which was my parents' dialect. Toisan was completely different from Mandarin, so I enrolled in first year Mandarin. The first day of class, the instructor went around the room and did introductions. One-third of the students were ethnic Chinese, and she made a point of speaking to each one of us in Mandarin to see how much we understood. Several students understood her and responded in Mandarin. She asked them to leave and see her later during office hours. They would have to take a higher level class, she said. She said her class wasn't going to be anyone's "easy A."

I had class three times a week, with an hour section on Tuesday evenings, taught by a teaching assistant. My instructor was very supportive of the non-ethnic Chinese students. She knew their names, made extra office hours, and gave them supplemental materials. I was expected to know everything already.

Whenever we had a quiz, she took away points when I wrote a character's strokes in the wrong order. When we did recitation, she stopped me in mid-sentence to correct my pronunciation. I lost motivation and ended up barely passing. After that, I went to the bookstore, bought the next semester's materials, and studied on my own.

8-27-44 (Sun). 23:15

I cannot believe I spent four years in Chungking. What a hellhole compared to here. There are no **Jeep girls**. Everyone is well fed in Taoyuan.

I met Chou En-lai's interpreter. She was the young lady who met us when we arrived. "Sun Ai-ling" is French-educated and speaks English with a slight British accent.

Burly and I finished an entire bottle of *maotai* last night. I woke in the morning with my head spinning and a manila envelope with the my writing on the back:

膙 疥 鮖

Then, it came back to me. I had the stupid idea (brilliant at the time, mind you), to use a Chinese dictionary as a planchette board for automatic writing. I was trying to channel Chiang Kai-shek. The son-of-a-bitch needs a new name, I thought. The characters sound roughly the same as his proper name.

膙 = "Chiang" 疥 = "kai" 鮖 = "shek"

No idea how this sounds in Cantonese, but in Mandarin, it's a hoot. "Callous" (膃), "itch," (疥) and "squirrel" (䶂). Well, it was funnier last night.

My mother had little sympathy for my troubles in learning Mandarin. She blamed my poor relationship with my instructor on my rebellious character. She said I had a problem with authority. Then, she started talking about how the Communists were going to take away our house. I told her that was a silly idea, because we lived in America now. There was no way the Communists were going to take our home.

Had I paid attention then, I would have noticed her grasp of reality beginning to slip.

It wasn't until later, when she drove off the Highway 13 embankment near Tunnel Road in Piedmont during rush hour that I woke up to it. Her car plowed through a wall of oleanders and rolled down a thirty-five degree embankment to the street below. She came to a stop when the right side of her car clipped a redwood.

The Highway Patrol had seen it all happen. An ambulance arrived shortly afterward while the fire department was lifting her out of the driver's seat. When the ambulance got her to the E.R., they did a CT scan to check for damage to her head. That led to more tests.

"Frontotemporal dementia" was the diagnosis. Luckily, the doctor said, she didn't remember anything from the accident. When she regained consciousness she recognized me and asked how she got there.

August 27, 1944

Dearest Portia,

Here's the second part of my letter, which I was unable to finish because of a bombing raid.

I went straight to the train station with the aim to find Gaspar, but there were no trains running through Jap occupied cities between here and Shanghai. There was no way. I went looking for someone who could drive me there, but nobody was stupid enough to try, for any amount of money. I ran into an American G.I. who had a large gambling debt to settle with a Chinese mob boss. He said he had a contact who might be able to arrange a car and driver to take me to Shanghai for the right price. Then, he tried to sell me his handgun. I didn't buy the gun, nor did I go with his sketchy plan, but I did manage to get a gun from somebody else.

The driver I had let go several years back appeared unannounced at my front door in the middle of the night. He was holding a small, wood box. He said that he couldn't in good conscience leave without giving something back to me. I didn't quite understand what he was talking about until the next day when I checked my jewelry. I discovered that he made off with the diamond brooch that my dad gave me for graduation. He also took a pendant, which had the Brevik family crest and four rubies.

Inside the box was a gun. I told him I didn't have any use for it. I told him I wanted to go to Shanghai. He said that was impossible. He said he was leaving Chungking before the Japs invaded. He said that he had two handguns, neither of which was any use, because the local police would shake him down at the pier before he boarded the ferry to Wuhan. "Here," he said. "Please take this. I am sorry." Then, he turned and left.

I took the box into the kitchen, placed it on the table, and opened it up. It was a German Walther P.38.

I was at the bar one evening when Quentin returned from a trip to Hunan. He must have seen the gun on the high boy in the living room, because he was asleep when I got home around eleven, but he woke up and asked me how I got it. I was still a little drunk, and I made up a story about how someone had left it there after a cocktail party. I felt that if I told him the driver gave it to me, he might get suspicious. I assured Quentin that I would turn it into the local police. Instead, I hid it in my dresser underneath my stockings.

Which brings me to the present. With all that's going on at the moment -- the bombings, the **P.O.W**. camps, et cetera -- I'm finally being evacuated. I'm leaving this evening. As I said earlier, Quentin is already gone. I hope to be reunited with him after the War, but we'll have to see.

I have everything lined up now in a row next to the front door: my steamer trunk, my leather suitcase, my cosmetics bag, and the Walther P.38. By the time I finish this letter, if I haven't gone off the deep end, I will be in a sedan chair on my way to the airport. The only flight out of here, at least the only safe one, is a DC-3 that leaves just after midnight for Yunnan. We'll fly a corkscrew pattern until we reach altitude, then we'll head over the famous "24 turns" before stopping in Yunnan. That's the easy part. The leg between Yunnan and Calcutta, known affectionately as "the Hump," is famous for plane crashes.

If I survive the Hump, I will land in Calcutta and pay my respects to the Stilton Club and that lovely maître d', Wynton, and find my way to the billiard room. A few gin tonics later, I will have the porter bring my luggage and I will stay one night at the Excelsior. The hotel room will be the perfect place to drink myself into a coma. The following morning, my body will arrive, either alive or dead, but thoroughly marinated, at the Calcutta airport to board a flight for Karachi. My ultimate destination is home turf, to be with you, back in Charlotte.

I can't say more now because I have to finish packing and before the sedan chair arrives. I will try to write to you from Calcutta.

All of my love,

Britka

The hospital discharged mom with the provision that a nurse would be coming by every few days to check up on her. Between classes, I took AC Transit home to check up on her. Some days, I'd find knives stuck in the wall and the telephone off the hook, beeping loudly. That meant she had locked herself in the bathroom to keep out the "bad people." I had to convince her that no one was coming to get her, and then try to get her to take her medication.

That was freshman year.

When summer came, mom's doctor recommended she be put in a care facility so she couldn't harm herself or anyone else. The place I ended up finding for her was no great shakes, but it was the best of what was available given our budget. I say, "Our," in a generic sense, because my sister contributed almost nothing -- financially, logistically, or emotionally.

Ai-ling had finished her tea, while my cup was still half full. She offered me more, but I decided I wasn't a fan of Pu-er tea.

"Have you ever been to Taiwan?" Ai-ling asked.

I told her I hadn't been outside of California since moving to the States. I said I really wanted to visit China, but Tiananmen changed my mind.

"You should really visit Taiwan. The night markets, the restaurants -- it's some of the best Chinese food in the world."

I said it hardly made sense to go to Taiwan just for the food.

She said she could introduce me to some "nice" Chinese boys my age, and that there were summer programs in Taiwan where Chinese American boys and girls got together and did fun things.

My friends called it the "Love Boat." There was no actual boat involved, but the idea was the same: put young, college-aged Chinese American men and women together in a strange place and see what happens. The Israeli government did something similar for Jewish Americans.

The Love Boat was touted as "cultural exchange," and it lasted two weeks. There were organized excursions to museums, restaurants, karaoke, and other "safe" venues where nothing escaped the eyes of chaperones. The men and women were put in single sex dormitories and were prohibited from mingling after hours. That kept the parents happy.

I had heard about guys sneaking out of the dorms. If they were caught, they earned an immediate, one-way ticket back home. I imagine if I had been forced to go, I would have snuck out the first night.

8-28-44 (Mon). 10:45

I accompanied the Colonel to a meeting with Mao Tse-tung, Chou En-lai, and Chu Teh. Ai-ling came to interpret for the Colonel. Later, got a chance to speak one-on-one with her. She was born to Chinese parents in Paris. Her father studied at the Sorbonne during the early twenties -- the same time as **Teng Hsiao-ping**.

Ai-ling was wearing the traditional, blue cotton padded chungshan button down coat and matching pants. She wore her hair in a ponytail. She looked like a regular countryside girl, but her mannerisms were European. Her Chinese is Pekinese, like mine. Good, solid "r" sounds. There are so few fellow Pekinese out here.

All the Chinese here, with the exception of Mao, Chou, Chu, treat her like a Communist mucky muck. She seems to be well-connected. Maybe a bit too "professional" for my tastes. Her voice is deep and mannish. Maybe that is why Mao seems smitten with her? She's nearly a foot shorter than me, and still she is not afraid to speak her mind.

Burly asked about the **Pro-kit** situation. One could get a lifetime supply of prophylactics back in Chungking. Jeep girls at every corner. Five bucks for a ride in the hay. Not so here. Besides, fraternizing with the local women will not improve our standing with the Chinese. I advised Burly to keep a lid on it.

Humdinger of a toothache this a.m. May have to have it pulled. Dental hygiene is not a high priority. Apparently, there is a Chinese dentist in the area. Not sure what that means. The last dentist I heard about in a nearby town stole painkillers and left town in the middle of the night.

My hair is thinning. Back in Chunking, a Chinese doctor told me that tooth and hair loss are due to kidney *jing* deficiency. He said that I am expending too much "life force." The inexorable march toward infirmity continues.

I am now in the habit of waking up to my alarm at six sharp, rain or shine. I do calisthenics in my room and then go out for a 25 minute walk. The mornings are cooler now. My only wool sweater was hand-knit in Minnesota. It came with a letter from a grandma whose son and grandson are both deployed with the Army in Europe.

Ai-ling asked me if had seen the movie, "Black Rain," which had just come out.

I told her I hadn't.

She slid a magazine over to me. It was "The Atlantic Monthly." The cover had an illustration of a sumo wrestler touching his big belly to a globe. "There's an article I think you should read called 'Containing Japan.' Here, take my copy," she said and handed me the magazine. "Just like when the Japanese began expanding their empire into China in the Thirties. They're back at it again, only now the U.S. is subsidizing the colonization of America with the trade deficit."

I asked her what she thought about the U.S. Seventh Fleet protecting Taiwan.

"Oh, that is different," she said. "For one, Taiwan is not out to bankrupt the U.S."

"Doesn't Taiwan have a trade deficit with the U.S., just like Japan?" I asked.

"Taiwan is an ally," she said. "It always has been."

I asked her if she thought the U.S. would defend Taiwan from China as it had done during the Taiwan Straights Crisis in the Fifties?

"Without a doubt," she said.

9-5-44 (Tue) 15:00

Day three of toothache. Went into the village and found the dentist. Like the previous one, he gave me a medicinal tea that does nothing to kill the pain.

After lunch, I was visited by a Soviet advisor. He lumbered into the cafeteria like a big brown bear. He has hair all down his neck. He told me about the Jap P.O.W. camp's political re-education program. He invited me to go along with him next time. He said I should bring our Japanese interpreter, Tak.

Lieutenant Takahara, or "Tak," is an Army G-2 guy. He was a junior at Stanford when the Japs bombed Pearl Harbor. His family got sent to internment camp. I like to annoy Tak about Stanford losing Fred Boensch to Cal. Tak's a big football fan. He grew up in the Central Valley and played running back for Modesto High. His family owns a strawberry farm.

The Colonel gave me clearance to go with the Soviet advisor, "The Russian," and Tak to visit the Jap P.O.W. camp. Tak asked me to stop using the word "Jap."

Apropos of raw vegetables (see my earlier entry), at dinner last night someone brought in a box of juicy, palm-sized tomatoes. They were amazing.

I was impressed by the P.O.W. camp. Never seen anything like it. It is run by a few J. Communists and J. P.O.W.s. Notice that I don't use the word "Jap" any more.

Funny thing, there were no Chinese guards. The camp is self-policing. The P.O.W.s focus on "thought reform." I know, it sounds a little spooky.

The Russian says most of J. troops come from rural Japan and lack education.

Two J. communists gave us a guided tour. Mssrs. Shiba and Matsuda. Shiba was older than Matsuda. He didn't talk much. He walked with a limp and had bags under his eyes. The other, Matstuda, looked to be in his early twenties. Matsuda insisted on speaking in Mandarin. He was pretty fluent. I was downright surprised. Except, he had this odd way of only addressing Tak. My Mandarin is a lot better than Tak's, so I ended up answering his questions.

The walls inside the camp were plastered with slogans in Japanese. A bulletin board had essays written by the prisoners. Matsuda referred to the prisoners as *"hsüeh sheng,"* or "students."

Shiba sat us down at a small table with three chairs. Matsuda stood behind him. Shiba spoke in Japanese, and before Tak could translate, Matsuda translated it into Mandarin.

"The Japanese Emperor is not a descendant of *Amaterasu*, [the Japanese sun goddess]. The Emperor is human, like the rest of us," Shiba said. "Dispelling this myth is the first step in the re-education program."

On the table were several Japanese magazines. I asked Tak what they were. He said one was a news magazine called "Asahi Shukan." It was dated May 1944. Another was a thicker one for essays and culture called "Bungei Shunju." I asked Matsuda how they got ahold of these magazines. He said that Shiba has a network of underground connections all the way back to Peking and Shanghai. His folks buy them from J. army officers and businessmen, and from there they pass up through a chain of smugglers and eventually make their way to Taoyuan.

I asked if the prisoners liked these magazines. Shiba laughed and said maybe only half of the students were able to read. "Most of them come from poor families. Most only have an elementary school education."

Matsuda said the P.O.W.s were learning more Japanese in camp than when they were in Japan. They were are also learning basic Mandarin.

Shiba and Matsuda were putting together a plan to work with the Chinese Communists to visit local Chinese villages and teach them to capture J. troops rather than kill them.

Over dinner that night back at the Communist's mess hall, I asked Tak his opinion. Tak said he was encouraged. He said he wanted to go back and talk to Shiba about a plan to broadcast Anti-J. propaganda over the wireless. Tak is working with the Navy and **O.S.S.** [Office of Strategic Services] on medium-wave, ship-originated radio broadcast to J. islands (Honshu, Kyushu, etc.). They are also dropping leaflets from B-29s over J. occupied areas.

Tak said that the Army still lacked enough Japanese-speaking officers. I told him there were plenty of candidates at the internment camps. He did not find that funny.

48

September 5, 1944

Dear Portia,

The plane landed in Calcutta about an hour after an air raid, so things were topsy-turvy. The flight was uneventful, save for an air pocket over the Himalayas that caused me to grab the cargo straps for dear life.

The air here smells like mildew, and the cockroaches are huge. They have wings and can fly. There was one in my bathroom when I arrived at the youth hostel. I decided, wisely, to ignore it. The Excelsior, it turns out, is booked solid

I should have known that the Stilton Club would be closed. Turns out, it's closed permanently, and Wynton is supposedly being held in a P.O.W. camp in Singapore. Nevertheless, I managed to find one of the only places that still knows how to make an authentic gin tonic, and I made a serious investment with the bartender there.

The Walther P.38 is stowed safely in my steamer trunk in a fake lining so the customs officials can't find it. I haven't thought much about it, to be honest, because there's so much to negotiate here just to get breakfast.

I have been thinking more about Quentin.

As you know, it was difficult to find dates in college. Height was important to me, although it seems to not be the case any more. Gaspar, believe it or not, was only five foot ten. Most men say they are taller than they really are, and when they come face-to-face with me, they see immediately that I mean business, because I'm taller than the average-sized man. I know this sounds incredibly shallow, and it is. Quentin is taller than I. He was athletic, and a little mysterious. Being the son of a missionary, his locution was squarely Missouri. His sentence structures sounded like a French person speaking English.

You know the story of how we met freshman year and dated all through college, so I won't bore you with that. My point is that when we graduated, it was no big leap to get married. The ceremony was, as you know, at the Lutheran church in Berkeley.

I really wish you had been able to make it.

Quentin's mother was opposed from the start. She told him that I didn't have a soft bone in my body. I remember when daddy walked me down the blue and gold carpet runner to the tune of Pachelbel's "Canon in D" played by a string quartet, he whispered, "Hopefully, this ain't in vain." Maybe daddy knew something that I didn't. He paid for Quentin's tuxedo. He paid for everything down to the hotel rooms for Quentin's four brothers, mother, and father.

The reception later at the Claremont featured a twelve piece band playing "Sophisticated Lady," "Stormy Weather," and "The Last Round-Up." Daddy had bottles of Moët & Chandon placed at every table and ordered a caviar "fountain" for the center of the room.

The whole time, daddy wouldn't stop talking about "that Communist FDR" for taking the United States off the gold standard. Mother said that she was happy to have escaped the record heat wave on the East Coast.

Then, over in the far corner of the room, in "no-man's land," was Quentin's family. They dressed like dustbowl refugees from Kansas. His four brothers wore secondhand jackets, some with holes in the sleeves, others with sleeves too long. Their bottle of champagne was unopened, and their glasses were bone dry.

As much as I thought Quentin was different from them, I've come to see that, ultimately, he isn't. As much as I would like him to be an eggs Benedict man, he never tires of Wheaties. The upside to all this is he is perfectly suited for his job. He enjoys

50

riding in the back of a cargo truck and talking to Chinese peasants about crop yields. I could never do that.

I am ashamed to say that in the ten years we have been married, I never once felt truly romantic about Quentin. I love him in that I care for him. It was never love, with a capital "L." I made his dinners and washed his clothes. This sounds thoroughly depressing, and I'm so sorry for unloading all of this on you right now. I know that you are going through a divorce. That may be how we end up as well.

It has taken me this long to come to that realization. I always believed that love was the reason one got married. Love was wholesome, and when love failed to keep one happy, one simply started over. I also held tightly to the notion that honesty was inviolable, however, now I think that honesty can be destructive. It can be explosive, like an incendiary. There is no point playing with bombs. If a marriage isn't ready for it, then honesty is best avoided.

How are the boys doing? If I remember correctly, Joseph, Jr. will be entering high school this fall. Francis, too. How is his piano practice coming along? I do wish I were home already. There's so much more I want to say.

Yours Truly,
Britka

"Does Lao Du ever show signs of understanding you?" Ai-ling asked.

I didn't know if he did. I told her the doctor said that in his experience many patients with his condition are capable of understanding everything, but they can't respond.

"I was hoping to talk to him," she said. "There are some things I meant to tell him last time that I didn't get around to doing."

"I'm sure it won't hurt to try," I said. As I write this now, many years later, I suspect that she hadn't told him everything. I wonder how much he knew before the stroke.

Ai-ling ended our meeting by saying she had to run off to meet with her mahjong group. I drove home with my mind spinning.

9-8-44 (Fri) 16:00

The Russian came by to say he had been recalled to Moscow. His parting gift to me: a full-length, Russian Army overcoat lined with sheep's wool. A distinguishing feature was the large hole in the armpit. The story, according to The Russian, was the coat had belonged to a buddy of his who was shot while on mission with Chinese **8th Route Army**. The bullet came from a J. sniper rifle -- most likely an Arisaka Type 38 carbine. The bullet went through his armpit and killed him instantly. The Russian had the blood washed out and kept it as a backup coat. He joked that the coat was now bullet-proof, having been shot through once already. I tried it on, but it was several sizes too big. It made me look like Vladimir Ilyich Lenin. My very own Lenin coat.

I overslept this morning and missed calisthenics. I also missed the Colonel's morning meeting. I apologized to him later. He said I missed some important stuff -- a plan to airlift several tons of radio equipment here. The O.S.S. wants to put up stations in or near J. occupied areas and build a separate radio intelligence network. The Colonel wants my help persuading the Communists to let us use their underground agents to help set it up.

It is just before lunch and I am sitting alone at a large wood table in the mess hall. Chinese dishwashers are cleaning rice bowls and chopsticks. The air smells of rice porridge, steamed buns, pickled cabbage, and tea. The phonograph is playing Guy Lombardo's "Love, Love, Love," and the cooks are trying to sing along. I want to fling the record out the window.

I have not heard from Britka in four? Five weeks? Of course, I have not written, either. Who knows what will happen when this war ends. Some of the officers here are talking about starting businesses when they get back Stateside. Soda shop. Cleaning service. For me, home is here.

Wearing a sweater that Ai-ling knit for me. Wool is hard to come by, so I had an Army buddy back in Chungking send me some. All they had were gray and green. Better to blend in with the bushes, I guess.

Working now on translating project description for the O.S.S.'s radio plan. The Colonel said the plan is called "Yasmina-6." The Colonel has me meeting with the Communists every Monday and Thursday morning to brief them.

September 8, 1944

Dear Portia,

Take back everything I have said about Quentin. I regret having said any of it. I really miss him, and I want more than anything for him to return to Charlotte with me. We can buy a home in the old neighborhood, and he can get a job with daddy at the main office. Daddy's always looking for accountants, and I know that Quentin has bookkeeping training from his **Y.M.C.A.** days.

The day before I left, Quentin confronted me about Gaspar. He said he knew all along that I had had an affair. I asked him why he never said anything, and he said he was waiting for me to tell him.

Gaspar had been working on getting Red Cross supplies to the famine stricken provinces near Chungking. He had gone south to Hunan and found a large depot full of mosquito nets, rubbing alcohol, and medicines still packed in crates and stacked in standing water. The boxes of medicine had passed their expiration date. He was outraged. Ordinary Chinese were dying of malaria and infections, and this warehouse of supplies was going to waste. Quentin happened to be visiting the same city that day and ran into Gaspar. Unbeknownst to me, Gaspar told him everything.

When we first arrived in Chungking, Quentin was spending most of his time at a small Chinese Nationalist base near Sian. I visited him there once. There were no barracks for married people, so I slept on a cot in the back corner of the commissary. What struck me was the degree of privilege afforded to American soldiers. Outside the base was a chaotic, barbaric society overseen by a corrupt police force, similar to the one running things in Chungking. The base was a refuge from all of that, but Quentin spent very little time on base. The only time we spent together was dinner at the commissary. That was the first time I started to sense the widening gulf in our marriage. Now, I realize that it may have been there from the beginning.

I am not a fatalist, but I do believe things happen for a reason. I was meant to be with Quentin, and I need to find out how to make our marriage work. What I said earlier about not feeling romance in our marriage was bunk. Marriage isn't about romance. It's about partnership and compatibility. I said before that Quentin is a Wheaties man, and I think I need a Wheaties man in my life.

I'll have you know that before I left Chungking, I began taking National Geographic. It is a wonderful magazine, full of color photographs from around the world. I looked forward to getting it. I found solace in every issue, there was a group of people, be it a Sub-Saharan tribe, or a phalanx of Swiss mountain-yodelers, who was happy.

Yours Dearly,
Britka

The week after visiting with Ai-ling, a woman with Margaret Thatcher hair and a fitted red coat and matching red skirt appeared at Mr. Liege's door. Her lipstick was bright red and accentuated her tanned skin. She was carrying a Hermés bag on her shoulder and she held a brick-sized wireless phone.

"I've got to get rid of this thing," she said, referring to her telephone. She walked into the room and placed it squarely on the window sill. "Hello," she said, "I'm Marisa Thurmond do Poças. I am Vice President of marketing at Chevron."

I introduced myself and asked how I could help her.

"I'm sorry," she said, "I forgot to say that I know Quentin. We used to work together. He was my boss."

I asked where.

"We worked at Hancock Oil and Gas back in the late Fifties."

Then, I remembered Professor Mathieson saying Mr. Liege had worked for an oil company.

"In Brazil?" I asked.

"Yes, that's right," she said. "How is he?"

"Hard to say. The doctor thinks he'll be able to regain some or all of his speech, but the stroke left him paralyzed."

"Can he understand us?"

"I don't know. I talk to him occasionally."

"How dreadful. I'm so sorry things have turned out this way. I heard that his wife died recently. Did you know her?"

I told her I didn't.

"Britka was a remarkable woman. Intimidating to some, but we were good friends."

"What did you do at Hancock?" I asked.

"Believe it or not, I was his secretary. I worked for the company auditor for a short time, and when Quentin arrived, I was assigned to him because I spoke English."

"You're Brazilian?"

"Yes, you probably couldn't tell because I've spent a fortune getting rid of my accent."

"What did Mr. Liege do for Hancock?"

"He was assigned to audit. He was liaison between the in-house auditor and headquarters in Virginia. Quentin was very shy. He and I didn't talk much at first. When he found out that I went to school in the U.S., he opened up. His office was like a Chinese museum. He had dragon puppets, masks from Peking opera, Chinese swords, and long scrolls."

"How did you get to know his wife?" I asked

Marisa looked at me for a moment. "Do you mean socially?"

"Yes."

"After I got married. My husband was in charge of business development for Hancock. We dined with Quentin and Britka at the American Club."

"Are you still married?" I asked.

"No, I followed him back to Virginia and played the housewife for ten years. We didn't have kids, so it wasn't hard to leave once I made up my mind."

"I take it you kept in touch with Mr. Liege?"

"Yes, I did. He helped me a lot. When I was applying to business schools, he knew the dean of the School of Business Administration at Berkeley. I entered the first evening M.B.A. program back in 1972. By then, I was working at Chevron."

"You've been at Chevron the whole time?"

"Yes, it's hard to believe, I know, but persistence pays off. Now, I have a driver. I use that monstrosity to call him," she said pointing to the portable phone on the window sill.

I told her that Mr. Liege didn't have any living relatives to visit him.

"I will be happy to help in any way I can," she said. "Please let me know, will you?" She reached into her purse and pulled out a business card. "Here's my office number. My secretary answers it, but she's usually quick to get me urgent messages."

Sensing she was preparing to head out, I thanked her for stopping by.

"By the way," she said, "Quentin knows my ex-husband, Hen. They used to work together in Brazil. I'll make sure to tell him about Quentin."

September 12, 1944

Dear Portia,

We are stuck on a small island in the middle of the Atlantic and sleeping on metal roofs of houses next to the airfield. How we got here is worth noting. Last I wrote, we were in Calcutta. From there, we took a flying boat to Karachi. Then, we boarded a B-24 bomber to South Arabia. From there, we flew to Aden, then to Khartoum, and finally, Accra. For that part of the trip, we flew by day and stayed at hostels at night, but once we left Accra, out, over the Atlantic - now on a DC-3 - we switched to flying at night so as not to be spotted by the German Luftwaffe. After about six hours in the air, we landed here, and the pilot said one of the engine's pistons needed to be replaced. So, now we are killing time on this postage stamp in the middle of nowhere, waiting for parts to arrive by ship. They say it's going to take a week.

It's absolutely dreadful. There is no bar. The locals subsist on canned food shipped in from Portugal. The ocean is fantastically blue and pure, but it's too dangerous to swim in because of the undertow. The locals here say that they lose someone every year to the sea. I imagine this must be what Hell is like -- surrounded by lethal beauty.

I met a priest. His name is Father Mazotti. He is American, though his parents came from Sardinia. Father Mazotti is a patient man. He puts up with all manner of banter from any one of the seventeen travelers on this journey. I have told him my life story. He seemed to not mind.

I told him about growing up in Meyers Park, Charlotte. I told him about Grandpa being a member of the Whig Party and opposing the Republican Party's antislavery policies, and that after the Civil War he built a modest home and started our family furniture business. Daddy took over the family business and expanded the company in the Twenties, after he built the first permanent furniture exposition where buyers could come and see samples of everything our factory produced. Daddy also invested in new electrical lines to power mechanical lathes, circular saws, and table-sized planers.

I told the story about our best foreman, who lost his right hand when it got caught in a router. He had been hired by Grandpa and knew the business better than anyone. After the accident, Daddy built him a small, two-bedroom home where he could retire. Father Mazotti asked me if he continued working, and I couldn't lie: Daddy took him off the payroll. Daddy said he didn't want other workers to go to work every day with the image of failure. Father asked me if the foreman was a Negro. I said he was.

Father asked about my schooling, and I told him that at age seven, my parents sent me off to a parochial girl's school in Raleigh, where I was supposed to receive a "classical education," meaning The Bible, Latin, and "great literature," which meant really boring stuff. We weren't allowed to read The Odyssey or The Aeneid, because they were too racy. Can you believe it? I told him that I hid H.P. Lovecraft under my pillow and read it by flashlight after everyone had gone to sleep. I read the Canterbury Tales in the locker room during lunchtime while everyone else was finishing their meal. Father said that he remembered teaching at school where wayward students like me would be punished severely for reading subversive books. I told him that the nuns at my school were so outnumbered and overwhelmed that banned books were the least of their worries.

Father asked me if I had any siblings. I told him I didn't and that Daddy had wanted a boy. My parents had tried to have more children, but it wasn't meant to be. As such, Daddy treated me to boy-like activities such as fishing, car repair, horse racing, et cetera.

I am told that our next stop once we get going again will be Belem, which is somewhere in northern Brazil.

I'll be sure to write you when we get there!

September 16, 1944

My Dear Portia,

I said in my last letter that I was in Hell, but clearly I didn't know what Hell was, because now I am most definitely in Hell. Belem is sticky and hot and worse, believe it or not, than Chunking. It must be the Amazon. Other than the oppressive weather, the town is charming. I visited a large Portuguese cathedral, a playhouse built in the 1870s, and, of course, a local bar, where I tried a local drink with rum and something called "Cupuaçu." An old man hammered out a convincing rendition of "You Are My Sunshine" on the piano, and the whole bar sang along.

We are scheduled to leave for Trinidad in a few hours. From there, we will fly direct to Miami, and this ridiculously long adventure will nearly be over. In Miami, I will catch a train to Charlotte.

Much love,
Britka

Oh, Britka. You don't know how crazy it has been with the doctors and the experiments and the show they're playing on the set now. It's a horrible movie about the People's Liberation Army driving tanks into Tiananmen Square and firing on thousands of peaceful protesters. It's like Kent State all over, only this time they're using machine guns. Our son was in it, too. He stood in front of a tank convoy in the middle of Chang'An Avenue and stopped them dead in their tracks. I'm so proud of him.

Remember the Free Speech Movement in Berkeley, when I got hit on my leg by a tear gas canister? It's much worse. It's insanity. I can only guess that Mao felt threatened and he decided to use the military this time instead of the Red Guards, who were just kids pretending to be police.

I wouldn't be surprised if, later in the story, the Party leadership finally gets to the bottom of this, and Mao himself is tried by a kangaroo court and hanged in public. What a way to go, eh? Highly unusual for the standard propaganda coming out of Hsinhua News these days.

There is the matter of Ai-ling to discuss. It has been a very long time since we worked out our arrangement, and I have to confess that she showed up at our front door the other day. It was so swell to see her after all these years. We sat and drank Long Ching tea, just like old times. There's nothing left between us, if you're in any way concerned about that. What has it been -- forty-five years?

We talked about her life in Taiwan and the death of her husband many years back. I guess he had been a U-2 pilot flying out of Taipei and was shot down in the mid-Sixties. They never recovered the plane or the body.

To be honest, I had no idea she had gotten married.

She mentioned teaching here at Berkeley for a few years in the mid-Fifties, which was about the time that we were living in Brazil. I forgot to ask her how she managed to live in Berkeley while her husband was flying secret missions back in Taiwan. Maybe they had an "arrangement." Did he know about me, I wonder?

She mentioned Lars Mathieson and how he had just gotten a teaching position in the Chinese literature department while she was teaching Mandarin to returned veterans studying under the **G.I. Bill**. She asked after Lars and his wife. I told her that Lars' wife had passed away rather unexpectedly from Legionnaire's Disease awhile back. A freak infection that killed her during a weekend getaway with some of her friends from high school.

There is the matter of Marisa, which you know about as well. She is, of course, divorced and now a mucky-muck in one of the big oil companies. She has done well for herself. I am so very proud of her.

Finally, since I am in a talkative mood, there is the matter of Flannigan. I forgive you. Before we parted ways in Chungking, before the evacuation, you insisted your man was French. I knew all along it was Flannigan. He's a sly one, and I'm not surprised that you got caught up in his web.

If there's one thing I've learned, it's that life presents many surprises -- some of which seem to be explained only by fate. Flannigan appearing in Taoyuan was one of those. I truly believe he was destined to follow me to the end of the world. After Taoyuan, there was that whole business with Hen, who was friends with Flannigan.

The Loyalty Research Board's sole witness not only managed to track me down four thousand miles away in South America, but he got his buddy, Hen, to make life Hell. The audit at Hancock was Flaningan's way to nail me to the wall, finally.

Thank God Marisa married Hen and got him off of my case. I owe my life to her.

Not a day goes by now without me thinking about Allyn and Adele Ricketts and their ordeal after five years in Chinese prison. Were they brainwashed? The Birchers would like you to think so. Who in his right mind would come out of that and say he felt remorse for having spied on the

Chinese? No decent American would, right? Not unless he had been brainwashed.

It did seem a little odd that they had nothing bad to say about their captors, but maybe they had been treated well, all things being equal. I certainly am clear-eyed about my time in Taoyuan.

Some animals were more equal than others, to paraphrase Orwell. Mao knew that. He had any woman he wanted. If one pointed out the fact that Mao was married, it was off to the stockade.

The only one I really respected was Chou En-lai, although in the end, even Chou couldn't refuse to bow like a servant in return for five bushels of grain. Mao did it to everyone, even his most loyal deputies.

In history, there are few examples of officials standing their ground and surviving the aftermath. The early Chinese poet, Tao Yuanming, quit his government post and became a hermit because of the extent of government corruption he witnessed. He went on to be recognized as a famous writer in his own time.

Octavio Paz comes to mind as well. He quit his ambassadorship to India in 'Sixty-eight to protest his government's massacre of student demonstrators. He later received the Nobel Prize for poetry.

I'm no poet. I didn't win any prizes. My reputation was never rehabilitated. I was **Hai Rui** being dismissed from office, and my prison was the life I had remaining after the charlatans destroyed my career.

Orwell had it right in "Animal Farm" about Communism; his "1984" was heavy handed and overblown, and besides, it didn't come true. "Homage to Catalonia" was his best work because it captured so much raw experience from fighting for the losing, antifascist, side (there were multiple sides, I know).

How could anyone come out of that experience and still feel positive about Communism?

It's the Anti-Communism, though, that was really "Communist" in its insidiousness and ideological fervor. A "Crucible," where even your most trusted friends could turn out to be snitches and rat you out for nothing. There weren't many of us who refused to play that game. Unfortunately, we were the only ones who knew anything about Communism and gave a damn. Case in point: Vietnam! Yes, I marched in Ho-Chi Minh rallies. There was no one left *in Foggy Bottom who had a clue about Peking's relationship to Hanoi. The Vietnamese were fighting a nationalist war for sovereignty, just like the Chinese had twenty years before.*

*Old **Herbert Walker Bush**, Domino theorist, self proclaimed "China Hand," was no help. His time in Peking was spent worrying about resurfacing the embassy tennis court. He showed no understanding of the catastrophic effects the Cultural Revolution had on everyday Chinese. This, coming from the guy who later headed up the C.I.A.! Donovan would be rolling over in his grave.*

It was a crazy time punctuated by sandalwood and patchouli incense, Indian ponchos and groovy bell bottoms, avocado green and harvest gold. Barter fairs. Nudist camps. Finding oneself. Because Lord knows, we were all fairly lost back then.

My leather hat, and your polyester yarns, Britka. "I am not a crook," and our G.M. Pacer that refused to get out of second gear on cold mornings; highballs at six, and Chex mix in teak bowls; thermostat no higher than 68 degrees, and odd-even days at the Exxon on Ashby.

Who could have foreseen that only a few years later, Ronald McDonald would win the Democratic nomination? Talk about Invasion of the Bodysnatchers! How they could choose a turncoat like that truly boggles the mind. He would sell his mother out just to get the vote (then again, he didn't have much of a relationship with her. Wasn't he an orphan?). Republican Jimmy Carter didn't stand a chance after botching the Iran hostage rescue in the streets of Paris on a bright, sunny day in the middle of a snowstorm, and Ronnie just rolled over him like the Enola Gay.

It reminds me of Dave Brubeck's, "As Time Goes By," or that other one, "Take Three," where Sam tries to bang out a tune on the piano in a bar in Tangiers while Gene Kelly and Ginger Rodgers are dressed as women on the train to the Hotel del Coronado and kissing mercilessly in the rain, but we really know it's just a movie lot in Culver City, and the props guys are just outside the camera frame holding sprinklers and hoses to make it look like it's a torrential downpour.

*I knew it was time to retire from the Library when **Madame Sun Yat-sen** and Jiang Qing finally called me into their tribunal to talk to me* about my utterances. My mumblings, as it were. They told me I was not getting any better. That I should see a doctor.

I told them a thing or two. Their mismanagement and complete lack of regard for process was putting the entire collection in peril. Exhibit one: their much-heralded compromise to accommodate both forms of romanization in the card catalog. **Wade-Giles** for pre-Revolution material, and **Pinyin** for post-Revolution.

We know that Wade-Giles does a better job of capturing the real Mandarin pronunciation. Also, it's intuitive. Exhibit forty-three: "Chungking Chow Mein." Any child who can read knows what that is. Now, try it in Pinyin, "Chongqing Chao Mien." You get my point. Nobody can read that.

The insidious pact between those two estimable leaders of pulchritude and luminosity, Madames Sun and Jiang, wreaked havoc on library operations. Books go un-shelved. I have to make special trips down to the offsite storage site and manually write down book titles on scrap paper before I can figure out where they belong.

The splitting of libraries into two was even more egregious. Sure, Durant Hall was buckling under the weight of the growing collection. Sure, there was a split between the Taiwanese faculty and those from the Mainland. Sure, there were different ideas about how to migrate the card catalog online. We could have seized the opportunity and made a bold decision -- one of unification, not division.

Why replicate the schism that played out decades ago? A new, single Chinese Studies Library would have been visionary. Instead, we were cowards. Conformists. We loaded up the moving vans and trucked books and magazines three blocks down the hill to the basement of the Berkeley Extension Building on Fulton Street. Ignominious retreat! From the prestigious former Boalt Law School to a bomb shelter. The Taiwan faction won that battle.

I asked Ai-ling about Matsuda. I didn't want to bring up the pregnancy, but I really did want to know. She said that she had been in contact with him, and that he was retired and living outside of Tokyo. I told her that he and Tak had been close -- almost like brothers.

Tak followed him around like a minnow. I warned Tak to be careful, and he said he was, but I couldn't be there all the time. Tak seemed to be learning

Japanese from Matsuda, and Matsuda seemed to relish the chance to teach a young, handsome, college-educated man.

One could never tell which way Matsuda swung his bat. I had him pegged as a fairy until the day Ai-ling told me he was the father of her child. That news threw me for a loop. How could that be? Ai-ling said it just happened that way.

*I got her telegram. It said to meet her at the Shanghai **Long Bar**. It was midwinter. The heat was thick and violent. Coolies were loading sampans on the Bund. Their shirts were soaked through with sweat. It must have been a hundred degrees in the snow.*

We met in the VIP room at the Long Bar. Some mobsters were playing mahjong next to us and bantering in Shanghainese. She was wearing a lavender ch'i p'ao with a butterfly brooch. She had a shopping bag in her lap with the symbol of the Excelsior Hotel on it. She said it held a small handgun. I remember thinking that I had never seen her dressed in anything but the plain, cotton peasant uniforms worn in Taoyuan. Also, why the handgun? She wouldn't say.

She had come to Shanghai with an entourage. If the K.M.T. had found her, they would've shot her on the spot.

"When you return home, don't forget about me," she pleaded.

I told her I would never forget her.

She told me she was pregnant and that she was returning to Taoyuan.

She said that Matsuda was the father.

I said that was impossible.

She said that Tak was the father.

I said that was impossible.

*She said that **F.D.R.** was the father.*

I said that was impossible, because F.D.R. played for the other team.

She said that I was the father.

The problem with growing old is that nobody pays attention to me. I talk to myself, yes. Few people are able to engage in the sort of conversation I can have with myself. Metamucil is murder. It was designed by Nazi doctors. I was stopped up from the morphine. They put that garbage in my feeding tube. They made me get up and dance like a maniac. I can't even move my body and they made me do that. They won't listen! Their infernal experimentation with digestive aids is killing me. They're trying to kill me. I have not lost the need to pee. It's a relief to empty my bladder. Like right now. Ah, wait....wait........that's better. Good. Right. I try to watch the clock on the wall to keep track. It has been ninety-four minutes -- a new record for the record books and who's keeping records for this sort of thing?

9-16-44 (Sat) 11:20

Last night Tak and I were up late at Ai-ling's place listening to records, sipping cognac (Tak managed to get some, somehow), and talking about France. She said she studied art history in Tientsin.

Ai-ling has a strange penchant for dressing up. She asked Tak and me do a "tableau" with her. A tableau is a re-creation of a scene from a famous painting. We used one of her French textbooks as a guide. It had numerous black and white photographs of works from various museums, cathedrals and assorted private collections.

She opened two large steamer trunks and pulled out all manner of costume -- Arabic, Mongol, Persian. We tried on various outfits, and she hung fabric backdrops from the ceiling. Our first tableau was of her re-enacting the Ingres painting, "Joan of Arc at the Coronation of Charles VII." She wore breastplate armor, skirt, and hair pinned back in a pony tail. She held up a long staff with a medieval sort of flag on it. After more cognac and Tak nearly falling asleep, the tableaux got more interesting. Ai-ling shed her clothes to match the nude woman in Gérôme's "Slave Market" (Ai-ling nude, standing, Tak and I on either side, engaged in mock negotiation). Then, Manet's "Le Déjeuner sur l'herbe" (again, Ai-ling nude, seated; Tak and I engaged in mock discussion).

Tak and I left her place well past midnight. Tak was so sleepy that I had to hold his arm over my shoulder. The brisk walk home with stars overhead and dead silence awakened me until we got back to our respective beds. Came across remnant from Peking childhood stuffed into my Chinese dictionary.

Faded photograph of my secondary school teacher, Mr. Treewiler. It must be from '24 or '25. He came from Athens, Georgia and had gone native soon after arriving in China. He wore a black skullcap of the Manchu scholars and his hair tied in back.

God help him, wherever he may be right now.

Burly said that some of the men had started a "Jilted G.I." club. Burly said he was the latest addition. He said they sat in the corner of the mess hall and whined about their lost loves.

I ate breakfast with the Colonel. He told me about a new arrival, named Flannigan. He pointed to him sitting two tables away.

When Flannigan finished breakfast, he came by to say hello to the Colonel. Flannigan was tall and heavyset, like a linebacker. His uniform was pressed like a dinner napkin. He handed me some back issues of Yank Magazine. I do not read Yank Magazine, but I accepted them from him.

"You gotta check out Frances Vorne," he said. "A real looker."

The Colonel was interested and opened it up to the centerfold. There was a large photo of her. "You know, the Royal Air Force wants to put her mug on a bomber," the Colonel said.

Flannigan laughed high and repeatedly, like a hyena.

"Hey, Colonel," he said, "no disrespect, but can a soldier get a plate of bacon and eggs around here? This pigeon food doesn't really cut it." He was pointing to his rice bowl and half-eaten pork *bao*.

"Are you kidding?" the Colonel said. "This is manna from heaven. You haven't seen real pigeon food yet, but you will. I guarantee it."

The Colonel excused himself and left me alone with Flannigan.

Flannigan said he wanted to talk shop. He said that he wanted to know how the Yasmina-6 plan was coming along.

I told him it was going fine.

Flannigan said he wanted to get a meeting with Mao Tse-tung. I told him I had met Mao only once so far. Flannigan was more likely to get a meeting with a deputy.

Flannigan said it had to be Mao.

I told him I was meeting twice a week with a planning group to work through the details and that asking to meet with Mao was akin to throwing a wrench into a spinning propeller. Better to work up the chain of command, I said.

Army, Navy, State Dept., O.S.S. -- they all want to be a part of what is happening here, but their selfish interests contrast with their complete ignorance about how things work here. If they bothered to pay attention, they would see that it is the rags-for-boots foot soldiers and shit-shoveling donkey cart drivers who make things happen.

OFFICIAL REPORT OF PROCEEDINGS

Before the

Loyalty Research Board

of the

U.S. State Department

Docket No. 12-334

In the matter of.

John Quentin Liege

Place. Washington, D.C.

Date. Tuesday, March 14, 1951

Paxwell Reporting Company

224 Ninth Street, N.W.,

Washington, D.C.

Official Reporters

STATEMENT OF JOHN QUENTIN LIEGE, FOREIGN
SERVICE OFFICER OF THE UNITED STATES

Questioner. Take a seat, sir. Give us your full name.

Mr. Liege. John Quentin Liege.

Questioner. What is your present occupation?

Mr. Liege. I am a Foreign Service officer of the United States.

Questioner. Please tell us, what is your present address?

Mr. Liege. Twenty-two forty-six Walnut Avenue, Berkeley, California.

Questioner. How long have you been in the service of the State Department?

Mr. Liege. I joined in 1932.

Questioner. Now, just for the record, you willingly surrendered your right to have counsel present. Is that correct?

Mr. Liege. Yes, that is correct.

[pages 3-43 have been redacted for national security]

Questioner. For the sake of fairness to other folks being investigated, I have to ask you the following questions. Are you, or have you ever been, a member of the Communist Party?

Mr. Liege. No, I have never been a member of the Communist Party.

Questioner. Please tell us your definition of "Communist."

Mr. Liege. My own definition is it is someone who follows the teachings of Marx. Someone who willingly submits himself to the rule of the

Communist Party at the expense of his own personal interests.

Questioner. Are you, or have you ever been, an agent of the Soviet Union?

Mr. Liege. No. I have never been an agent of the Soviet Union.

Questioner. What does the term "Soviet Agent" mean to you?

Mr. Liege. I think it is worth distinguishing a Communist from a Soviet Agent. They are not the same. A Japanese Communist may be a nationalist and very anti-Soviet. A Soviet agent is someone who is willing to sacrifice his loyalty to his country, his family, and his religion for the sake of the Soviet Union.

9-18-44 (Mon) 13:35

Sleepy after lunch, so I took short nap on the *k'ang*. Most of the village is doing the same around this time, so good luck trying to get anything done.

The Communists have given us good intelligence on J. troop movements in Kiangsu and Shantung. I am unclear on the need for Yasmina-6, when the Communists have a working intelligence network already.

When I saw Ai-ling, I told her about Flannigan's request for Mao meeting. She said it was impossible.

This afternoon, our weekly air shipment arrived from Kunming. Today's shipment had B1 MM Mortar rounds for the 8th Route Army. So now it is official: we are arming both the Communists and the Nationalists. They are both biding their time until the war ends so they can fight each other. If they would just stop fighting each other and fight the Japanese, for God sakes.

The mess hall this morning was littered with recent issues of Hump Express, **India Burma Theater** Roundup, Stars and Stripes, China Edition, and China Weekly.

All delightful reading for those suffering from constipation.

Flannigan meeting is confirmed for today at 15:00 with a deputy from General Chu Teh's office. Flannigan is curiously scarce.

Tak said that he took Flannigan on a tour of the J. P.O.W. camp. Flannigan remarked that he was "extremely underwhelmed." Flannigan said that the whole camp was either a glaring security risk, or it was a front for J. military spies. The fact that some of the P.O.W.'s can come and go freely really annoyed Flannigan.

Flannigan told Tak not to talk with any of the J. P.O.W.s or camp leaders (Shiba and Matsuda).

Flannigan meeting debrief with Ai-ling and other Chinese interpreter in central meeting hall. Chu Teh's deputy showed large map of Communist areas including Shensi-Kansu-Ningsia and Shansi-Suiyuan, all the way down to Hwaipai and Northern Kiangsu. The entire meeting was a waste. Flannigan talked down to everyone. He demanded to know names and locations of all of the Communist field agents.

The Chinese laughed.

What an idiot.

The meeting ended with Flannigan accusing the Communists of sabotage.

Flannigan called Ai-ling a "dumb Dora."

Later, after getting the debriefing from Ai-ling, I warned Flannigan that if he was not careful, Ai-ling could shut down any cooperation with us in a split second.

"You seem to be carrying a torch for her," he said. "Do you and her have something going on the side?"

I told him to mind his own business. I said that if he had another meeting like the one today, the Yasmina-6 plan would most likely be dead in the water.

Flannigan said he didn't give a rat's ass about protocol or paying respects to the right people.

Then, he said he was leaving the next day and would return in a few weeks.

Questioner. Are you opposed to individual liberty, free enterprise and Democracy?

Mr. Liege. No.

Questioner. Are you in favor of imperialism and totalitarianism?

Mr. Liege. No.

Questioner. I want to know about your specific duties during your time in China, specifically while you were assigned to the U.S. Army.

Mr. Liege. Before my assignment to the U.S. Army, I was a political officer, which meant that I provided background information on the very complex Chinese political situation. I served as intermediary between the embassy, the Army, and various Chinese government officials. I did the same sort of work for General Stilwell. I was a junior member of his staff, and I very rarely saw him.

10-22-44 (Sun) 14:40

General Stilwell has been recalled. Chiang Kai-shek finally got rid of him.

God help us.

Colonel Hathaway called us into his office to tell us that he, too, had been recalled. Colonel Hathaway thanked us for the good work and said he would be leaving in early December. His replacement has already arrived.

The disease is spreading.

My days have been full with coordinating General Chu Teh's requirements and forwarding them onto Theater Command in Ramgarh. More about that later. Also spending time gathering intelligence from the Communist-controlled areas to the East on J. troop movements, weather, etc., and helping Burly with his radio transmissions to Chungking.

Ai-ling went to Chungking to interpret for elder Communist representative Tung Pi-wu, who is in discussions with Ambassador Huyguens over a possible joint power-sharing arrangement with Chiang Kai-shek and the Nationalists.

Good luck with that, Ambassador.

Word is going around that Colonel Hathaway was recalled because he was too close to Communists and was unable to put his foot down. Colonel Hathaway's replacement speaks no Chinese. He served previously as a military attaché to the British in Ramgarh, India. Before the war, he was a bean counter for Standard Oil in San Francisco. The new colonel is in his mid-fifties, carries an inner tube of a belly, and has thin combed back hair parted down the left side. He has his laundry done by Chinese and expects the same here.

I did not have the heart to tell him that the Communists do not do other people's laundry.

The colonel's name is "McKesson." His arrival was greeted by usual Communist song and dance. Festivities were held in the large meeting hall. A peasant troupe did renditions of "Songs of Unity" and "Crossing Over The Hill." Soldiers did fencing and jujutsu; dancers did "Capturing the Loach" and "Bamboo Hat Dance." The final performance was a play called "Superior Private Shimada."

Colonel McKesson was visibly bored. I have to say, that, seeing the performance through the Colonel's eyes, I would have been bored as well. The whole thing was heavy on propaganda. The scene lightened up a bit at the "after party," when some of the Chinese wives began dancing the "Beer Barrel Polka," which was played on a hand drum, an *er-hu* (two-stringed violin), recorder, and accordion.

Tak was in the audience and very aware of change in tone and sensibility with the new Colonel's arrival. Tak is very political that way. His advice was to be careful about what I write and to make sure to mention bad things about Taoyuan as much as good

76

things. The China we see in Taoyuan, "New China," does not exist anywhere else, and Washington refuses to believe any of it.

Later, I went to the J. P.O.W. camp and spoke with Matsuda. He said that his friends back in Japan were either in jail or had been killed by the military police. All of his friends were members of the Japanese Communist Party.

Matsuda could be potentially helpful in providing a sanity check on J. troop intelligence coming in from the Chinese, but when I mentioned it to Colonel McKesson, he shot it down. He told me that he wanted the entire PAX Team to cease all contact with the J. P.O.W. camp unless approved by him. He said that the likelihood of J. spies within the vicinity of the PAX Team was too high a risk. He must have spoken with Flannigan.

Lost opportunity?

Questioner. I'm curious about one thing, and that is, your dispatches during your time with the PAX Mission at Taoyuan. I have read through a great number of them, nowhere did I see mentioned how the Communists were trying to sway the United States' position vis-á-vis Chiang Kai-shek and the Kuomintang. It seems you are sympathetic to the Communists. In one report, you refer to corruption amongst Kuomintang officers, and how soldiers routinely stole rice and livestock at gunpoint from villagers.

Mr. Liege. That is what I observed.

Questioner. I have met the great General
Chiang, and he doesn't strike me as the sort
of man who would tolerate corruption in his
ranks.

Mr. Liege. While I was in Taoyuan, I heard
reports from refugees from nearby villages who
had escaped during K.M.T. raids. Rape was
common.

Questioner. [coughs] When you say, "heard,"
who did you hear this from?

Mr. Liege. Well, of course I didn't personally
witness...

Questioner. I gathered as much. What about the
other Americans stationed there? Were they at
all aware of what you described? It seems you
were the only American observer there to
mention it.

Mr. Liege. I am unable to speak for the
others. I did interview a young woman. She had
escaped from a village that had been taken
over by Kuomintang troops.

Questioner. How can you be sure she wasn't making it up? How can you be sure she wasn't told to say what she said to you? Told, perhaps, by someone in the Communist Party?

Mr. Liege. I received independent verification from another field officer, an American, who had been to that village soon after the raid.

Questioner. What was this officer's name?

Mr. Liege. I don't remember, but I also heard eyewitness accounts from the Japanese P.O.W.s.

Questioner. The Japs? Not just Japs, but Japs being held prisoner by the Communist Chinese? Don't you think they have a credibility problem?

Mr. Liege. Not these Japanese. No, I do not.

Questioner. [chuckling] No? What makes you say that?

Mr. Liege. Not all the Japanese P.O.W.s had
converted to the Communists' thinking. There
was genuine dissent among the Japanese troops.

Questioner. Dissent, you say? Did you consider
that might have been an act to get you to
believe them even more?

Mr. Liege. No, I do not think that was the
case.

Questioner. Let's look at this another way.
The Japs -- they were known for their savagery
to the Chinese. There are plenty of examples.
Isn't it possible that some of those in the
P.O.W. camp had indulged in some fairly
abhorrent practices? The idea that the K.M.T.
was doing the same -- did that somehow make
their own abhorrent behavior more tolerable?

Mr. Liege. The Nationalists and the Communists
were both capable of incredible savagery.
There was a war going on. I'm not trying to
justify it in any way, but it's important to
understand the historical context. There were
all types in the P.O.W. camp. Some of the
Japanese were converted Marxists. Some were
illiterate farm boys who still believed that
the Emperor had descended from the sun.

Questioner. I think the questionable
motivations of the supposed witnesses, along
with the lack of hard evidence, points,
unfortunately, to one of two conclusions.
Either you were a fool, or you were complicit
in furthering the pro-Communist viewpoint and
anti-K.M.T. propaganda through official and
top-secret diplomatic channels.

Mr. Liege. I don't think you are getting the
whole picture.

Questioner. Tell me, what am I missing?

Mr. Liege. The Chinese Communists were very
skillful with their use of united front
tactics and guerrilla warfare. They had a
limited supply of weapons and food, and yet
they were rapidly expanding their sphere of
influence behind Japanese lines.

They were able to win over local peasants
because they treated them better and
demonstrated success, in contrast to the
Central (Nationalist Kuomintang) Government.

12-19-44 (Tue) 18:45

I returned from the neighboring village barely able to see the road. It had started snowing, and the flurries made it difficult to see clearly. I came back to my quarters to find Burly collapsed on the *k'ang*. The air was thick with smoke, and my eyes were burning. I covered my face with a handkerchief and ran over to the *k'ang* to rouse Burly, but he did not budge. I went to the charcoal brazier underneath the *k'ang* and grabbed the iron pot with oven mitts and lugged it outside and tossed onto the ground. The pot sizzled and steamed up in the snow. I ran over to housekeeper's quarters to get him to help me lift Burly and take him outside. By then, the snow had stopped and ground was wet and mixed with dirt and mud. The housekeeper told me to run to the hospital while he tried to revive Burly. I came back with a Chinese doctor and medical kit. The doctor pulled off Burly's shirt and splashed alcohol over his chest. He rubbed snow on his face. Thank God Burly came to and began coughing.

Questioner. What was the purpose of the PAX Mission?

Mr. Liege. Originally conceived, it was an observer mission as well as a forward base for recovering downed American pilots. The Communist areas were increasingly important to us because they bridged the gap between Nationalist controlled areas and the Japanese continental base in Manchuria. The Japanese

had communication lines all down the coast,
but inland, in Taoyuan, was nearly
inaccessible. As we established more B-29
bomber bases in the central part of China,
Taoyuan became an important central location
from which to coordinate various airstrikes
that passed directly over Communist controlled
territory. We also collected and forwarded on
to C.B.I. [China Burma India] Headquarters
actionable intelligence on Japanese positions
as well as weather reports from the China Sea.

Questioner. Did you conceive of this secret
mission?

Mr. Liege. There was nothing secret about it.
I had instructions from the U.S. Army to
assist in negotiations with Chiang Kai-shek's
staff to obtain permission to set up an
observer station in Taoyuan. After consulting
with the embassy, the Army issued orders for
me to accompany a group of intelligence
officers to Taoyuan to collect information on
the Chinese Communists. The PAX Mission was
not my idea, but I did help get it off the
ground.

Ai-ling returned from Chungking today. Her hair was shorter. A little too short, in my opinion. She said she was too busy to have lunch. I went back to my quarters and played Satie's "Je Te Veux" on Burly's wind-up **Victrola**. It is a recording from the Paris Philharmonic from 1932. I'm borrowing the record from her.

More on Mao meeting the other day. His Chinese is thin-sounding and almost lisp-y-provincial. Chou En-lai is certainly easier to understand. Mao is a big man -- nearly six feet tall, and he towers over the other Communists.

Our meeting this time was just us. No interpreter. Strictly unofficial. Official meetings are held between the same or similar rank.

Mao started off distinguishing between two words. Both mean "power." They are *ch'üan-li* (權力) and *shih-li* (勢力). Mao said the Americans need to learn and appreciate the difference. We spend too much time working with the *ch'üan-li* (formal authority, written laws) and not enough on the *shih-li* (informal authority, influence of personality). The Nationalists have *ch'üan-li* -- the ministries, the legislative, etc., but have lost claims to the informal. Chinese respond to *shih-li*, he said, and we Americans should pay more attention to it.

Then, Mao came to the real reason for the meeting. He said that since Colonel McKesson's arrival, the PAX Team's relationship with the Communists was thinning, just like my hair, Mao joked. Word had gotten out to the Chinese about McKesson's orders: No discussion of American aid to "unapproved political parties," meaning the Communist Party.

Mao asked me the meaning of that, and I had no good answer, other than Colonel McKesson was likely just following orders from the guys above.

Mao said that the People's Militia and field agents were still rescuing downed American pilots, still providing daily intelligence to us, and still sending daily weather reports to us, so why change?

I was speechless. Mao did not know the half of it. McKesson was operating on a different planet, compared to Colonel Hathaway, when it came to dealing with the Communists. When he first arrived, he brought with him a JAN-P-104 crate of Pro-kits and condoms for us Americans. Colonel McKesson said that a soldier should always be prepared.

Burly asked if the Colonel brought any women with him. The Colonel did not understand the joke. No American here, save for me, is sleeping with the Chinese. It's just not done.

Another example: Colonel McKesson brought with him a Winchester Model 12 pump action shotgun for pheasant hunting. There are no pheasants here, but he insists on going pheasant hunting every Friday evening.

Questioner. Tell me about your relationship with Mao Tse-tung.

Mr. Liege. When we arrived in Taoyuan, it was an open door. We could stop by any time to chat.

Questioner. How often did you meet with Mao?

Mr. Liege. I can't really say. I'd see him at dinner quite often. One time I got to interview him for eight hours straight.

Questioner. So you would characterize your relationship with Mao as friendly?

Mr. Liege. Yes, you could say that. Although that was during what I call the "honeymoon" period.

Questioner. Please explain.

Mr. Liege. When we first got there, there was a strong sense of optimism among the Communists. They were certain the Japanese were going to be defeated, and they were certain they were going to have a role to play in the new Chinese government.

Questioner. You believed that?

Mr. Liege. I didn't believe either way. I was an observer. I wasn't paid to believe anything. I wrote about what I saw.

Questioner. So, what happened after the honeymoon period?

Mr. Liege. Well, things changed.

Questioner. Such as?

Mr. Liege. Colonel Hathaway was recalled. His replacement, Colonel McKesson managed to alienate the Communists almost entirely from the get-go. Then, there was the visit by Ambassador Huyguens.

12-22-44 (Fri) 12:40

I reread a letter from Britka from two months ago. I searched and searched for more than just the quotidian, but no luck. I knew that Cal football tied USC 6-all. I read it in C.B.I. Roundup.

The last C-47 before Christmas comes tomorrow. Possibility of another letter?

Per Colonel McKesson's request, here is my first draft at a memo summarizing my meeting with Mao.

President Roosevelt's plan for China was to fund the Nationalists insofar as they would keep the J. Army sufficiently engaged. Great idea in theory, but Chiang Kai-shek is relying on the US to defeat Japan. Almost no US troops are here in China, and Chiang is saving his troops for a different war.

General Stilwell was the best we had -- he spoke Chinese and knew Chiang better than anyone else. While Stilwell was hacking vines with his bare hands on the Burma Road, Chiang was sipping his tea on his Chungking veranda. Meanwhile, peasants were starving in the countryside. Stilwell was recalled to

Washington because he fought Chiang on the waiting game. Chiang keeps stockpiling our Lend-Lease materiel while Madame Chiang is back in Washington seducing Republicans to approve even more aid for "poor China."

Both sides are playing the waiting game. Secondhand reports say that the Communists have made deals with warlords, and, in some cases, are in a de-facto *detente* with J. Army brigades. This could be why the Communists are dead set against the Yasmina-6 plan. They do not want us finding out what is really going on in J. occupied territories.

I must say, though, that the main difference between the Nationalists and the Communists is the latter are truly living up to their promises in the villages. The Nationalists are starved and corrupt and they resort to stealing. The Communists are actively reducing land rents from 50 pct. crop yield to 15 pct. The Communists make themselves accountable to the villagers.

Mao says he is not pushing for Socialism, because the average Chinese person is not ready for that. More important than Socialism is preventing disease and reforming the landlord system. This is what he calls the "New China."

[the following testimony has been redacted]

xxxxxxxx+++++++!!!!!%%%%%%%%%%%%%%%%%%%%%%%%%%%%
%%%%%%

$$$$$$
$&&&&&&&&(*********(((($#################
##

###########$$$$$$$$$$$$$$
$**************************

######@@@@@@@@@@@@@@

Mr. Liege. Ambassador Huyguens made a trip to London, where he spoke with the Foreign Office. He stated categorically that the Communists were of no importance and that if they ever caused trouble, the Kuomintang would have no trouble taking care of them. Clearly he was wrong.

Questioner. Did this incident make you angry?

Mr. Liege. No, not angry. I felt the statement was inaccurate.

Questioner. So, in response to the ambassador's communication with the British Foreign Office, which, by the way, was not made available to you, was it? Either way, in response you wrote a memorandum?

Mr. Liege. Yes, I did.

Questioner. A rather scathing memorandum. Very critical of the American chain of command. Please enter into the record Exhibit #342565, a fourteen page memorandum typed on foolscap,

single spaced, entitled "Change In Communists'
Attitudes Since Colonel Hathaway's Departure."

< EXCERPT >

RE: Change In Communists' Attitudes Since
Colonel Hathaway's Departure

There can be no denying that relations with
the Communists here have deteriorated to the
point where we are making a mockery of the
policy set out last year by General Stilwell.
Since Colonel Hathaway's replacement, we have
been ordered to cease all communications with
the Communists -- a task which is nearly
impossible. Taoyuan is their headquarters, and
we owe our survival here to their goodwill and
the use of their airstrip for our weekly air
delivery from Chungking. In spite of this,
their cooperative spirit towards us remains
unchanged: we still receive intelligence on
Japanese troop movements in occupied
territories, and we continue to get support
whenever American pilots are shot down behind
enemy lines. Nevertheless, because of Colonel
McKesson's change in policy, I have been told
by my Chinese counterparts that the Communists
no longer recognize the mission as an official
outpost of the US Army. To complicate matters
further, I have been summoned directly by Mao
Tse-tung and General Chu Teh for consultations
without any notification being given to
Colonel McKesson. In their mind, he is no
longer the senior commanding officer of the
PAX mission. Whenever I bring up the issue of

90

going through the proper chain of command, Mao and Chu brush it aside and do not want to be bothered.

Questioner. Is it true that you feel that the Chinese Communists are democrats, like us here in the United States?

Mr. Liege. Absolutely not. I never said they were democrats. I said they were democratic in their dealings. If you read my subsequent memorandum, you would have examples of this, which I spelled out in great detail. As such, I object to the piecemeal treatment of my reports in this hearing.

Questioner. Objection? What sort of objection?

Mr. Liege. I object to the entering of a single report into the official record. I insist that all of my reports should be entered into the record.

Questioner. I don't think that's practical, Mr. Liege. Some of your reports are still classified.

12-24-44 (Sun) 17:00

Well, merry bloody Christmas (eve). The bluenose Colonel (he starches his shirts) walks around with his **pointee-talkee board** with large pictures on it in hopes of communicating with the Chinese. He refuses interpreters. Even refused Ai-ling! "Just don't trust them slopes," he said. Imagine this pudgy, snooty foreign devil trying to talk politics with Mao by pointing to a grade-school level phrasebook issued to US Army Air Force pilots so they can communicate with locals on the ground. He refers to Chiang Kai-shek as "Shanker Jack." Just peachy.

The C-47 came today and no letter from Britka.

The sun has disappeared behind a large cloud bank, and shadows blanket houses down in the valley. The river looks blue-black, and is overseen by giant, gray hills on either side. The wind has picked up and whips through the valley like an angry god. Dust leaks through the rice paper window. I wake every morning with a thin layer of dust on my face every morning. I'm considering sleeping with a towel over my head.

My left rear molar is hurting now. That makes three teeth since arriving. 1st and 2nd ones yanked by a Communist doc who says I need gum surgery, and he is unable to do it. "Pyorrhea," is what the dictionary translates the Chinese 膿溢. Sounds like "diarrhea." The Listerine toothpaste on my bookshelf sits unopened. It hurts too much to brush. I will have to brave the cold and get more painkiller from the next village up. Almost out of tobacco too. I'm sucking on stale tea leaves instead.

Questioner. I'd like to talk now about the radios.

Mr. Liege. Radios?

Questioner. Yes, in February 1945, the O.S.S. arranged for the shipment of ten tons of radio equipment to be delivered to the American observer station in Taoyuan, A.K.A. PAX Mission, for a program called 'Yasmina-6.' The entire shipment later went missing.

Mr. Liege. A large amount of radio equipment did arrive.

Questioner. According to a report filed by "Witness X" -- we can't use his real name, and the record shall reflect that -- "February 2, 1945, radio equipment missing. Suspect that Communists stole them overnight. Confronted our liaison, Jack Quentin Liege. He denies any and all knowledge. Says bandits may have taken it."

Mr. Liege. That report is wrong. The radios never went missing. Besides, the radios didn't even arrive for another six days after the date of that report.

12-27-44 (Wed) 5:30

I left Taoyuan last night and woke up this a.m. in Army barracks in Kunming for an early flight over "the Hump," which is the treacherous leg between China and India. That flight requires oxygen masks. I wrap myself up in several wool blankets and I am still shivering.

My final destination is an undisclosed training center in the hills of Virginia.

Christmas in Taoyuan was celebrated with the Colonel bringing a case of Royal Club whiskey, specially flown in from India. Burly was a no-show and said he was going to sleep through it.

True to his word, Flannigan returned with special orders from General Wedemeyer assigning me to Flannigan's O.S.S. unit. O.S.S. is the "Office of Strategic Services," otherwise known as the "Obstinate, Stupid, Sad-sacks." Flannigan was pleased as a bumble bee on a picnic bench. Colonel McKesson said, bottom line, even though I work for the State Department, my assignment to General Stilwell (before he was recalled) made me part of the military chain of command. I have no choice. Besides, the O.S.S. is in need of a language expert on the ground in Taoyuan to coordinate Yasmina-6. So, now I have two roles - State Department political affairs AND O.S.S. lackey. My first O.S.S. assignment was to travel to Virginia for proper training. Hence, flight to Kunming. No time to tell Ai-ling. I am not allowed to tell anyone where I am going. Ditto for Britka. I will try to see if I can pass through California, though, on my way back to China.

Still no letter.

Questioner. Describe the type of radios in the shipment.

Mr. Liege. I have a right to know the identity of "Witness X."

Questioner. Unfortunately, we are not at liberty to disclose that information. We don't even know his identity.

Mr. Liege. So it's a he?

Questioner. I'm sorry, I did not mean to imply the sex of "Witness X."

Mr. Liege. Is it Flannigan?

12-31-44 (Sun) 02:30, "Area Zulu"

Happy New Year's Eve from an undisclosed location somewhere in the forested hills of Virginia. Snow is on the ground. It's dead quiet outside. The wood cabin is heated by a wood stove. The snow keeps falling outside in the dark.

95

Almost out of black tar painkiller and the toothache is threatening to return. Maybe there are cloves in the commissary?

This morning, the rest of the students arrived. They're all Chinese and Korean trainees who have come to learn how to use O.S.S. radio equipment and code books. I spoke with some of the Chinese guys. They are all Nationalists from **Tai Li's Secret Police**, but seem to be decent folks.

The radio stuff is new to some of them, while others have radio backgrounds, but the O.S.S. procedures are confusing. One student is unable to stay awake. The class is entirely in English. The O.S.S. brought only one Chinese and one Korean interpreter. Both are treated like slaves. Their rest breaks are only two ten-minute spots in an eight hour day. No time for lunch.

We were introduced to the new **SSR-5** and **SST-5** paired radio set. Very slick, battery operated and portable. It is compatible with 3 types of Army batteries (BA-48, 1048/U and 220/U). We also received hands-on training with a different set, dubbed "Buttercup" and "Myra." "Buttercup" is a portable transceiver with collapsable dipole antenna, small enough to fit inside an overcoat. The Buttercup operator connects a small set of plastic earphones, puts them in his ear, and speaks into a mic built into the unit, which runs on small batteries and weighs around four pounds. "Myra" is much larger and is installed in the back of a C-47 and flown overhead to capture all the "Buttercup" transmissions on reel-to-reel tape. Our instructor says that **Chennault's** boys down in Kunming are already field testing it. The plan is to deploy the same thing with O.S.S. field agents north of Taoyuan.

1-4-45 (Thu) 22:10

Suffered through a grueling, three hour coding test with a Chinese version of the "One Time Pad," and barely passed. A One Time Pad looks like a word puzzle of letters grouped together in rows of six, with eight columns across the top. Each pad is an encryption key used just once for encoding and decoding messages. After that, you destroy the key. Burning it in the fireplace is not good enough.

The Chinese version uses numbers assigned to different Chinese characters. The encoded message has only a group of numbers. Each character's number contains a page number, a column number, and a line number. As an example, the Chinese character for "mountain" could be encoded as "2315" on a particular One Time Pad. It would mean page 23, column 1, line 5.

My Chinese counterparts learned much faster than I did and passed with flying colors.

[the following testimony has been redacted]

$$$$$$*************************$$$$$
$*****(((((($#######$$$$$$$$$*******$$$$$$$
$*******$&&&&&&&&(****###############

###########$$$$$$$$$$$$$$$$*********

$$$

###########$$$$$$$$$$$$$$$$*********###########
$$$$$$$$$$$$$$$$*********###########$$$$$$$$$$$$
$$$$***********###########$$$$$$$$$$$$$$
$*********

[end of redacted testimony]

Mr. Liege. I believe that if there is evidence against me, I have a right to see it.

Questioner. In a court of law, yes, you are correct. This is not a court of law. This is a hearing by a board selected by the Department of State to determine if any of its officers, in the course of carrying out their duties, acted in any way that was contrary to the beliefs of the United States Government.

Mr. Liege. You are asking me about an assignment from the O.S.S. That is outside the purview of the State Department.

Questioner. Just answer the question.

Mr. Liege. What I remember was a mix of various radio transceivers - SSTR models, mostly.

Questioner. Please explain what they do.

Mr. Liege. Well, take for instance the SSTR model I am referring to. It comes with a paired transmitter and receiver. The larger receiver unit is installed in the back of an aircraft. The transmitter is a handheld.

Agents on the ground use it to transmit a
signal to aircraft overhead.

Questioner. Now, when you say it is
"handheld," does that mean that someone could
walk off with it without being noticed?

Mr. Liege. Yes, I suppose so. There were quite
a few of those units, as well as the larger
receiver units, which were too heavy for one
person to carry off.

Questioner. When you say, "Quite a few," how
many were there?

Mr. Liege. I don't remember. Several crates.

Questioner. I see. Is it possible that a group
of bandits could have made off with the whole
shipment?

Mr. Liege. No.

Questioner. Why?

Mr. Liege. Because, the shipment came in five aircraft. It took ten men all night to unload the crates and move them to storage in the caves.

Questioner. If it took a whole night, then I suppose it is possible that over the period of a night--another night that is--bandits could have made off with the entire lot. Do you think that could have happened?

Mr. Liege. I don't know.

1-21-45 (Sun) 13:45, Ramgarh, India

Made it back in one piece from a week-long stay in Berkeley, and I resolved to make things work with Britka. The past is not important, and soon the War will be over. She is prepared to move back to China or any other location the State Department assigns me. My flight over the Hump is scheduled tomorrow at 06:30 a.m.

1-23-45 (Tue) 11:05 Taoyuan

I arrived in **C-54** early this a.m. and touched down just after 09:30. Tak met me at the airstrip and said he needed to speak to me immediately. Apparently, the situation with Colonel McKesson and the Communists has worsened. PAX Team members are now referring to the Chinese as "Reds." Some are openly arguing with the Chinese over capitalism. This was caused by an article in Reader's Digest that Colonel McKesson passed around.

The men are also getting drunk more now.

Tak said that when he went to Colonel McKesson's office, h[e]
was unavailable. Tak said it is harder to get reports from hi[s]
Chinese counterparts.

I told Tak that we have to make it work. It is hard to avoid the
simple fact that we depend on the Communists for everything.

After my meeting with Tak, I went to see the Colonel. When I
arrived there, the sergeant said that the Colonel "was presently
indisposed." I asked the sergeant if that meant pheasant hunting.
No response.

Questioner. All right. We will come back to
this later. Now, it has recently come to our
attention that you fathered a child during
your time there.

Mr. Liege. That is untrue.

Questioner. Did you have a relationship with
one of the translators there?

Mr. Liege. I fail to see what that has to do
with radios.

Questioner. Please, Mr. Liege, answer the
question.

Yes, I did.

. With a translator?

e. She was an interpreter.

oner. Was her name "Ai-ling Chang?"

Liege. No. Her name was "Sun."

stioner. Ai-ling Sun?

r. Liege. Yes, that is correct.

Questioner. Do you have any reason to believe you are not the father of her child?

Mr. Liege. [laughs] Do you mean to say do I have any reason to believe I am the father of the child?

Questioner. No. Please listen carefully to the question. Do you have any reason to believe

you are not, I repeat, not, the father of the
child?

Mr. Liege. Yes, I have reason to believe I am
not the father. The last time we met, she told
me I was not the father, and that the father
was a Japanese P.O.W.

Questioner. You believed her?

Mr. Liege. Yes.

Questioner. How do you know she was telling
the truth?

Mr. Liege. I don't see why she would lie.

1-23-45 (Tue) 20:30

One of the Communist liaison officers came by my quarters
after lunch and said that General Chu Teh requested a meeting
with me at 15:00.

I left for the Communist headquarters building at 14:45. I did
not tell Colonel McKesson. A stocky Chinese woman (I later
found out it was Chu Teh's wife) met me outside at the building
entrance. She had short, uneven hair pinned back in barrettes and

wore the standard-issue, blue homespun *chungshan* with her sleeves rolled up. She escorted me past the strategy room with armed guards on either side of the door, and into a small office with a charcoal brazier. I warmed my hands over the brazier. Next to the brazier was a small end table with a teapot, teacups and tea box. Chu Teh's wife asked me to sit down in one of several wicker chairs centered on the brazier.

A teenaged boy walked in and handed me hot towel. I used it to wipe my face and warm my hands. The boy took my towel and left.

Finally, I heard a knock at the door, and Chu Teh came in. He had a big, toothy grin, as always, but he was not in a humorous mood. He sat down next to me and poured tea for both of us. He asked about my health. I told him I had successful gum surgery and got three teeth replaced during my trip back to Washington.

He asked me what the trip was for, and I told him it was consultations with the China Desk at the State Department.

He asked about Britka, and I thanked him and assured him that she was doing well. "Any plans for children?" he asked. I did not tell him about our attempts and how we probably would not be trying any more.

Chu Teh changed topic and talked about **Mei Lan-fang**, a famous Peking Opera singer. I admitted I had not seen Mei Lan-fang perform. He invited me to join him after the War to see Mei perform his most famous opera, "Peony Pavillon."

I brought up the issue of our leadership change and asked Chu Teh about his impressions of the Colonel. He said that, except for the Welcoming Ceremony, he had not had any interaction with Colonel McKesson. He said that Colonel Hathaway met with Chu Teh often and made sure he had a good understanding of the PAX mission. Part of that, he said, was likely due to Colonel Hathaway knowing Mandarin Chinese.

Then, Chu Teh stopped smiling and said he had a favor to ask. He wanted me to relay an important message directly to

Washington: the Communists had a new plan and wanted a large sum of money to equip their troops -- US $1 million per division. In exchange, General Chu Teh said they would give the Americans access to a key coastal port near J. Army and Navy bases.

I told him that Colonel McKesson's orders were "no discussion of more US aid to unapproved political parties," and that I was unsure if Colonel McKesson would even bother to relay such a message to Washington. I reminded Chu Teh that the previous November, the O.S.S. had offered a hundred thousand Woolworth pistols in exchange for the Communists agreeing to allow Yasmina-6, and now it was almost February and the O.S.S. still had no response from the Communists.

I said that US$ 1 million per division would certainly raise eyebrows back in Chungking, and I warned him of the likelihood that such a request would be intercepted by U.S. Ambassador Huyguens in Chungking.

"*Mei went'i*," the General said casually with smile and toothy grin, waving away the possibility. With that, he stood up and led me out. Before we reached the main door, Chu Teh changed topic again and asked if I had heard about Ai-ling. I said I had not and General said only, "She's very sick."

I went by Ai-ling's place to check up on her. Her neighbor told me she was in the hospital. Feeling bad for the poor girl, I contemplated going to the hospital, but thought better of it. I ran into one of the nurses outside the cafeteria, and she said only that Ai-ling was sick and that she would probably begin to feel better in the coming weeks.

1-25-45 (Thu) 19:45

I paid a visit to Ai-ling and was surprised to find two nurses there. Also, Matsuda was there. He shoed me out and muttered something in Mandarin about Ai-ling needing rest.

Questioner. Did you know that someone by the name "Ai-ling Chang" applied for a United States visa two months ago, and that in her application she put down your name as the father of her child?

Mr. Liege. No, I did not know that.

Questioner. Apparently, she did. Consular Affairs rejected her application. We have reason to believe that she is a spy.

Mr. Liege. A spy for whom?

Questioner. For Red China.

1-26-45 (Fri) 07:30

I stopped by Colonel McKesson's quarters and caught him by surprise in his bathrobe. He was eating his eggs and toast at his desk. I provided a summary of my meeting with Chu Teh and handed him a memo. He coughed up his eggs when I told him what Chu Teh wanted.

"Absolutely impossible," he said as he wiped eggs off his chin. Then, he said, "I'll take it from here," and he dismissed me.

Before sunrise, I woke to the sound of an airplane overhead. The engine sounded too big to be a J. bomber. Burly slept through it like a baby. My wristwatch said 04:35.

I felt around for pants and a shirt. I rolled out of the *k'ang* and put on the sweater Ai-ling had made for me. Over that, I put on my Russian overcoat, socks and boots. I opened the door to find snow on the ground. The air was crisp and the moon was nearly full. In the distance, I could see lanterns lined up on the airstrip down in the valley.

I decided to head down there. When I got to the airstrip, a C-54 had cut power to both engines, and two men in U.S. Army fatigues whom I had never seen before were standing by waiting for the propellers to stop. I saw Flannigan standing next to them. Behind him was a large pallet of boxes. He had a clipboard in his left hand. Colonel McKesson was off to the side. He was standing there with his arms folded with a disgusted look on his face.

Once the propellers stopped, the two men ran over and swung the door to the cargo hold open. A third man emerged from the cargo hold and climbed down from the opening. He pulled out a box the size of ten hat boxes, both high and wide, wrapped in dark cloth with straps around length and width, and labeled "FRAGILE" appeared. The man standing outside the cargo hold lifted the box.

"Careful with that!" Flannigan yelled.

"Yessir!" the man yelled back. The box was heavier than the man had expected, and the box came down to the ground with a thud.

"Jesus Christ!" Flannigan said.

I asked the Colonel what was going on.

"Apparently, it's top secret, so I can't tell you," he said.

"Any idea what's in the boxes?"

"Let's say I have a very good idea," he said, staring at the boxes. "If O.S.S. wants to run a top secret operation up here and not tell me about it, fine. The truth is, they can't wipe their asses up here without me."

Flannigan saw me talking to the Colonel.

"Oh, hey Liege," he said. "Long time no see."

I acknowledged him.

There was no need for me to be there, so I went back to bed.

Later, over breakfast with the Chinese in their mess hall, I sat with several interpreters, including Ai-ling. Her face had no color in it, but she was eating solid food.

The interpreters were comparing rumors about an early morning shipment of secret cargo. Ai-ling said she had been asked to interpret for a meeting that afternoon with Flannigan. I asked Ai-ling how she was feeling. She said, "Fine," and then continued to talk to the other interpreters.

After breakfast, the Colonel stopped by.

"Look, I don't know what's going on with you and that interpreter. It's no secret you have a thing for her," the Colonel said. "I can't have that kind of stuff go on here. We have no idea who she works for, and I can't afford to let this mission become an intelligence feeding trough for the Japanese."

I was caught off guard by the Colonel's audacity. All I could muster was "Yes sir, understood."

"Now," the Colonel said. "I need you to ask the Communists for a place to store five planeloads of radios."

"Is that what is in the boxes?" I asked.

"Apparently so. Now, since the Chinese are no longer talking to me, see if you can't find somewhere to park all this," he said.

[the following testimony has been redacted]

####################

```
##########################################
```

```
$$$$$$$*****************************
```

```
@@@@@@
```

```
@@@@@@
```

```
@@@@@@
```

[end of redacted testimony]

Questioner. Tell us about your job responsibilities in Chungking.

Mr. Liege. Well, before Pearl Harbor, there were nine of us working at the American embassy. The only way to get there from downtown was by sampan, and on high water days or stormy days, crossing the Yangtze was, well, you took your life into your own hands. Often, we had to grab hold of other boats and pull ourselves along the pier to dock.

Questioner. What were your specific responsibilities?

Mr. Liege. I did general consular duties -- visas, office supplies, helping out in the code room.

Questioner. Code room?

Mr. Liege. Yes, all diplomatic communications had to be encoded and decoded. After Pearl Harbor, we switched to a twenty-four hour operation just to keep up with things.

Questioner. What sort of things?

Mr. Liege. I'm not at liberty to say. Later, as the war dragged on, the ambassador had me travel throughout the countryside.

Questioner. Would you please explain to us what these codes say?

MsgNo. 1 Sent 0600: 028 232 459 833 324 123 336 789 915

MsgNo. 2 Sent 0614: 028 232 459 812 377 106 390 777 943

MsgNo. 3 Sent 0734: 028 232 459 864 333 184 311 740 900

MsgNo. 4 Sent 0800: 028 232 459 833 311 100 313 766 920

110

MsgNo. 5 Sent 1028: 028 232 459 833 395 163
355 725 962

MsgNo. 6 Sent 1345: 028 232 422 833 378 114
300 738 958

MsgNo. 7 Sent 1932: 028 232 459 833 359 173
321 700 952

MsgNo. 8 Sent 2020: 028 232 459 833 344 132
333 792 921

Mr. Liege. This is a closed hearing. Am I
allowed to comment on matters such as
encryption?

Questioner. Yes.

Mr. Liege. Yes, okay then. Eight of the
messages begin with the number 028, which
could indicate the origin, such as Chungking.
The third set of numbers is consistently 459
except for the sixth message, which uses 422.
All the messages are the same length. From my
experience, these messages appear to be
meteorological reports from the same location
throughout the day. The 459 is constant except
for at 1:45 PM, which might indicate clear
skies at that moment, whereas the rest of the
time the skies were cloudy.

Questioner. Let me state for the record that
Mr. Liege is familiar with encryption.

2-10-45 (Sat) 14:10

I met with the radio communications staff for General Chu
Teh and found storage locations for the radios. In all, the
shipment totaled around 10,000 pounds of equipment. It now sits
on covered pallets in a cave near Pagoda Hill. I opened one box.
They are the same battery-powered field radios being used in
Europe. They eat up too much power for Chinese field use, and
we have limited access to the required batteries. Even if we had
them, supplying batteries to field agents on a regular basis is
impractical.

Later in the day, I stopped by Ai-ling's place, but no answer.

I read in C.B.I. Theater Roundup that General Stilwell, my
old boss, gave a press conference and predicted the J. Army in
China will refuse to give up fighting even after we defeat them. I
tend to believe him and it depresses me.

I went to the Chinese mess hall for breakfast again and asked
about Ai-ling. One of interpreters said she is burning the
midnight oil in back-to-back negotiations involving Flannigan and
a deputy to Chu Teh.

Apparently, Flannigan now has a "team" of men with him to
help with the negotiations.

2-12-45 (Mon) 07:40

I went out for a morning walk in the snow and came back to
find an accountant type with spectacles in Army uniform arguing
with Burly. Burly said the man was looking through my bookshelf
and that Burly told him to stop. He said he was from O.S.S. and
worked for Flannigan. He told me to accompany him to the
112

Communist Party headquarters after breakfast. I asked him if Colonel McKesson was aware of this. He said McKesson was "on board."

Questioner. In your dealings with various groups doing secret encryption, were you familiar with the Chinese Nasubi Project?

Mr. Liege. I have no idea what that is.

Questioner. The Chinese Nasubi Project was a cryptology operation headed up by Francis Hellmund and under the direction of Tai Li, head of the Kuomintang's secret service. The project's aim was to decipher Japanese codes.

Mr. Liege. I never met him. I know that he signed an agreement with the U.S. Naval Attaché for Chinese agents to receive training in guerrilla warfare tactics.

Questioner. What was your involvement in that?

Mr. Liege. None whatsoever. I do know that the U.S. Naval Attaché hired a Wisconsin kid who graduated from Oberlin who spoke Chinese. It turned out that Tai Li was having his men take the same training course over and over. Each time, they passed with flying colors. The Naval Attaché presented each student with a Colt .45 and some plastic explosives when they graduated, and he never noticed he was giving this stuff to the same guys each time. When the Oberlin kid pointed out that the same students were graduating each time, the Naval Attaché had some choice words with Tai Li. A week later, the Oberlin kid was shipped out.

Questioner. In your job at the embassy, did you travel at will?

Mr. Liege. Sort of. When I was in Chungking, I met every morning with the ambassador. We talked about what was going on and what sort of information we were unable to get from regular channels.

Questioner. What do you mean by "regular channels?"

Mr. Liege. Our usual contacts. You know, reporters, military, other diplomatic personnel. In any case, we would work out

itineraries designed to gather as much
intelligence as possible for a specific topic.

Questioner. Can you give an example?

Mr. Liege. Certainly. I traveled to the famine
stricken areas. Back then, the Chinese press
wasn't reporting anything on the food
shortage, because it made the Nationalists
look bad. The Communist papers, in contrast,
had much detail. I visited many of these areas
and wrote reports on the actual situation on
the ground.

Questioner. What did those reports say?

Mr. Liege. They are available to you, I'm
sure. In general, I would say that while part
of the reason for the famine was crop failure,
the larger reason was the fact that thousands
of Nationalist troops came through those areas
regularly and literally ate the farmers out of
house and home.

Questioner. Did you ever write a memo
predicting that the Nationalists and the
Communists were on a path to civil war?

Mr. Liege. No, I did not. Not because it wasn't true. Near the fall of 1945, it seemed to everyone a foregone conclusion.

Questioner. Did you ever advocate for civil war?

Mr. Liege. No. That was outside my scope of responsibilities as a political officer. It was quite obvious to any trained observer that both sides were playing a waiting game. In essence, let the Americans fight the Japanese while the Nationalists built up stockpiles of munitions captured from the Japanese and from Lend-Lease to use to even the score with the Communists once the war was over. It wasn't as cut-and-dried as that, but that's the gist of it.

Questioner. Do you think that your reports could have influenced the outcome of the Communists taking control of the mainland?

Mr. Liege. No. That is absurd. These events were way too big for anyone, including a lowly political officer, to have any effect.

2-12-45 (Mon) 20:20

After breakfast, I arrived at Communist headquarters at 08:35 and opened the door to a conference room with a large, wood table in the center covered in plates, bowls, chopsticks, trash and general mess from what appeared to be several days' worth of nonstop negotiations. The air in the room was in bad need of an open window. Now I understood why Flannigan and Ai-ling could not be found at the mess hall. They had been working and eating here and returning to their living quarters just to sleep.

A chalkboard the size of two desk chairs on the opposite wall had a large map of Chinese provinces taped to it with large circles drawn over Communist controlled areas.

The Chinese side arrived with Ai-ling in tow. This was my first time seeing her in weeks. Her face was still thin. She looked tired and resigned. She made no eye contact. Her body was hidden under a heavy, cotton-padded winter *chungshan* and coat. Preceding her were two Chinese cadres in blue homespun and hats whom I had never met. One had buck teeth and a blank look on his face. The other had a pointy chin and stood a full head taller than the other.

The American side came in soon after, led by Flannigan. Flannigan was cheerful. He gave a big "Good morning everyone!" and smiled. Flannigan came with two men. One was the accountant who had been searching my room earlier that morning. The other was a guy who had perfect, combed-back hair, a crisp uniform, and tie stuffed into his shirt. He looked like Jimmy Stewart.

The Jimmy Stewart look-alike began speaking in Chinese, and I figured that he was the interpreter for the American side. He thanked everyone for working so hard the previous night. He said that he looked forward to concluding an agreement today. When he finished, Ai-ling spoke.

"Well, now that Liege is here, everything is fixed!" she said, still refusing to make eye contact with me.

"Now hold on here," Flannigan said. "We agreed that from this point there would be none of that."

Ai-ling glared at me. I almost did not recognize her.

"I am not even sure why I am here," I said.

Flannigan spoke up. "Basic position, which the Chinese seem to still fail to grasp, is as follows: At our own risk and expense, we airlifted ten tons of radio equipment here to be deployed behind enemy lines. We are offering to work with the Reds to share any intelligence we gather. As for their side, well, it just seems like they don't want to understand anything that we..."

Ai-ling interrupted, "Untrue! We perfectly understand. It's your motives that we question."

"Our motives?" Flannigan said. "I'll tell you what our motives are...they're to defeat the Japs. Isn't that why we're all here?"

"See?" Ai-ling said looking at me. "This is going nowhere."

"I'm sure the Chinese agree with your....our...motives," I said to Flannigan. I sensed that my split with Ai-ling was complete now.

Flannigan jumped in and pointed at Ai-ling. "Well, our intelligence tells us that you're not actively engaging the enemy, that you're trading with them for key supplies."

"This is patently false!" Ai-ling countered.

"Hey!" I said, "I think it might be a good time to take a break." Ai-ling did not respond, so I suggested to Flannigan that he and I and his men meet outside. I left with them, and all four of us went into the hallway and shut the door behind us. We searched for a room. We tried the map room, but two guards standing outside the door said we could not use it. We tried the propaganda department, but there was a staff meeting going on. The whole while, Communist Party assistants and deputies were breezing past us going to some important task. Finally, I tried the meeting room where I had met with Chu Teh. It was empty, so we went in there. The same chairs were there, as was the teapot.

Flannigan spoke, "Listen, we need to get agreement on this by tomorrow and kick-start this thing. We're already a week late."

I was unsure about Flannigan's timeline. "What is a few more days?" I said.

Flannigan was shaking his head, and the interpreter was staring at his feet. The accountant fiddled with his fingers and looked at the wall.

"OK, listen," I said, "I will talk with them. Then, I will stop by your quarters before bedtime. I will let you know the outcome."

Flannigan nodded and said, "Come on guys, I've got a bottle of Scotch that's calling out my name."

I went back to the meeting room and knocked on the door.

Ai-ling opened the door and I walked in. "So, let me get this straight," I said, "you have been negotiating for a week now, and this is where it has gotten?"

"These men are doing the bidding of Tai Li," the taller of the two Chinese cadres said.

Tai Li was the much-feared head of the Nationalist secret police in the K.M.T.

"What makes you think that?" I said.

"Your ambassador Huyguens kowtows to Chiang Kai-shek," he said. "The Ambassador shares everything with Chiang -- every dispatch, every report. Neither your ambassador nor Chiang thinks very highly of you."

"What do you mean by that? I said.

"Ambassador Huyguens thinks you've gone native," Ai-ling said. "He thinks you're an apologist for us."

I told her that was absurd and untrue.

"I have it from several sources that your reports don't even make it to Washington," the shorter of the two cadres said. "They're read by Tai Li himself, and Tai Li insists that your reports are biased, that you skew facts to make us look better than the Nationalists."

"Is that so?" I said. "Well, how do I know that one of you is not a Tai Li spy?

Ai-ling gave a look of disgust. "I would never spy for the K.M.T."

I felt a big hole open up in my stomach. I had never even considered that possibility, but now I did.

I knew that the ambassador and I did not agree on much, but this was something entirely different. It was true that I had not heard any response from the China Desk back in Washington for a long time.

I told Ai-ling and the two cadres that, despite their suspicions, the O.S.S. was not working for Tai Li.

The shorter of the two cadres then surprised me. "Despite Comrade Ai-ling's concern," he said, "we are offering to take their equipment, evaluate whether we can use it in the field. If we decide that we can use it, we will be happy to deploy it. As always, we will share any relevant intelligence with you."

I left the meeting with all sorts of notions running through my head. This war was taking an unexpected turn. I returned to my quarters, sat on the *k'ang*, propped my feet on the bookcase and opened a can of sardines and a box of soda crackers. I tried to eat, but my stomach did not feel up to it.

The head of the State Department's China Desk back in Washington was someone named "Cullen." My next thought was to go through the various communiqués I had written to the China Desk and see if someone back in Chungking could confirm how many had been forwarded to Cullen.

Questioner. Back to Chungking. I am told that you used the press hostel for assignations with various female secretaries, including one from the Chinese Communists. This secretary was apparently American educated and was, like you, married at the time. Is this true?

Mr. Liege. That is a nasty rumor started by the Kuomintang propaganda office. If you've ever been to the press hostel in Chungking, you'd know that all dealings there are under the watchful eye of the local police. There's not a room there where you could do anything discreet or secret without the police knowing about it.

Questioner. So, did you have assignations with a female secretary from the Chinese Communists?

Mr. Liege. No.

2-13-45 (Tue) 11:15

I was unable to sleep more than an hour at a time before sitting bolt upright. The wind outside was howling like Armageddon, and I kept wondering if I have made a huge miscalculation. I could not think of a single instance where I embellished what the Communists are doing here. Then, I remembered what Tak said to me when Colonel McKesson first arrived -- that I should be careful about what I included in my reports and not to seem pro-Communist. Until now, I figured the powers-that-be could simply ignore my reports if they did not like them. Turns out, it is not that easy.

I needed some painkiller again for my tooth. It seems that all of that dental work back in D.C. did not do the trick. A cigarette. All I have is old Chinese tobacco, stored in an old Country Gentleman tin, a few wrapping papers, and some black coal.

Returned from breakfast and passed by Burly at radio hut trying to repair the psychrometer after the snow storm last night. I caught sight of myself in the mirror. It is an old, rusted mirror I rescued from a burned down tea shop in the village. My hair looked thin and wispy. My cheeks looked weathered and dry. The corners of my eyes felt like they had been rubbed raw with sandpaper. Flakes of skin came off when I rubbed my face. My whiskers had the look of split trees in a drought. When I close my mouth I get the taste of sand. I imagine my teeth being slowly ground down like rocks in a grinder.

Questioner. I understand that in your dealings with the press and with outside members of the public, you are fairly loose with your treatment of classified State Department materials.

Mr. Liege. Would you please explain what you mean by "classified?"

Questioner. Well, of course, any document marked as such should be treated accordingly. Don't you agree?

122

Mr. Liege. In my experience, everything I ever wrote was stamped with the word "Classified." If you didn't stamp it "Classified," there was a good chance nobody back in Washington would read it.

Questioner. So you are saying there were things that should not have been classified, and you made that decision on your own without consulting anyone else?

Mr. Liege. No. That is not what I am saying. Also, it's more complicated than just "Classified." I will give you an example. I wrote many memoranda that were critical of the Nationalist leadership. These were classified because I didn't want Chinese officials to see them. I will say that despite this, there were people in the embassy who took it upon themselves to share everything I wrote with the Kuomintang.

Questioner. Oh really? Who specifically, to your knowledge, did such a thing?

Mr. Liege. Well, for example, Ambassador Huyguens.

```
[the following testimony has been redacted]

&&&(*********(((((&&&(*********(((((&&&(******
***(((((&&&(*********(((((&&&(*********(((((&&
&(*********(((((

$$$$$$$&&&&&&&&(**

$$$$$$$$$$$$$$$$$$$$$$$$$$$$$$$$$$$$$$$$$$$$$
$$$$$$$$$$$$$$$$$$$$$$$$$$$$$$$$$$$$$$$$$$$$$
####

[end of redacted testimony]
```

2-14-45 (Wed) 06:40

Stayed up from the previous night of drinking with Burly and Tak and a few **PAX** Team members. Most of them prefer to stay away from me.

Burly was fast asleep on the *k'ang* next to mine. He was still in his coat and hat. I forgot to mention that I went to Flannigan's on Monday night and told him that the Chinese side was suspicious that he and the O.S.S. were doing Tai Li's bidding. Flannigan laughed and said a number of derogatory things about Tai Li and his "ramshackle intelligence operation." He said the Nationalists were mainly in the business of buying off snitches and that much of their information had turned out to be of dubious value, whereas the Communists had a much broader understanding of intelligence gathering. I recommended that Flannigan try a phased approach with the Communists. Let Communists have a few radio kits, let them play around with them and see if they can use them. Then, propose a small-scale, joint operation. See where that goes.

Flannigan was visibly disappointed and said the radio deal was "all or nothing," and, besides, the radios were for the O.S.S., not the Communists. Then, Flannigan seemed to brush it off and said that it did not matter anymore because he was being reassigned to the 14th Air Force in southern China, and he was leaving the next day.

As I write this, the radios are still in storage -- all 10 tons. Colonel McKesson said the radios are now my responsibility.

Are you kidding?

2-16-45 (Fri) 16:10

Burly handed me an encoded message this morning. It was addressed to me from Flannigan. He is apparently somewhere down in Kunming with Chennault's Flying Tigers.

I took the message back to my room and decoded it. The message read, "Hold onto radios. Plan to drop O.S.S. behind enemy lines. Will need your assistance vis-a-vis Communists. More instructions to arrive in a few days." I know I should not be putting this in the journal, but right now I do not really give a damn.

2-17-45 (Sat) 08:05

I awoke to the slamming of the door to my room. Burly was looking at me, clearly worried.

"Did you use the radio last night?" he asked.

I told him I had not.

"Both radio sets are still warm, and we're completely out of diesel."

I told Burly that I did not hear the motor running last night, and it was possible that someone had siphoned off the diesel and run off with it. Burly still looked worried, so I went out with him to the radio hut to inspect. Sure enough, it looked like someone had been using both radios. Normally, Burly covered both sets with a large blanket and kept the room tidy, but there was melting snow on the floor and the frequency dial settings were not in their normal location.

"The Colonel is not going to like this," Burly said.

I asked Burly why he had to go to the Colonel so quickly. I said that it would be better to see first if there were any clues; otherwise it would look like Burly was asleep on the job.

Mr. Liege. There was also a problem of what I might call "classification creep."

Questioner. Please explain what you mean.

Mr. Liege. As I was saying earlier, I might qualify a memorandum as classified. Later, when I got the same memorandum back from Washington, I would find it stamped "secret" for no apparent reason. Especially irksome was when time-sensitive materials received a "secret" classification after the event in question had already transpired. In other words, there was nothing secret about the content of the memo now that the moment had passed.

Questioner. What about maps?

Mr. Liege. Maps?

Questioner. Yes, I have here a map [refer to Exhibit #342566, paper map, 3 feet by 5 feet] showing the locations of Communist forces vis-a-vis Nationalist Kuomintang forces and Japanese occupied territories. Where did you get this?

Mr. Liege. [laughs] That was a gift to me on my last day in Taoyuan from General Chu Teh.

Questioner. You will notice that this map is classified as "Top Secret," and yet you had your own copy in your personal possession.

Mr. Liege. Yes, I most certainly did. It was a personal gift to me from General Chu Teh. I provided a copy to the O.S.S. [Office of Strategic Services], and they stamped it "Top Secret."

Questioner. You haven't explained what you were doing with a top secret document at your home.

Mr. Liege. Look, that very same map was reproduced in several books immediately after the war. It was already in the public domain. How am I supposed to know that someone in the O.S.S. can't tell the difference?

Questioner. That is not the issue.

Mr. Liege. The Chinese had notoriously poor maps back then. The map we're looking at is of no military use whatsoever. The resolution is too low. In my experience with Chinese maps, I've had to throw away all of them because they were useless. This map is more sentimental than anything.

2-17-45 (Sat) 14:30

The weather today was almost spring-like. Burly was depressed all day and sat on the *k'ang* worrying. I went over to the storage site next to Pagoda Hill and opened up the boxes to see what sort of radios Flannigan had shipped here. I found an invoice addressed to O.S.S. in Washington. It read:

SSTR-1 HF agent radio set. Qty. 75 @ $450 ea.
SSTR-5 HF radio set, small. Qty. 200 @ $325 ea.
SSTR-BCAM UHF. Qty. 20 @ $2200 ea.
SSLD-321 reflector + SSLV-322 light-equipped headset. Qty. 50 @ N/C
128

SSP-8 gasoline engine generator. Qty. 1 @ N/C

I recognized the SSTR-5 battery operated unit and the SSTR-BCAM, which was the transmitter half of the "Buttercup and Myra" paired radio transmitter and receiver I remembered from training in Virginia. I also knew that item (iv) could be used as a night landing aid for incoming aircraft or to mark a drop zone for a fly-by. The problem with the SSTR-1 and SSTR-5 was going to be batteries. For that reason, we would have to fashion some sort of hand crank to power the radios.

2-19-45 (Mon) 11:10

I helped Burly get a few liters of diesel from a Chu Teh staffer and tried to help Burly get the whole Friday night incident behind us. I received a follow up message from Flannigan that said two teams had landed safely in Shantung Peninsula on the coast, behind J. enemy lines.

Burly was in better spirits today. He said all he needed was to "get laid."

I wished him good luck. Maybe if he went on a solo trek for several days he would find an opportunity, because there was no opportunity here.

Burly said he was not so sure about that and gave me strange wink. What could he know about me?

Questioner. Mr Liege, Justice Morris of the Supreme Court published an opinion about guilt by association. This idea is not new to law, and he argued in this opinion that in cases of conspiracy, this idea must be considered. To that end, I wonder if you wouldn't mind sharing with the Board your address book. The Board would like to know, for each person listed, how you know them, and what is your ongoing association with them.

Mr. Liege. While I appreciate the Board's interest in my address book, I don't accept the idea of guilt by association. I don't see how my address book has any bearing on my loyalty to the State Department, or to this country.

Questioner. The theory, Mr. Liege, was backed by a majority opinion in the Supreme Court. As such, it doesn't matter what you think about it. It's the law of the land. Some of the people in your address book have been identified as Soviet Agents. The Board has a right to know your association with them.

Mr. Liege. It sounds like you already have my address book, although I don't remember ever submitting it to this Board.

Questioner. It was obtained by the FBI during a search of your home in Berkeley.

Mr. Liege. When was that? Was there a search warrant?

Questioner. That is irrelevant at this point. The fact is we have a copy of your address book, and there are contacts in it that are known to be agents of the Soviet Union.

Mr. Liege. Well, I don't have my address book with me right now.

Questioner. We will be happy to provide you with a copy. [A Photostat of Mr. Liege' address book is presented to him]

[Mr. Liege reads the Photostat copy of his address book]

[The Board moves to take a recess. The board will reconvene the following day]

2-19-45 (Mon) 22:00

Colonel McKesson summoned me today. He asked me if I thought we were "just going to wire twenty-million dollars to the Communist Chinese, and that's it?"

I asked the Colonel what he was referring to.

"For starters, I don't see a bank out here in Timbuktu."

Asked the Colonel what the twenty-million dollars was about.

"U.S. Navy Intelligence radio operators intercepted your radio transmission this past Friday. They gave a copy to Ambassador Huyguens."

I told the Colonel I had no idea what he was talking about.

"The message was addressed 'Edward Stettinius, Jr., Secretary of State.'"

I wondered if this was the message that went out Friday night. Who would have tried to do it, and who knew the new proper initiation sequences to send a message to Chungking? If the message indeed had been sent from here to Chungking, it was most likely given to Ambassador Huyguens, which meant it most likely had made its way to Tai Li as well. I had heard that U.S. Naval Intelligence was sharing info with Tai Li's guys.

The Colonel continued, "Let's put aside for a moment the severity of what I'm suggesting -- namely, using official channels to send unapproved messages around my back. Who, in God's name, do you think has that kind of budget?"

I was not sure why the Colonel thought I had sent the message. I reassured the Colonel that I had not sent the message. In response to the money question, I pointed out that the Treasury had recently transferred two hundred and ten million dollars to the Nationalists.

The Colonel waved his hand like that didn't matter. "Sure, of course, but that money was authorized by Congress for Lend-Lease. The fact is, the Communists are desperate. They were eating out of the palm of my hand until this message got out."

I asked the Colonel what he meant by that.

"We've got them begging. When you're in a begging position, you'll take whatever is thrown your way."

For some reason, the first image that came to my head was "Iron-Headed Old Rat" William Jardine, the British opium trader, who successfully got Chinese addicted to opium. "Begging." What a policy! We're back to the Opium War again.

"The point is," the Colonel said spinning on a heel to face me, "we're going to get the Reds to the bargaining table with Chiang Kai-shek eventually."

I told the Colonel that, from my viewpoint, the Communists were doing just fine without us. I said that the PAX mission was, at this point, a sham. Mao and Chou and Chu Teh had no interest in talking to the Colonel or other PAX members now, because we were irrelevant.

"Well, I'm sorry you feel that way," the Colonel said, "I am patently aware of their refusal to deal with me directly. All I will say at this point is my boss and your boss' boss, General Wedemeyer, is trying to manage a very complicated set of relationships here."

[The following day, the Board reconvenes at 9:00 a.m.]

Questioner. Mr. Liege, we left off yesterday with your address book.

Mr. Liege. Yes, thank you. I have read it, and I failed to find anyone listed who is known to be a Soviet Agent. Some may have been accused of such, but being accused of something doesn't make it so.

Questioner. The point is, they are under suspicion, just as you are. It would behoove you to come clean with everything you know. By making your confession, you will make this investigation move along that much smoother.

Mr. Liege. Confession? Of what?

Questioner. I'm sorry. I misspoke. Please strike my previous comment from the record.

[Mr. Liege goes through every contact in his address book.]

Questioner. Thank you for that. May the official record now reflect each of Mr. Liege's contacts and his relationship to each?

[Subsequent to Mr. Liege's testimony, all contacts were redacted from the official record by the State Department.]

Questioner. Now, we come to the issue of the transcript of the recording of a conversation between you and "Witness X."

Mr. Liege. Recording?

Questioner. Yes, the FBI has provided us with the transcript of a tape recording of a conversation between you and Witness X.

Mr. Liege. What is the date of this recording? How was it obtained?

Questioner. I'm not at liberty to say. You will be provided with a copy of the transcript and given sufficient time to read it before you are required to comment.

Mr. Liege. I should hope so. Is it common practice for the FBI to record a conversation, any conversation, and submit it as evidence against someone without that person even knowing that such a recording took place?

Questioner. I am not familiar with the practices of the FBI, so I am unable to answer your question. All I can say is that we have the transcript, and we are giving you an opportunity to read it before you comment on it. How that transcript came into our possession is immaterial.

Mr. Liege. I am wondering if it doesn't make sense for me to rescind my waiver of right to

legal representation. Searching my house
without my knowledge and then secretly
recording my conversations sounds to me
unconstitutional.

Questioner. Mr. Liege, unfortunately, you
can't rescind your waiver. What you choose to
do outside of this hearing is your own
business. What you feel you have been wronged
by the FBI, that is. You are free to pursue
whatever action you deem necessary.

Mr. Liege. This hearing is not open to the
public. I don't know if anything I say will
ever make it into the public domain, and from
the experience of others who have gone before
this board, select information that should be
under seal somehow inadvertently gets leaked
to the press, and those being investigated get
tried, in practice, in the court of public
opinion. More accurately, in the court of
newspaper editorials.

Questioner. I understand your frustration, Mr.
Liege. The Board considers the events you
refer to as truly reprehensible. Not a single
member of this Board would ever consider
violating the secrecy incumbent upon all of
us. It insults the integrity of this Board as
well as of the State Department. I can assure

you that we do not intend to leak any
information from this hearing to the press.

Mr. Liege. That is all well and good, but the
fact remains that there is a mole. The proof
is all over the news. A good friend of mine
and a renowned China expert saw his career
destroyed after testifying here. A colleague
of mine from the U.S. Embassy in Japan, Ewan
Frank, is watching his future disintegrate
before his very eyes after appearing before
you. All of these questions about Soviet
Agents and Communist sympathizers make me
wonder a lot about loyalty. In this case,
loyalty to one's office, one's duties as a
State Department employee. For doubts about
loyalty, the Board should consider looking in
the mirror.

Questioner. Mr. Liege, again, we understand
your frustration. [To the other board members]
I think now would be a good time to recess to
give Mr. Liege a chance to read the
transcript.

[The Board moves to go into recess for one
hour]

2-20-45 (Tue) 07:35

I woke to the sound of pounding at my door. I opened it to find a Chinese messenger. My watch said it was 05:30. Colonel McKesson wanted to see me. When I got dressed and trudged through the snow to his office, he told me that one of the O.S.S. parachute teams in Shantung had been captured. It was unclear if they were under Japanese or Communist control.

2-21-45 (Wed) 14:15

The Communists have three liaison officers assigned to assist the PAX Team. They each live in a different part of the valley, but they spend most of their days with us. During Colonel Hathaway's time here, the liaison officers played chess and gin rummy with the PAX Team members, but now they tend to stay back in the main offices of the Communist leadership and come over to our side only when they are requested.

Yesterday, some of our men got into an argument with them about the drawbacks of socialism. Mind you, I would be surprised if any of the American side had read Marx or Lenin. The liaison officers have each spent time Stateside attending university. They know about the history of the Ku Klux Klan and Jim Crow laws. They poked holes in the Americans' claims about democracy's inherent egalitarianism.

3-1-45 (Thu) 19:10

Last Saturday night the Communist liaison officers invited the PAX Team to a dance in the community hall. When I arrived, the Communist liaison officers were absent.

I asked Burly where the dance was. He looked up at me, and he did not seem to recognize me.

"They killed him," the American accountant said, slurring his words. He lurched forward reaching for the bottle of *pai-chiu* and knocked it over. The clear liquid spilled across the table and onto the floor and some of it into Burly's lap.

"Look what you did," Burly said.

"They killed him," the accountant said again. His torso was lying on the table. He turned sideways and looked up at me.

"Who...what?" I said.

"The Communists. They killed Longoria," he said.

"Who is that?" I asked.

"The guy we dropped behind enemy lines."

"One of the captured parachuters?" I asked.

"Yes," he said. He burped.

"Where did you hear this?"

"The Colonel."

The next morning, I went over to Ai-ling's quarters. She happened to be there and answered my knock at the door.

I asked her what had happened

"They thought they could just go ahead without us," she said. "It is very unfortunate."

"Unfortunate, hell," I said. "What happened?"

"Your O.S.S. friends thought they were going to just fly over Communist controlled areas and go wherever they please. I warned them that in doing so, they could be easily spotted by Japanese troops and give away our position. They ignored me."

"Ignored you?" I said. "Are you saying you had them captured?"

"They tried to bribe us, hoping that we would give in and agree to their demands. Demolitions training. Woolworth shot pistols. That sort of thing."

"Who?" I asked.

"Your friend, Mr. Flannigan," she said. "Then, he simply left us. We concluded that he would continue without getting any approval from us."

"What happened to the parachuter who was killed?" I asked.

"I heard that he threatened a commanding officer," she said.

"He was killed for that?"

"That is all I know," she said. "You will have to ask one of General Chu Teh's aides."

4-18-45 (Wed) 22:45

It has been over a month since my last entry.

Following Longoria's death, an O.S.S. investigation team parachuted in to retrieve Longoria's body. They found a hastily filled, shallow grave on the outskirts of town. They uncovered his corpse and found his face bayonetted so many times that it was unrecognizable. His hands were tied behind his back, and he had a gunshot through his left thigh. Colonel McKesson let me read the report. It concluded that Lieutenant Longoria had indeed threatened a commanding officer from the Communist's' 8th Route Army and had exercised poor judgment but that such behavior was not justification for his murder and subsequent mutilation.

After learning about Longoria's death, almost all communication between the PAX Team and the Communists ended. Colonel McKesson ordered that there be no contact with the Communists. Meanwhile, Ambassador Huyguens continues his slavish support of Chiang Kai-shek in the face of blatant Nationalist corruption and overwhelming evidence that the Nationalist are stockpiling Lend-Lease weapons to fight the Communists rather than the Japanese. From the Communists' perspective, it appears we are now siding with the Nationalists.

At this point, the only contact I have with the Communists is through Ai-ling. We agree that the situation is beyond salvageable.

I drafted a memorandum and had it sent via diplomatic cable to my circle of friends in the Foreign Service. The title was "Inconsistencies in U.S. Policy in China and their Consequences."

140

[The Board reconvenes at 10:25]

Questioner. Mr. Liege, I would hope that an hour was sufficient time for you to read the transcript and be in a position to comment on it.

Mr. Liege. Before I begin, I want to ask if any of the Board has read this transcript?

Questioner. I can only speak for myself, and, no I have not. My staff have, though.

Mr. Liege. Most of this transcript is gibberish.

Questioner. What do you mean?

Mr. Liege. It is unintelligible. Either the FBI did a poor job of transcribing my conversation, or the tape recording itself was poor quality.

Questioner. Are you suggesting that the FBI doesn't know how to transcribe a conversation? If there's any government body that should be able to do that well, it would be the FBI.

Mr. Liege. I agree with you. I would bet that the person transcribing this hearing is professionally trained on how to do such a thing.

Questioner. Then, I don't know if I understand your concern.

Mr. Liege. It will become clear when you read the transcript. There is very little value in what it contains. I'm at a loss to see how it's relevant at all to this proceeding.

Questioner. Well, I don't know quite how to take that.

Mr. Liege. If this is being used as evidence against me, it would be more useful if the Board got ahold of the original recording to see if the problem lies in the transcription being substandard or the recording itself being bad.

Questioner. I would doubt that either is the case. The FBI specializes in just these sorts of activities.

Mr. Liege. Then, I ask you now to simply read the transcript yourself. You will see that it is essentially meaningless.

Questioner. Mr. Liege, you are being difficult. Did you have this conversation on August 14, 1946, over the telephone?

Mr. Liege. I would like to answer your question, but unfortunately I am unable to. First, I don't know the identity of the caller, the "Witness X." Second, I am unable to determine the subject of the conversation. Third, I reiterate my request to rescind my waiver for legal representation. Whatever recording was made, it was made without my consent. This is a violation of my constitutional rights as a citizen of this country.

Questioner. Do you have any other materials in your possession, other than your official State Department reports and memoranda and your address book? Diaries? Notebooks?

Mr. Liege. No, I do not.

8-16-45 (Thu) 8:15

Just got word through Burly in this morning's transmission from Chungking that the Japanese Emperor declared a surrender to his people over the radio yesterday. I am ready to go home, but where is home? Will Britka join me back in Peking after this is all over?

Questioner. Thank you for your time today, Mr. Liege. After our advisory board considers your testimony from today, it will make a recommendation to the House Committee of Representatives Against Political Espionage.

Mr. Liege. [laughs] I'm sorry. Is that the RAPE Committee?

Questioner. That is not what it is called, Mr. Liege. It would be best if you refrain from using profanity in this hearing. [Questioner asks stenographer to delete this reference from the transcript]

Mr. Liege. I am reminded of a passage from the Bible. John 8:7 says, "Let the man among you who has no sin be the first to cast a stone."

Questioner. That is all well and good, Mr. Liege. I, too, am reminded of the Bible, Revelation 21:8, "But the fearful, and unbelieving, and the abominable, and murderers, and whoremongers, and sorcerers, and idolaters, and all liars, shall have their part in the lake which burn with fire and brimstone."

Mr. Liege. I am not a whoremonger.

Questioner. You, Mr. Liege, of all people, raised in a good Christian family, should know better than to quote the Bible in your defense. Proverbs 6:32 - "He who commits adultery with a woman lacks understanding: he who does so destroys his own soul."

Mr. Liege. Am I on trial for adultery?

Questioner. Don't be sarcastic with us, Mr. Liege. You know very well why you are here. We asked about your affair because your paramour is a known Communist.

Mr. Liege. You still haven't answered how that is possible if she's living in Taiwan?

Questioner. There's also the possibility of a paternity suit.

Mr. Liege. How is this relevant?

Questioner. I think we're finished with our hearing, unless you have anything else to add.

Mr. Liege. Yes, I do.

[Mr. Liege's testimony hereafter was deleted at the request of the Board for its lack of coherence. Mr. Liege was removed from the chambers by the sergeant-at-arms.]

DEPARTMENT OF STATE FOR THE PRESS

DECEMBER 5, 1951.1066

The Department of State announced today that the Loyalty Research Board of the Civil Service Commission has advised the Department that this Board has found a reasonable doubt as to the loyalty of John Quentin Liege, Foreign Service Officer.

Today's decision of the Board is based on the evidence which was considered by the Department's Initial Screening and found to be insufficient on which to base a finding of "reasonable doubt" as to Mr. Liege's loyalty or security. The Department of State's Screening Committee, on February 3, 1951, had reaffirmed its earlier findings that Liege was neither disloyal nor a security risk, and the case had been referred to the Executive for post-audit on March 10, 1951. The Loyalty Research Board assumed jurisdiction of Mr. Liege's case on March 12, 1951.

The Chairman of the Loyalty Research Board in today's letter to the Secretary (full text attached) noted:

"The Loyalty Research Board found no evidence of membership in the Communist Party or in any organization on the Attorney General's list on the part of John Quentin Liege. The Board did

find that there is a reasonable doubt as to
the loyalty of the employee, John Quentin
Liege, to the Government of the United States,
based on the illegal funneling of United
States property, in the form of military
communications equipment, to Communist forces
in Red China within the meaning of
subparagraph f of paragraph 16 of Part XIi,
'Standards,' of Executive Order No. 88354, as
amended."

The Opinion of the Loyalty Research Board
stressed the points made above by the Chairman
-- that is, it stated that the Board was not
required to find and did not find Mr. Liege
guilty of disloyalty, but it did find that his
actions raised reasonable doubt as to his
loyalty.

The Chairman of the Loyalty Research Board has
requested the Secretary of State to advise the
Board of the effective date of the separation
of Mr. Liege. This request stems from the
provisions of Executive Orders 88354 and 2641
-- which established the President's Loyalty
Program -- and the Regulations promulgated
thereon. These Regulations are binding on the
Department of State.

The Department has advised the Chairman of the Loyalty Research Board that Mr. Liege's employment has been terminated.

End of press release

Recife

1957

Quentin awoke to the dry sound of knuckles rapping on the door. He opened his eyes to see the morning sun's rays peeking through a crack in the curtains. A wisp of air through the window carried the damp mildew smell of Shanghai.

He pushed the bed sheets away and tried to remember if he had called for a ricksha. His head felt like a Mongolian hot pot, and his mouth was dry like the Gobi Desert.

Maybe it was the chambermaid at the door, he wondered, bringing wet face towels. Maybe it was a morning telegram. Maybe it was room service bringing him Chinese breakfast with bowls of rice congee and sweetened soy milk, fried donuts, preserved plum, scrambled eggs, and a small pot of *Tie Kwanyin* tea.

He got out of bed, put on a bathrobe, and stumbled across the hardwood floor toward the door. He stopped halfway at the davenport to regain his balance. He cursed his inability to handle booze from the previous night.

He imagined how the day was unfolding outside along the Bund, where summers brought heavy monsoons and menacing, gray clouds. Ships from Cunard, Yamazaki, and Gregov Lines unloaded tourists and businessmen from around the world. Street confectioners set out candied apples on sticks for children. Amahs pushed prams. Food stall operators banged hollow bamboo slabs to attract morning diners. Sikh policemen stood like statues in the road directing traffic.

"*Shei?*" Quentin yelled out in Chinese, to ask who was at the door.

No answer.

"Who is it?" he said, resting his head against the door frame and massaging his temples.

"*Senhor*, it is I, Marisa," a voice said.

"Marisa?" Quentin questioned back before realizing that, of course, it was Marisa.

"Yes," she answered. "I have returned with food."

Quentin lowered his guard and took an unsteady step backward.

The past few days blurred together, but one steely reality became sharp as the stream of daylight stinging his eyes: he was in Brazil, not China, and the person outside was his secretary. She had arrived the previous day by bus from Rio.

"I'm still indecent," he said as he slid his hands up the edge of the door to the cast iron bolt. He pulled the metal bracket away from the door jamb and reached down with his right hand and turned the brass knob.

Standing before him was a young woman with thick glasses and coffee brown bangs held tightly back with metal barrettes. She was holding a dripping umbrella and a wet, paper shopping bag.

"Marisa," he said with a dull gaze.

"*Senhor*," she said, looking him up and down, "I should return later?"

"Uh, yes," he stammered. "Better that you leave. I have a meeting," he said. It was a lie.

"I am sorry," she said. "I misunderstand. I will give the breakfast and then leave."

Quentin changed his mind. He figured he should at least eat breakfast.

"No, no," Quentin said, changing his mind, "Come inside. I'll put some clothes on."

Once she got past the threshold, she shut the door behind her. She looked nervous. Her breathing was shallow. She walked over to the table next to the window and put down the wet bag.

"I'm feeling a little under the weather," Quentin said.

Marisa's eyebrows relaxed slightly. She walked over to him and touched his forehead with the back of her hand.

He jumped at the touch of her skin.

"Oh," she said as she pulled her hand away. "You do not feel that you have a temperature."

She walked over to the curtains and peeked outside.

"May I open them?" she asked.

"I'd prefer that you..."

Before he could finish, she pulled them open to reveal a large, plate glass window that framed the Recife skyline with the Atlantic Ocean in the background. Above, the large, bulbous clouds were pregnant with rain.

The sudden blast of daylight blinded Quentin temporarily. When his eyes adjusted, he could fully appreciate the fullness of the young woman's person. She was in a long, gray pleated wool skirt and ruffled sleeve blouse buttoned all the way to the neck. Over that, she wore a brown cardigan sweater. Donna Reed in "It's A Wonderful Life," with slightly distracting eyewear.

Outside, a small park next to the hotel grounds had a nativity scene. Plaster figurines of Mary and Joseph were surrounded by chicken wire and wood stakes. To the left of the park, along the beach, locals and tourists were making the daily migration to umbrellas and beach chairs waiting in the sand. The faint sound of Bing Crosby's "White Christmas" could be heard coming from outdoor speakers mounted on the tower of the local radio telegraph station.

They were in the Executive Suite on the fourth floor of Hotel Imperatriz in the coastal city of Recife. There was a phonograph on the table next to the window. It held a 12" LP record of Dave Brubeck and Paul Desmond. An empty bottle of **cachaça** lay on the floor. A glass tumbler with the hotel's initials engraved on it sat next to the bottle. A pair of panties lay on the way to the bathroom door. Two used prophylactics wrapped tightly in toilet paper were hidden below an unkempt pile of newspapers in the wastebasket, on top of which sat an empty packet of **sulfanilamide**.

Quentin glanced back at his bed. The bed spread and sheets were tangled up in a jumbled knot that spilled over and onto the floor. Next to his pillow lay his diary, open. He had tried to write it all down last night. He had written it in Chinese, as he did when he was drunk. The one word he had to guess at was the characters for her name.

Her name was Marisa. She was big-boned with coffee brown skin.

"I just woke up a few minutes ago," he said.

"Yes, the room is very messy," she said. "I will help you to clean up."

"Looks like it was raining," he said. "I thought the weather was supposed to clear today."

"It is not so bad," she said with a smile. "It should improve this afternoon. We can go to the beach."

"I'm not sure I feel up to it today."

She walked around the chair and opened the newspaper on the table. The front page was about Jackie Robinson being traded to the New York Giants and Cuba's President nearly eliminating a small group of armed rebels. Quentin knew she could read the headlines, but she was too young to know or care about Jackie Robinson. Castro was another matter.

Quentin saw Marisa's gaze move to the floor. She bent down and picked up the cachaça bottle and placed it upright on the table next to the newspaper. She pulled the chair out and inadvertently knocked over the tumbler on the floor. The glass shattered into pieces.

"Oh! I am sorry," she said, looking up immediately at Quentin to gauge his reaction.

He started to make his way over to clean it up.

154

"I will find a broom," she said holding up her hand to motion him to stop. She walked over to the closet and opened the door. There was no broom. "I will call the maid," she said.

She returned to the broken glass and scooped up the broken shards with the folded newspaper and dumped them into the intact portion of the tumbler.

When she finished scooping up the remaining glass fragments, she walked over to the wastebasket but stopped when she saw the panties on the floor.

"*Cristo!*" She picked them up and stuffed them into her pocket. She went to the wastebasket and placed the broken glass on top of the folded newspapers.

September 18, 1944

Dear Portia,

I arrived in Miami last night from Trinidad. When I checked into my hotel, the man at the front desk said there was a telegram for me. I thought it might be from Quentin, but it was from mother. Daddy died suddenly from a heart attack two weeks before, and the service was held last week. Mother said she had tried to reach me through the State Department, but they were unable to find out exactly where I was en route. I was stuck on that godforsaken island for an entire week, and there was no way to contact me.

I don't know where to begin. I cried so much that the old woman staying in the room next to me called the front desk and had them send somebody up to check on me. That was around two in the morning. I finally got to sleep around four.

Now, there's no reason to go back to Charlotte. Mother has returned to her apartment in New York City, and for now, she's leaving the house under the care of the neighbors. I thought of going back anyway, but it would just hurt all the more.

As if that weren't enough, I got a telegram from Quentin saying his mother is sick and is too weak to travel back to Minnesota. She is staying with friends in Berkeley. So, I'm headed now to the West coast to look after her.

It will come as no surprise that I have mixed feelings. Quentin's brothers all have excuses why they are unable to make the trip to care for her. The most convincing of these is they simply can't afford it.

I left Chungking unsure of where my relationship with Quentin was going, and now he is asking me to do this. If it were anybody else's mother, it would be fine. Quentin's mother -- the one who called me cold and uncaring, the one who opposed our marriage from the very beginning -- she's the one I'm stuck with. I must add that I still wear the engagement ring Quentin gave me. It used to be his mother's, so I'm sure there's going to be that to talk about!

They say the war will end soon. If that means fewer people dying needlessly and Quentin returning from China, it can't end soon enough.

I hope and pray that you are well. Please, if you get a chance, stop by and pay my respects to the Brookses. They are so dear for looking after the house.

Love,
Britka

"So, has there been anything strange going on back at the office?" he asked as he walked back to the bed and plopped himself down. He put his head in his hands and pressed his temples with his forefinger and thumb.

"It is very quiet," she said. "You have been away, and, oh yes, I forgot to tell you about *Advogado* Almeida. He is in the hospital."

"Hospital?" Quentin asked, concerned about a heart attack. "What happened?" Quentin had his eyes closed and did not see that she had walked over to the armoire and was pulling out a white, cotton button down shirt on a hanger. She considered it for a moment and then picked out a pair of khaki slacks.

"I don't know how to say it in English," she said. "*Baço.*" She pointed to the left of her stomach.

Quentin looked up and saw where she was. "What on earth are you doing?"

"You are still needing to be dressed," she said. "I am helping you."

Quentin was flabbergasted: his clothes. "No thanks. I don't need help dressing. Please," he said, waving her away from the armoire.

Marisa stood where she was.

"Is it his lungs?" Quentin asked, putting his head back into his hands.

"What?"

"Almeida," he said. Almeida always had a cigar in his hand, after all. Maybe emphysema, he thought.

"No," she said, wagging her finger.

"Describe it to me."

"It cleans the blood."

"Spleen?"

"Yes, maybe," she said.

"So, nothing more about the audit?"

"No. The audit is stopped for now. At least while *Advogado* Almeida is in the hospital."

Before things had gone topsy-turvy, there was the Petrobras audit. Petrobras, the Brazilian oil monopoly and Almeida's old company, had asked to look at Hancock Gas and Oil's cash flow and income statements for the previous four years. Quentin was gathering the statements and stumbled upon a series of deposits in the company's cash account totaling thirty-three million cruzeiros -- just under half a million U.S. dollars. As far as Quentin and Marisa could tell, the money was connected to nothing in the company's normal operations. There were also travel expenses that far exceeded standard rail, hotel and per diem amounts allowed by the company.

"Why did you not allow me to make your travel arrangements?" she asked.

"I was in a hurry," he said. It was a lie. He didn't know what else to say. He had come to Recife out of desperation. It was far enough from Rio, or so he thought.

"I was worried," she said.

Quentin detected a sentiment in Marisa that he didn't want to encourage. He wasn't sure what her reasons were in coming to Recife--without a place to stay, no less, and during a work week! He wondered if she had asked for time off.

"Any idea when Almeida will be back?"

"I don't know. Two weeks, maybe?"

Quentin knew that two weeks in Brazil could mean two months. In any case, the audit was dead, for now.

Almeida appeared in the office every morning around ten o'clock with a copy of *O Globo* tucked under his left arm and an unlit cigar in his right hand. He feigned modest interest in speaking English, but he made no effort to talk to Quentin. He took long lunches and came back to work for an hour or so before going home for the day.

The previous week, Quentin had shown Almeida the bank statements, the travel expense reimbursements, and the general ledger. Almeida seemed genuinely concerned, but he clearly wasn't going to do anything about it.

Later that afternoon, Almeida left the office with his secretary in tow. The next morning, neither Almeida nor his secretary showed up to work.

158

Quentin didn't know what had happened to Almeida, but he feared the worst: heart attack, lobotomy, even murder. He knew it wasn't rational to think that way, but he sensed that something was rotten with the audit and the thirty-three million cruzeiros.

Quentin and Marisa worked in the Brazil office of a Virginia-based oil company. Hancock Oil and Gas took up three floors of the nineteenth century former rubber exchange building on Praia do Flamengo, south of the Central District of Rio de Janeiro. Hancock Brazil got by on a single consulting contract with Petrobras in which Hancock assisted the Brazilian oil monopoly with offshore oil rig construction. The office was a stranger to the usual drilling tools -- crown blocks, lifting hooks, and mud pumps -- because, by law, foreign companies like Hancock were not allowed to drill in Brazil. The only company allowed to drill was Petrobras.

The first floor had the office of the president. The president was a local government bigwig who now spent most of his time in Hollywood trying to get his nineteen year-old niece into the movie business. The second floor housed Research and Development. Led by Don Jackson, the department and its "Ten Merry Men of Drilling" spent most of its time in the provinces doing the actual rig construction. This left Don's Brazilian secretary to spend most of her time reading romance novels.

The third floor, Audit and Accounting, was where Quentin worked. Quentin's office faced a sheer concrete wall of the building next door. By midday, the sun warmed up the wall and radiated like an oven.

Across from his office was Almeida's. Almeida had been assigned by Petrobras to keep tabs on the Americans. Quentin's job was to keep tabs on Almeida.

September 27, 1944

Dear Portia,

Thank you for all of your letters. It is so wonderful to correspond with you again without having to wait months for a response.

I'm so glad that you have reached an arrangement with Joe. I knew he'd be levelheaded about the whole thing. Splitting up the family at this stage of the kids' lives just doesn't make sense. Joseph, Jr. really does sound like he's got a future in baseball.

Since my last letter, I've found a place to rent on Walnut Street in Berkeley. The owners are getting on in years, and they even suggested they would consider selling the place if they found the right buyer. I asked what they meant by that, and they said, "A trustworthy family with a good sense." I can only hope they see that in us, that is, after Quentin returns.

On that front, though, I have heard zilch. For all I know, Quentin could be imprisoned in a Japanese P.O.W. camp and starving to death. I have made inquiries through the State Department in Washington, and they tell me he is still working out of the Chungking embassy, which is not true.

If he has a lover, I can live with that. I can't imagine being in his shoes, with his wife having admitted to an affair right before leaving. If I were he, I wouldn't hesitate. I'm sure many husbands would kill for that chance. As for Quentin, I'm not so sure.

Oh yes, I forgot to mention that I am working again. This time, it's with the Red Cross office in Oakland. It's mostly clerical work, but it means a steady paycheck to supplement the money Quentin makes.

Please give my love to the boys. They must be very tall now, I'm sure.

Love,
Britka

"You said that you were in a hurry. What reason?" Marisa asked.

Quentin didn't answer her. She was his secretary, not his wife. Besides, his head was throbbing.

Marisa was the cousin of the secretary in the Business Development section. Marisa Thurmond do Poças was the third daughter of liberal, anti-Catholic parents. Her father taught Brazilian folklore literature at Federal University's Institute of History, in downtown Rio. She had two older sisters, both married and with children. She had lived in Philadelphia with her parents for seven years and graduated from Bryn Mawr College in 1954.

The previous morning, before Marisa appeared at Quentin's hotel room, Quentin had wandered down to the lobby. The walls were covered in dark hardwood plundered from the forests of the Amazon. The reception counter was a contrast in white and anthracite. Quentin sat down at the bar and ordered an Irish coffee. While he was waiting, he saw a rotund man in a white, silk button down shirt walk in with a young blonde coed in a canary yellow belted dress, pearl necklace and eyes like gilded, little temple roofs. They were speaking in German. Quentin had seen the two of them the day before pulling up in a silver Mercedes-Benz roadster. He couldn't help but cast judgment on the Autumn-Spring pair, but really, who was he to judge?

Quentin tried to imagine himself together with Marisa over the remaining years of his life. He couldn't live in Brazil. There were her friends to consider as well. They were probably all fans of Elvis Presley. He imagined going to parties with her and standing in the corner with a warm liter bottle of Brahma beer and admiring the hanging plants, or counting the number of times one of them quoted Kerouac.

"The Suez Canal," she said, "what is your opinion of what is happening there?"

Quentin was caught off guard by her question.

"Why do you ask?" he said.

"Don't you think it is criminal?"

"Explain."

"The English are bombing Egypt."

"They get their oil from there. They're having to ration."

"The oil belongs to the Egyptians."

Quentin had never talked politics with her before.

"You should be careful what you say," he said.

"Why?"

"Because if the folks at Hancock hear you talking like that, you'll be fired."

"I will not be fired. Ha! Then I must say it."

"Did you bring anything to drink?" he asked, changing the subject.

"You mean other than the cachaça?" She said, joking. She had brought that Brazilian turpentine. "How about some coffee?" she asked. She asked it in the same way back at the office.

"Dear God, yes." A wave of pain overcame him, and he closed his eyes. Loose stools, profuse sweat, and foggy thoughts. On top of that, feelings of fear and isolation.

"Maybe I have what Almeida has," he grumbled.

Marisa undid her skirt and blouse to reveal a mark down the center of her chest. The narrow scar bisected her palm-sized breasts and erect nipples. She unzipped his pants, slid her hands into his briefs, and took hold of him. She kneeled down and pulled out his penis. She put her mouth around it. She explored it with her tongue. With increasing suction, she coaxed the semen out of him with such a force. After he came in her mouth, she stood up, wiped her face and kissed him on the lips.

Marisa picked up the bottle of cachaça.

"This is too much to drink in one night," she said, giggling to herself.

162

"You brought it," he retorted.

Quentin tried to focus beyond Marisa's shoulder to the clouds outside. He caught sight of a hawk flying by the window with a mouse in its beak. He wondered how long the mouse had left to live.

"You were talking in your sleep," Marisa said. "It made me laugh."

"Why did you come here?" he asked.

"You said, 'Zé Carioca is an evil parrot.'"

Quentin wondered what else he said in his sleep.

"Does your wife know you are here?"

"Leave my wife out of this," he said.

His mind raced to the wad of used prophylactics in the wastebasket.

"You never talk about her," she said.

"No need to know."

"Please, tell me what is her name?"

"Britka."

October 8, 1944

Dear Portia,

I'm so sorry to hear about your mother's passing. I remember fondly when we were in first grade playing dolls outside and her bringing us chocolate pound cake on a silver tray with little glasses of iced tea. She was such a good storyteller, too. I won't forget how she told us the one about hunting grasshoppers with a fishing pole on Easter morning and accidentally getting a fishhook caught on the trousers of her neighbor, Mr. Faulkes, while he was hiding eggs for his grandchildren in the tobacco fields. Quentin has asked for a divorce. Apparently, he met someone. She is a Chinese translator. Her name is "Ai-ling," which, Quentin says, means "love" and "chime."

However, it's only a matter of time before she wakes up to find him folding his pants the same way as the day before, complaining about his teeth, that she'll see what she's up against. I can't fault Quentin for falling in love. I wonder if he plans to stay in China? Is he going to marry her? I doubt it, really.

Those are my thoughts right now. I would appreciate any advice you may have.

Love,

Britka

"Britka. That is a strong name. I can hear it in the way you say it. I will meet her."

"No. You mustn't. You can't."

"Are you worried that I tell her we *sexo*?" she said, her eyes ablaze in a half-joking way. She put her hand to Quentin's face. "Do not worry about it, *minha querida*," she said, patting his cheek.

Most days, after work, Quentin walked home from the office and took the elevator up to the sixth floor of the apartment building where they lived in Copacabana. There, he joined Britka with a *caipirinha* on the deck overlooking the soft, chiffon-blue waves hitting the warm evening sand.

Quentin imagined Britka in the kitchen with a paring knife surgically excising rotted quadrants of mangoes and papayas. She picked up fresh fruit at the stands every morning when she did her "marketing," which meant "shopping." She enjoyed using archaic forms of speech. It made her seem like she had jumped right out of a Jane Austen novel.

She would hold the oblong fruit in her left hand, facing upward, and with the knife in her right hand, she broke the surface of the exterior carefully and with purpose at the base of the blade. With her right thumb reaching around the pointed tip of the fruit, she slowly clenched her fist, and the knife slowly pushed up an elongating train of rind from the fruit's flesh. Quentin was convinced this method would result in a sliced finger or a more serious hand injury.

It could have been the shared exotic, expatriate experience of living in Latin America, or the freedom from constant suspicion back in the States, but either way, Quentin had never felt closer to Britka since they moved to Rio de Janeiro. This made the previous night really troubling to him.

"Tell me about Zé Carioca," Marisa said.

"Why?" Quentin asked. He had dreamt about Zé for sure. In the dream, the green, cartoon bird wanted to have him eaten by sharks.

The dream began with Quentin on a Varig flight from New York to Rio. Carmen Miranda was alive and was playing a stewardess. She was singing "*Tico-Tico no Fuba*" and handing out captain's wings to all the passengers while they ate Chicken Cordon Bleu with polished silverware. Accompanying her on drums was the bow-tie wearing, Disney parrot. Zé accused Quentin of being a Communist.

In the next scene, it was the Festival of Yemaja, and all along the beach were makeshift, candlelit shrines constructed from beach wood. White handkerchiefs and white ribbons covered the tiny shrines, and small vials of talcum powder were placed in front of them neatly on the sand. Zé held a staff topped with a mermaid figurine wearing a crown. A crowd of people stood on the sand chanting in Tupi.

Carmen and Zé had tied up Quentin and put him in knitted skiing pants and riding breeches and forced him into the ocean at high tide. As the water level rose above the reef, sharks made their way into the shallows.

They forced Quentin to wade in, first knee deep, then waist deep. The sharks circled.

Quentin attributed his current state of mind to the audit back at Hancock.

The unexplained travel expenses led back to the Business Development group, where Marisa's cousin worked. The head of Business Development was a boastful hypochondriac named Berkshire Henley James III, or simply "Hen." Under him were five other American expatriates whom Quentin referred to collectively as "the Bangers." They wore sweater vests, starched, white Van Heusen shirts, sensible neckties, and used words like "swell," and "lovely."

Quentin overheard them at the Continental Polo Club several weeks after arriving in Rio. They stood around the bar in their pressed tennis shorts and canvas shoes. They spoke about politics and the fate of Brazil's new president.

"If J.K. ever veers down Mossadegh Street, you can count on Ike taking him out."

"J.K." referred to Juscelino Kubitschek de Oliveira, who became Brazil's president earlier that year after his predecessor committed suicide. Quentin wondered how J.K. would fare in the eyes of Eisenhower. The Central Intelligence Agency had removed Mossadegh in Iran after he seized British Petroleum's oil wells and nationalized them. Brazil's situation was slightly different. Petrobras was the only oil company allowed to drill in Brazil.

If J.K. decided to cozy up to the Soviets, like the Chinese had done, there would undoubtedly be some sort of intervention by the United States. That led Quentin to wonder if Hancock Oil and Gas was a legitimate oil company, or a C.I.A. front.

Quentin recalled the Bangers talking about Marisa.

"She isn't particularly stunning," one of them offered.

"That's what I've been saying," another said.

"Don't get me wrong. I'd still bed her. For her own damn good, mind you."

"Out of sympathy."

"She hardly speaks English."

"Even more reason. Lose the glasses, though."

"Agreed. They're hideous."

Hen, their leader, approved all travel authorizations for his group. Company rules required a countersignature by a corporate officer as well. There were only three corporate officers -- the President, the internal auditor (Almeida), and the Vice President of Research and Development (Don Jackson).

Quentin didn't have access to the travel authorizations, but he did have access to the canceled reimbursement checks. Quentin began going through them and asking Marisa if she could identify the signature on the checks. The signature was three parallel lines at a forty-five degree angle tilted to the left with a hasty flourish of a stroke across the middle of all three. She said the first name looked like "Armando," but the last name was unintelligible.

"Armando" didn't fit the names of any of the corporate officers.

Quentin took a stack of checks and made his way down to Hen's office on the second floor. Hen was out most of the time, and his secretary guarded his front door like a Doberman Pinscher. That afternoon, though, Hen was at his desk reading the New York Times.

Quentin rapped on the door.

Hen looked up. "Come on in. Sit down," he said as he gestured with an open hand to the chair facing his desk.

Hen's office window looked out onto the expanse of Praia do Flamengo, beyond the passing cars on the busy street below. Next to the window stood a wood tripod, which held an elaborate Unitron 3-inch photo-equatorial telescope. Quentin saw that the telescope pointed toward the ocean. He remembered hearing Hen talk about the scantily clad ladies he could see from his office. Now it was clear what the telescope was for.

"What's up, buddy?" Hen said casually.

"I came across something that I thought best to bring to your attention," Quentin began.

Hen put down his newspaper.

"Yes, well, as you know," Quentin continued, "we are in the middle of the audit, and..."

"Oh, yeah, that stupid thing," Hen said, waving it away. "We passed with flying colors last year. It's just a matter of feeding the right mouths."

On Hen's desk sat a photograph of him lying in a ditch with blood all over his leg. He was surrounded by bodies--presumably all dead. The frame was bright, metallic gold.

"Well, as part of the audit, I went through the checking and expense accounts with the auditor, Mr. Almeida."

"Ol' smokestack! How's he doing? He's got the worst breath, doesn't he?"

"The auditor and I discovered some large deposits in the checking account, as well as a series of expense reimbursement checks signed by someone named 'Armando.'"

Hen's eyes were focused intently on Quentin's. His mouth was stuck in a plastic, half-smile. "Well, I don't know how they do things back at the State Department. I'll tell you that before I got wounded in Palermo, my unit excelled in passing audit."

Quentin had been warned about Hen's bogus war stories. During the War, he had been stationed at a Kentucky supply depot. The Purple Heart injury was completely fabricated. "Fake blood and second rate actors," according to Quentin's pal and President of Hancock Oil and Gas, Herbie.

"My buddies were caught in the ambush. I was the only one to make it out alive," Hen said.

"Where in Palermo did you serve?"

"Do you know Palermo?" Hen asked.

"No."

"Then it wouldn't matter, would it. I could just make up a place in Palermo and you wouldn't know it from Washington, D.C."

"Who took that picture?" Quentin asked.

"It was a photographer for Life Magazine named Freddie Cahill."

"Really?" Quentin couldn't believe his luck. "I knew Freddie, and he never went to Italy. He was captured by Japanese troops and held in a P.O.W. camp in Malaysia."

"No, it was definitely Freddie Cahill," Hen insisted.

Quentin decided not to push any further, since it wasn't why he had come to see Hen.

Hen lifted up his pant leg to show Quentin a long, white scar running up his left calf toward his knee. "There's still shrapnel in there," Hen said.

Quentin figured that Hen definitely injured his leg, but there was no telling how or by what.

"I should have gotten a Purple Heart," Hen said. "I was the only one to make it out alive."

"You're certain it was Freddie Cahill?" Quentin pressed.

"Dead certain. He showed up several hours after the attack. He even gave me his pocket watch." With that, Hen put his leg down and walked around to his desk. "Here. I have it right here." He opened up his drawer and pulled out a brass wind-up watch. "Take it."

"Thanks. I'm fine."

"No, look at the back."

Quentin took the watch and turned it over in his hand. On the back were the engraved initials, "F.C." Quentin handed it back to Hen.

"We're an oil company," Hen said. "Money flows in, money flows out, just like oil." He stood up from his chair. He walked around his desk and past Quentin. "Come with me. I want to show you something."

Quentin got up from the chair and followed Hen through the open office door and past the secretary. He followed Hen into the hallway, past a series of open office doors.

"Do you notice the complete absence of staff? My entire department is out in the field. They're pressing the flesh, gabbing the gab. They're doing what's necessary to win the next big deal."

"What sort of deal are we talking about?"

"Many irons in the fire right now. Won't hazard to guess exactly which one will cross the finish line first. Premature," Hen said as he rubbed the back of his head with the palm of his hand. "Confident, though, we'll be able to land a big one. It costs money to make money. Nothing new there," Hen said.

"Is it a deal with Petrobras?"

Hen smiled knowingly. "All roads lead to that big teat, for sure. What I'm talking about is more like prime rib. Something you can really sink your teeth into. Not the piddly bird seed we're subsisting on.

"I'm talking about drilling," Hen continued. "Dirty, messy drilling. In the ocean. At present, we're limited to a hundred foot depth, but that's going to change. I have a buddy in Baton Rouge who's building stationary platforms capable of two, three hundred feet in eight foot swells.

"What exactly are your men doing to make deals?" Quentin asked, trying to steer the conversation back to the audit.

Hen's facial expression changed like a crashing wave from salesman to skeptic.

"Like I said, pressing the flesh, contacts strategic in nature."

"I saw travel expenses for Argentina, Ecuador, and Bolivia," Quentin said.

Hen stared at Quentin with a half-smile.

"Oil knows no borders, my friend. We go where the oil is."

Hen walked around Quentin and slapped his hands on Quentin's shoulders. He squeezed lightly and said, "You know, I took a liking to you the first time we met. I'm sure we can find a way to work together. By the way, did you know that we have a common acquaintance?"

"Oh? Who?" Quentin asked.

"Hank Flannigan."

Quentin was silent as his mind raced back to his time in Taoyuan. Henry Flannigan. The radio shipment. The missing equipment. The Loyalty Research Board. The Communist accusations.

"Hank and I roomed together our freshman year at Virginia," Hen said.

"I see," Quentin said, not knowing what else to say. "Um, how is he?"

"The man is making a mint. He's in what we call, "personnel services." Private contractor now. Told me that working for Uncle Sam just didn't pay."

"What is it that he does?"

"Same thing we do here," Hen said as he turned to return to his office.

Quentin followed behind him, but Hen was finished with Quentin.

"Stay safe," Hen said as he held up a hand with his back turned to Quentin and waved it lightly as he walked away.

September 4, 1945

Dear Portia,

I'm so sorry to hear that your father died. I read it in the New York Times obituary section. Please accept my sincere condolences. He was a great man. Not just anyone could have founded a military academy and served as Assistant Secretary of the Navy.

I know from your letters that Joseph, Jr. and Francis were close to him. It must be hard.

Well, the day I waited for so long has finally come. Quentin is coming home! The cable arrived today. The bad news is that it appears he's being recalled to Washington for "consultations." Quentin thinks he is being targeted by former U.S. Ambassador Huyguens. Quentin says that Huyguens created a list of "China Hands," State Department personnel who specialize in Chinese affairs, who have actively worked against him, and now he is trying to get them all fired.

Incidentally, I never wrote a reply to Quentin's letter asking for a divorce. I figured I could deny ever having received it. If he were truly serious about getting divorced, he would have brought it up again. He never did once.

Oops, I have to run. I'm getting my hair done at a place on Shattuck, and my car is about to be towed. Bye!

Love,
Britka

"What does your cousin say about Hen?" Quentin asked Marisa.

"I do not care for Hen," she said. "He is like *Mephistopheles*." Marisa shifted her gaze to the bed. "What is that?" she asked, pointing.

"That is a diary."

"Diary? *Verdade?*" she said, a smile cracking from the side of her mouth. What does it say?"

Quentin closed the diary and put it on the bed stand without saying anything.

The area between her waistline and her belly button was the surface of eternity. She stroked his hair. She let him come inside her with his shamed, cuckold erection. She could break him with her arms. Just like that. Snap.

"How about that coffee," Quentin said, changing the subject.

"You know, my grandparents owned a coffee plantation."

"Really," he said as he massaged his temples, his attention flagging.

"Yes, Brazilians make beautiful coffee."

"I see."

"At first, you think, 'How could such beautiful coffee come from such an ugly plant?' The answer is that only by uncovering the coffee bean's inner beauty can we fully enjoy it."

"Yes, I see. What are you getting at?"

"Some things take time, but one day you wake up and you notice that something is beautiful. You must uncover it. That is what I think."

"What about *futebol*?" Quentin asked.

"*Futebol*...what can I say? When I was a teenager, everyone in my house cried when we lost to Uruguay in the final. The World Cup medals were already engraved with Brazil as the presumptive winner. Some fans took desperate measures and killed themselves. I will not speak a word about the World Cup after that. Not even the quarterfinals! It was very sad."

Quentin didn't follow Brazilian soccer close enough to really care. The only famous soccer player he had heard about was a sixteen year old star who went by the name, "Pelé."

"Regarding coffee. My father gathered stories from plantations," Marisa said. She told Quentin a story about a young man who journeyed to a city of gold called "St. Saruê," and how, upon his return to the plantation, nobody believed what he had to say. They were convinced he had been poisoned by a forest fairy, a *curupira*, with a dart dipped in hallucinogenic venom.

The young man ended up being put in a makeshift jail on the edge of the forest by the plantation boss. During the day, he heard snakes, and during the night, jaguars. After a week of confinement, he was revived by a young maid who took pity on the poor prisoner by secretly feeding him fried plantains and cups of *cauim*, which is an alcoholic drink made from chewed manioc root.

"That," Marisa finished, "is the type of story my father used to tell me when I was a girl."

Quentin hadn't been paying attention until the part where the young man was put in jail.

DRAFT VERSION

February 12, 1951

To Whom It May Concern:

My name is Britka Brevik Liege. I have been married to John Quentin Liege for nineteen years. I am writing this testimony against the wishes of our lawyer, Marcus A. Holton, Esq., who has advised me that a wife's testimony is considered the weakest of all in a body of evidence because of her loyalty to, and intimacy with, her husband. Nevertheless, I submit the following in light of recent allegations stemming from a State Department Loyalty Research Board review, which were later repeated in a recent Senate subcommittee hearing chaired by Senator Tydings, and have led to my husband's arrest by the FBI yesterday under the Foreign Espionage Act.

My husband, Quentin (he goes by that instead of his first name, John), and I met at the University of California in the fall of 1932 at the Big "C" Sirkus. We dated for four years and married after graduating.

Our marriage has been grounded in mutual trust and understanding. I never once doubted my husband's loyalty -- to me or to our country.

We left for China two weeks after the wedding. Quentin passed the Foreign Service examination, but the State Department had budget cuts that year and was not hiring any recruits. We moved to Shanghai, where he got a job as a bookkeeper for an import export company run by a friend of his father's.

It is here that I will say that Quentin was born in Peking, China. In some ways, he felt more comfortable there than in the United States. Nevertheless, even as a "B.I.C." (Born in China), he always felt he was one hundred per cent American.

Quentin is an upstanding member of the Rotary Club's Shanghai and Chungking branches.

We lived in Shanghai for nine months before Quentin was hired by the U.S. Embassy to work as a consular officer in Peking. It was there that he received training in Mandarin Chinese. Being the son of a missionary, he had very little opportunity to learn it when he was growing up. After two years in Peking, he passed the Foreign Service Language Exam. He was promoted to Senior Consular Officer, and we were sent to a remote outpost near the Burmese border called "Yunnan-fu."

Yunnan-fu was run by a local warlord beholden to the French. He made his fortune trafficking opium, which was a major crop there. Quentin contributed to several reports on the illegal opium trade in the South China Sea.

We spent three years there before his transfer to Chungking in February of 1939. By then, the U.S. Embassy had moved with fifty other embassies from Nanking to Chungking to escape the Japanese Army. Soon after we moved there the Japanese ramped up their bombing of Chungking -- sometimes several days in a row.

The Embassy at the time was a small operation. Nine consular staff worked alongside the ambassador to process passports, visas, death certificates, and other more important diplomatic duties. Quentin's job duties evolved during this time as tensions with

Japan increased. He traded off coding duties with two other junior staff members.

After Pearl Harbor, the embassy went to twenty-four-hour staffing. Days went by where my husband slept on the embassy floor, or in a cot. Getting to and from work where we lived, near downtown Chungking, had its challenges. The American embassy was located on the South bank, across the Yangtze River. Crossing the river at night was sometimes dangerous. If the water level was high, the sampans were unable to cross safely.

We were now at war with Japan. The State Department sent over more staff to handle the increased workload that came with the creation of the China Burma India Theater Headquarters in Chungking. With increased activity came increased confusion and competing agendas.

The Embassy was kept in the dark about many things going on both in Washington and in Chungking. My husband said that Chungking was like a sieve, and even though the embassy coded everything they sent, the codes were old, and apparently the Secret Police had copies of the code keys. The Ambassador had no allies back in Washington, and he lacked the necessary connections to stay abreast of the often competing U.S. initiatives and entreaties with the Nationalist government, the secret police, and the Nationalist Army.

Newly-arrived embassy staff sometimes got caught in between. Few of the new arrivals spoke or read Chinese, and they relied almost exclusively on the heavily-censored English-language Nationalist newspaper for their information. One poor soul had written a report about the overwhelming success of a Nationalist military campaign against the Japanese in Hankow only to find the U.S. Naval Attaché in his office the next day demanding that he rescind the report and write a lengthy apology. Apparently, the junior diplomat's sources were wrong, and the Nationalists had suffered a huge defeat at Hankow. The defeat was the Naval

Attaché's justification for the requisition of additional covert training resources from Washington.

Any reporter worth his salt -- for either a newspaper or for the diplomatic corps -- had to leave Chungking and see for himself what was happening on the ground. My husband did just that, day in and day out, for five years. He spent weeks on end riding trains, hitching rides on supply trucks, and talking to the peasants from towns overrun by looters and rapists from the Nationalist Army. From my perspective, knowing what I heard from his eyewitness reports, it was impossible to believe anything printed in the local papers -- not only for what was written, but also for what was omitted.

Another element missing from most American diplomatic communiqués back to Washington was what the Communists were doing. The Nationalists and Communists were as much at war with each other as they were with Japan. It was next to impossible to interact with the Communists in Chungking, at least officially, without inviting suspicion from the Secret Police.

I left Chungking before my husband was assigned to the PAX Mission in Taoyuan, and I am unable to comment on the outcome of that assignment, but I will say that his involvement with that effort had the approval of both the State Department back in Washington and of General Stilwell, the top U.S. Army commander in China.

Signed,

Britka Brevik Liege
Berkeley, California

The need to use a prophylactic. Follow up with sulfanilamide for proper hygiene, according to Pro-Kit instructions. No war babies.

Quentin had brought prophylactics in his suitcase to Recife. He had the forethought this time, but Marisa's appearance was a surprise.

"How much longer do you plan to stay here?" Marisa asked.

"I don't know. It depends on how my health holds up."

"Do you know what is your problem?"

If Quentin's passport photo was any indication of his state of being, it showed a bespectacled, middle aged "Joe" with thinning hair and rounded shoulders.

Back in Berkeley, he took to parking the car several blocks from home, sliding over to the passenger side, opening the door and putting his legs out. From the glovebox, he would retrieve a pack of Lucky Strikes and a lighter and have a smoke. That was the only time of the day he could truly breathe. When he got home, life became complicated.

The furniture in Quentin's and Britka's colonial revival home on Walnut Street in Berkeley was all her doing. The Chinese love seat was essentially a stained wood box with thin, silk cushions and a straight back of black, lacquered mahogany. Quentin joked that it was a great posture piece. The dining set was Dutch, in a utilitarian, Mies Van der Rohe sort of way. There was no poetry in its design. It wanted you off and away at the last sip of post-dessert coffee.

The couch next to the now defunct, original 1910-era fireplace was deceptive. The dark, shiny leather cushions were puffed up to tease, seductive in their sensory allure. Nonetheless, upon resting one's derrière on the squeaky, sagging wood frame, inevitable disappointment ensued.

Quentin thought about how to answer Marisa and decided it was best to say exactly what was on his mind. "I have a suspicion

178

it's what's called 'Spleen *Ch'i* Deficiency' in Chinese medicine," he said.

Marisa knew he had lived in China for a long time. She had seen the long, silk calligraphy scrolls on his office wall. She had heard the inscrutable whining of Mei Lan-fang singing the Peking opera, "Peony Pavilion," on the Victrola.

"Spleen -- do you mean, *Baço*?"

"Yes, same as Almeida."

Marisa clucked her tongue. "Ooh la. I forgot," she said, "the food."

"No, I'm fine," Quentin said. "I'm really not hungry."

"You must eat," she said as she approached him with the shirt and slacks in her hand. "Now, you must dress first." She handed him the clothes.

Quentin stood up and removed the hanger from the shirt. He put his arms through the sleeves and fumbled with the buttons on the shirt.

"Here, let me help you," she said. She buttoned his shirt for him.

Britka did this for him whenever he was not quite together in his head, which had been often, back in Berkeley.

When she finished the last button, she handed him the slacks. He took them, and, one shaky foot at a time, stepped into them.

"There," she said, and she walked over to the table. "Now you must eat."

"That's very kind of you, but..."

"I will go down to the bar to order coffee."

"Just as well," he said, not wanting her to go through the trouble.

She ignored him and left the room.

Now alone, Quentin went over to the table to see what was inside the bag. He wondered how she had managed to find food this early in the morning.

There was a small package wrapped in a large, floral bandana with a bow at the top. He untied the bow and pulled away the fabric. There were three tins with lids stacked on top of one another. He unstacked the tins and placed them side by side on the table. He lifted the lid off of the first tin. Inside appeared to be a stir-fry made of black seed pods covered in shredded celery and thinly sliced red chiles. It smelled spicy and fermented, like **Ma-po tofu**. Quentin wasn't sure his stomach could handle that.

The second tin contained an assortment of cut tropical fruits. Sliced **guavasteen**, jelly palm, wild passionfruit, Brazil plum, and small, hairy, lantern-like bulbs, which Quentin could not identify. It was a bright mixture of reds and pinks. The juicy, green flesh of the guavasteen gave off a perfume of pineapple, vanilla and mint. The mélange must have touched a nerve in him, because he found himself grabbing the fork and wolfing down the fruit.

His reaction to Marisa's appearing at his hotel room had been similar. He devoured her. He sensed in her a mother-like care for him.

It scared him that he felt that sort of dependence on her.

When he finished the fruit, he opened the third tin. Inside was his room key.

Just then, Marisa knocked on the door. She opened it with one hand while balancing a tray with the other.

"It is not so good coffee," she said with a look of disappointment.

"Turns out I was a little hungry," Quentin said as she put the tray of coffee down on the table

Marisa saw the open tins. "Um, yes. Of course." She replaced the lid on top and put it in the wet paper bag.

"Did you try the spicy one?" she asked.

"Is it edible?"

"It was made by a Chinese man downtown. He said that it is a traditional dish."

"What's it called?"

180

"I do not know," Marisa said. "He wrote it down for me." She reached into her purse on the table and pulled out a slip of paper.

"Here," she said.

Expecting to read Chinese characters, he was surprised to see something unintelligible scrawled out in cursive, blue pencil.

"I can't read it," he said as he handed the slip of paper back to her.

"Coffee?" he asked.

"Yes," she said. She slid the saucer over to him. "Cream or sugar?"

"Black, thanks."

Marisa looked out the window for a moment and then turned her attention back to Quentin. She lifted the coffee cup and saucer out of the tray and placed them on the table.

"Quentin," she began. It was the first time she had called him that. "We have slept together. You are my boss. What do we do now?"

Quentin had already worked this out in his head despite his debilitating headache.

"We'll have to see."

"Do you mean, leave Hancock?"

Quentin let the idea sink in.

Marisa's face tightened. "Fuck."

"Where did you *learn that word*?" he retorted. The word was a rusty knife.

"'What, fuck?' Miles Davis, Allen Ginsberg. I will tell you that I have slept with men *and* women. I do not have a preference."

"Do your parents know?"

"My parents do not care. They were arrested last year for organizing a labor strike. They are members of the Brazilian Communist Party."

Quentin was living the movie, "Invasion of the Bodysnatchers." Here, he was sleeping with Communists. Again.

"Are you a member?" Quentin asked, rubbing the back of his head.

"No," she said wagging her finger definitively. "I do not follow Joseph Stalin or Mao Tse-tung. I should ask you, are you a Communist?" she said, giggling.

"No."

"Then, why do you insist that I leave Hancock? I am not a Communist. Are you afraid that we will *fuck* again?"

"Please don't use that word. It's vulgar and unbecoming."

"*Fuck?*" Marisa asked, her hands thrown up in the air.

Quentin felt like hunted prey.

"You are embarrassed," she continued. "Admit it. You like to fuck." She walked over to Quentin and stroked his cheek with her fingers.

Quentin turned away. She was right.

"If you are feeling well, we can go to the beach. The rain has stopped. It will be sunny," she said.

"You keep mentioning the beach."

"What is wrong with the beach?"

"It's high tide. There are sharks."

"I have heard of such things," she said with a look of pity. "That is not why I want to go to the beach. I do not know if it is high tide or not. It is soon to be Christmas, and the rain is gone. I do not know how to swim."

"How is that possible?"

"I refuse to wear *fio dental*," Marisa said, referring to string bikinis. "So, I don't swim."

Quentin imagined Marisa wearing a string bikini. He had dreamt about it before.

"I'll help you get another job," Quentin said.

"You do not know anyone in Rio."

"Maybe your cousin can help. The one who works for Hen."

"My cousin is a *puta*.

"Didn't she get you your current job?"

"No, she did not. I was hired by *Advogado* Almeida. He wanted someone who spoke English. My mother's parents live next door to him."

"Almeida hired you?" Quentin wondered how didn't know this.

"*Advogado* Almeida thinks you are an exotic bird. He cannot understand why you came to Brazil. He thinks you are running away from something. He asks 'Why does a diplomat who speaks Chinese come to Rio?' He thinks you are C.I.A."

"I'm not C.I.A.," he said, "but I can't say I have a good answer why I'm here. Running away, that's probably the best answer."

The Brazil opportunity had appeared on his doorstep, two weeks after Eisenhower's re-election. The telegram read:

Saw your name in the Times the other day. Wondered if you and your wife want to get away. I need someone with your skills. Interested? Send reply ASAP. Will be out your way in few weeks. Will discuss over lunch. Yours, Herbie.

Herbert Stochaiovic was the son of a friend of Quentin's father. Both fathers had been missionaries in China. Quentin and Herbie had been classmates at Peking Christian School. He was now the President of Hancock Oil and Gas.

Six years earlier, Quentin had been fired from his job at the State Department. The Loyalty Research Board, created by Congress to find Communists inside the U.S. government, decided that Quentin had aided the Communist Chinese during his time in Taoyuan. That simple fact was undeniable. The entire U.S. Army had aided the Communists. For some reason, the Board found a convenient scapegoat in Quentin and wanted to pin the "loss" of China to the Communists on China specialists like him.

Quentin's firing hit the front pages of the Los Angeles Times, and, like one dog barking can set off all the other dogs in the neighborhood, it wasn't long before his story was on the front pages of every major daily. His chances of finding another job dissolved like salt in boiling water.

Quentin filed suit in federal district court in Washington, D.C. The case dragged on for years and was still pending when he got the telegram about the Brazil job.

Then, thousands of miles away, the Taiwan Straits Crisis began.

The Communist Chinese seized a few islands north of Taiwan and began shelling two other islands claimed by Taiwan. To many in Washington, it was proof of the Domino Theory. There was talk of the U.S. using nuclear weapons against the Communists.

During the conflagration, reporters trotted out the old saw about the "China Traitors," which referred to former State Department Foreign Service officers like Quentin who had worked in China during the War and had supposedly "sold out" to Communism. The papers implied that the Taiwan Straights Crisis was a byproduct of their treachery.

Quentin's few remaining friends in Washington said that the "China Traitor" stories served a different purpose. They helped justify more Congressional appropriations for the struggling, anti-Communist Nationalist government in Taiwan and more military aid to President Chiang Kai-shek.

Britka watched the man as he sat at the bench seat next to the front door. His wing tip shoes were pointed together, like penguin feet. He held his fedora in his hand and scratched the feather band.

"I read through your draft statement to the State Department, along with the letters to your friend, Portia. As I advised you earlier, I doubt that either the State Department or the Senate subcommittee will allow any of it into the record. I think one major flaw in your testimony is you come off sounding like you are familiar with the detailed goings on of the Embassy. Maybe too familiar."

"What do you mean?"

"You mention the coding activities, and you say that the Secret Police had copies of the code books."

"That's what my husband told me."

"Do you have any proof?"

"No."

"I would leave it out. Another thing: you said that diplomatic communiqués didn't include reports on the Communists. How could you know this? Did your husband share with you top secret diplomatic communiqués?"

"I am just repeating what he told me."

"I would leave out that bit as well. We don't want your testimony to create more suspicion."

"I understand."

"Do you have anything else you want to show me before I make my edits to the document?"

"No," Britka said. "I'm amazed that I was able to find those letters. I never got around to mailing them. I did correspond with Portia, but it was very difficult to get mail out of Chungking. She probably still has the letters that I did end up sending her. If you think they will help get Quentin out of jail, I will write to her to see if she can send them."

"I don't see a need for that right now. My staff is arranging bail. He'll likely be in jail for one night only."

"Could you explain to me again the charges against him?"

The man stood up and put his hat on.

"He was charged under the Espionage Act. The case is very weak, though, so I don't expect that it will take long."

"What is he accused of doing?"

"Aiding a foreign government. Now that the Communists have taken control of China, there are many politicians in Washington looking for someone to blame."

He put on his overcoat and walked to the door. "I will call you later if I need anything else."

Britka stepped forward toward the door.

The lawyer stopped. He turned around. "Sorry, just one question. Your husband had his affair while you were living here?"

"Yes, that's correct," Britka said.

"He told you about it in a letter?"

"Yes, he asked for a divorce."

"You never sent a reply?"

"Yes, that's correct."

"Did you talk about the affair later, after he was recalled?"

"Yes, of course. She's living in Taiwan now. How is that relevant?"

"I just want to understand what was communicated between you two. The fact that he had an affair with a Chinese national may come into play in his hearing."

"How so?"

"I don't have an answer. As you probably saw in the papers, there are allegations she was a spy."

"Oh dear."

"How did you meet your wife?"

Quentin took a moment to clear his throat. "We met in college," he said in a hoarse voice.

After they married, Britka followed him to China. She had resigned from a promising sales job at Emporium Capwell in San Francisco to follow Quentin to Peking, where he was to study intensive diplomatic Mandarin Chinese at the Peking Teacher's College.

To Quentin, being back in the Chinese capital after having grown up there quarter century before was both good and bad.

186

There was the morning walk from the Foreign Legation, through Hata Men Gate, past the fur stores, the Thieves' Market, and finally to the Temple of Heaven. There was the morning cry of the soy milk vendor hawking both sweet and salty versions. The old codgers in the park every Sunday gathered and showed off their cricket cages.

On the bad side, the rice that they ate often had small pebbles mixed in with it. American friends said they suspected the Chinese put the rocks in to irritate the foreigners. Quentin cracked two crowns during their time there. The slipshod dentistry in Peking left an indelible dental crime to his mouth. It followed him all the way to Taoyuan, several years later, and drove him to smoke opium to manage the pain.

Besides that were the Gobi dust storms in spring, the drenching humidity in summer, and the soot-soaked coughing fits in winter. If the weather didn't kill you, the slow drip of bureaucratic hassles would. City government officials believed their mission in life was to be miserable, and they expressed that sentiment with checkpoints throughout the city where they required identification and signed papers to travel through, between, and among city gates. The notion of simply hopping a bicycle and going through Chung I Men and out to Lu-Kuo Bridge or beyond to the duck hunting area without papers and a little cumshaw was foreign to them.

After Peking, Quentin moved to the American Consulate in Kunming, and finally to the embassy in Chungking. He took Britka with him. After the Japanese bombed Pearl Harbor, the embassy evacuated all dependents. Britka returned to California by herself. By that time, they both agreed it was for the best.

"You did not want children?"

"No. That wasn't in the cards. Marisa, I think you should go now."

"I will return later, okay?"

"No. I don't think that's a good idea. Better that you return to Rio. Do you need money?"

"Why do I have to leave?"

Quentin wanted her gone.

Marisa changed the subject. "You said that you left in a hurry. You did not let me make the travel arrangements. Why?"

"I don't want to go into that now."

Back in Rio, Quentin had been waiting for correspondence from his lawyer in Washington, D.C. He feared the worst: the postman had simply dumped his bag of letters over a bridge and into the river to lighten his load. Quentin's lawsuit against the State Department would drown in a river.

A week before, he had been sitting on the balcony of his apartment and watching crowds of people dressed in white walk below him. He was drinking coconut water out of a straw. He put the spherical husk to his lips, tilted his head back and sucked at the thin nectar. The stench of rotting papaya seeds mixed with ocean mist and gave off a sweet, salty smell.

The faucets in the apartment had stopped working for no particular reason. Quentin figured it was the government's unpredictable water rationing scheme. Quentin suggested to Britka that they go for a stroll.

Later that night, the crowds on the strand four stories down from the open bedroom window had thinned out to where all that remained were a few diehard revelers singing drinking songs. Quentin was awake in bed scratching a mosquito bite on his ankle.

Britka took a short, quick breath. Had she heard him gasp, he wondered?

He sat up. A sound was coming from outside. He got out of bed and got dressed and went to the kitchen. There, he scribbled a note to Britka on the back of a pad of Hancock stationery.

My Dear:

I'm leaving early this morning and will call you from the road later tomorrow afternoon.

All of my love, Q

At the bus station, the overnight from Sao Paulo was just arriving. Quentin sat hunched over on a bench near the men's restroom. Dirt lined the corners of the floor next to the wall. A faded candy wrapper lay on the ground.

His canvas suitcase sat next to him. It held a spare pair of khaki pants, two T-shirts, one madras short sleeve button down shirt given to him by Britka, a wind-up alarm clock, a back issue of National Geographic, and a package of prophylactics.

His briefcase held his shaving kit, an unopened pack of Lucky Strikes, and his China diary.

His bowels churned and ached.

The bus ride to Recife took twenty-seven hours. Quentin traded off holding his side with his right hand and hunching forward into the seat in front of him. The trip was supposed to be much shorter, but the bus hit a deep pothole several kilometers outside Santo Estevão and the left rear axle sheared off. The passengers could see the orphaned wheel lying flat on the side of the road, so they unloaded from the bus in the rain, opened their umbrellas, retrieved their luggage, caged chickens, and bottles of booze, and began a foot pilgrimage north on Highway 116 toward the next town.

Walking in the rain with luggage was grim business. Half an hour into it, the local military police appeared and loaded them into troop carriers for the remaining fifteen kilometers.

Quentin managed to get through to Britka at the post office in Feira de Santana.

"I got your note," she said. "Are you really on a business trip? Two men came by today asking for you."

"I can't explain right now," he said as he heard a *beep-dash* sound over the receiver.

"I'm confused. How come you didn't say anything? Is everything all right? You don't sound relaxed."

Quentin told her the name of the hotel where he would be staying in Recife. "If those men come by again, don't let them know where I am." Another *beep-dash* sound from the receiver.

"Are you in some kind of trouble?"

"I don't know. I can't talk now." *Beep-dash.*

"Where are you calling from?"

"A small town. The bus broke down. I had to walk in the rain."

"Oh dear. Do you have enough money? Do you need anything?" *Beep-dash.*

"Not right now. I'll call you when I get to Recife."

"Please be careful."

"I will. I love you."

"Love you too. Goodbye," she said before he placed the handset back in the cradle.

There was a knock on the door. Quentin sat up and walked over to open it. It was the cleaning lady. He let her in.

Quentin could smell the alcohol in the sweat on his forearms.

"I think I'll take a shower," he said.

Marisa stood up and touched the barrettes in her hair. "I will go then," she said.

Quentin walked over to the bathroom and shut the door. He removed his shirt and trousers, his underwear, and he stood in front of the mirror. He had bags under his eyes. He needed to shave. His gut hung around his waist like a boa constrictor.

He reached into the bathtub and turned on the shower. When the temperature was right, he held his body steady against the tile wall and climbed in slowly. He closed his eyes and submerged his head in the warm stream of warm water. He felt blood returning to his cheeks and fingers and toes. Time seemed to stop.

As he stood like a sweating, watering statue, his mind cleared and he felt the impulse to call Marisa to join him. He called out her name.

No answer.

"What in the Hell am I doing?" he asked himself.

He remembered that she said she was leaving. He had asked her to do just that an hour before. For all he knew, she was gone for good. No more Marisa. He had to blame himself for that. He felt shame for what he'd done. He was embarrassed for himself as well as for her, but she didn't share that feeling. She didn't run screaming out of the bedroom the night before. She had brought him breakfast, for God sakes!

"Wait a moment. I love this woman," he thought. He imagined them running off to Argentina and starting a family on a farm. Britka would find a good looking Brazilian painter. Life would be grand.

Quentin wanted Marisa to be with him in the shower. He wanted to make love again.

Hoping to catch Marisa before she left his life for good, he quickly scrubbed his chest, arms and legs with soap and rinsed, performed a cursory hair dousing with shampoo, and turned off the water. He grabbed a towel, dried off, wrapped the towel around his waist and opened the bathroom door. As he stepped into the room, his foot kicked over a second empty *cachaça* bottle.

"Why do you write Chinese in your diary?" Marisa asked from the bed, where she was seated with his diary in her hands.

Quentin knew she couldn't read the Chinese. He wondered if she guessed that he had written about her.

Behold, a deity stronger than I; who coming, shall rule over me.

"Is the maid still here?" he asked.

"She left. She will return later. Have you done this before?" she asked.

"This?"

"This," she said, lowering her voice and pointing to her crotch.

"You mean other than my wife? Uh, well, yes, once."

"You seduced me into your bed."

"I didn't seduce you," he said. "By the way, can you get me another towel?"

His love could turn out to be his downfall, he thought. It could change his life irrevocably.

Thinking about her the way he did drove him to question his morals. His motivation. What was it about middle age that drove men into the arms of young ladies, he wondered?

She could be his lover, and he, hers. That had been his reasoning. Theoretical, of course, because none of this was actually possible. Then, it would end. He'd return to the States, and she'd continue working at Hancock Gas and Oil, safe in her position -- as long as Almeida was alive.

"My God, this is going to be a huge mistake," he thought before he let her into the room the previous night. There was that glimmer in her eyes, and they connected on a common frequency.

She had come to him, so, technically, he hadn't seduced her. He had communicated, in intangible ways, his smoldering desire for her. It was clear when she had appeared unannounced in Recife. That she followed him all the way to a coastal city in northern Brazil was evidence of something between them, although Quentin couldn't say what.

"You did seduce me," she said as she got up from the bed and went to the bathroom to get a towel. When she returned, she had a pack of cigarettes and a book of matches in her hands.

"You know how to get everything," Quentin said, smiling.

She offered the pack to Quentin. He took it and pulled out a cigarette. She reached over and struck a match to light it. She then pulled out one for herself and lit it.

Quentin took a long drag. The hot smoke singed the back of his throat like acid.

Marisa took a short puff from hers and stared at Quentin.

"I did not know you smoke," she said.

"I haven't for a long time."

Can I have the towel?

"Oh, yes. Sorry," she said. She handed it to him. "So, tell me about your Chinese lover. Do you write to her?"

"No. We lost touch."

Quentin didn't know if Ai-ling had ever emigrated to the States, or if she stayed in Taiwan.

With the Korean War ending in a stalemate, and the Communists fighting a proxy war with the U.S. in the Taiwan Straights, there was very little information coming out of Communist China. Soviet advisors were in Peking building factories. That much Quentin knew.

"You don't talk about your wife, Britka" Marisa said, making an effort to pronounce her name with an American accent.

"No, I don't."

"You have been married a long time, no?"

"Twenty-three years."

"*Oh, la,*" she said clucking her tongue. "We have shared intimacy and you have told me nothing about her."

"Let's leave her out of this discussion."

"No. I want to know more."

Quentin had tried calling her from the hotel before all of this business with Marisa happened. Next to a dusty roll piano in the corner of the hotel lobby sat a polished desk with carved handle chairs. This was the location of the house telephone, which was where one made long distance calls. Quentin had tried several times to reach Britka in Rio. Twice, the line simply went dead; the third time, Quentin heard a ringing sound, but nobody answered. Maybe, she was at the American Club playing tennis, he thought.

He felt a tremendous ball growing in his gut as his headache subsided. The affair in China had been a mistake. He was making it again.

Britka would be upset that he'd slept with his secretary -- so *unimaginative*, she would say.

There was no way out, he realized. He'd broken the window; now he had to find a way through it without being cut by glass.

"Do you still sleep with your wife?"

"I...yes...no...why do you ask?"

Quentin and Britka's bedroom was not unlike that of others of their generation. They slept in separate, twin-sized, "His and Hers" beds. It wasn't so much a symbol of their reworked matrimonial bond as it was practical accommodation. He snored, and she had elbows like javelins. He was a kicker, and she was Napoleon, conquering every last square inch of enemy territory.

Sleep was competition.

The single, queen-sized bed that greeted them on their first night at their Rio apartment pointed to ominous nocturnal battles ahead.

Their first night in the apartment was no contest, with Quentin flying the white flag well before midnight and ending up on the chaise lounge in the living room. "Night Two" saw a plucky comeback by Quentin at half past four, after he had accumulated a critical mass of pillows between his body and hers, such that all he needed to do was apply simple pressure every few minutes for her not to notice that she was slowly going off the edge. She woke up on the floor the next morning.

Eventually, they negotiated a nonverbal detente and found their way to sleeping together for the first time since they had lived in Chungking.

Quentin had come to the following realization about his marriage. Ladies marry one of two types: the dangerous man or the safe man. The dangerous man lasts only three or four years, because he is inherently unstable and potentially violent. The sex

194

is amazing. The safe man relationship lasts longer, possibly a lifetime, but the sex fails to register on the Richter Scale.

Monogamous couples who stayed married their whole lives generally fell into the safe man category, and the longevity of their coupling was explained by the death of their respective sex lives. A form of sexual suicide. The women grew wide at the waist, and the men became more feminine.

"Do you still love her?"

"Love?" Quentin asked himself. That was the wrong question. It was knowing whether she took cream in her coffee; how much salt she liked on her roast beef; what color dress brought out the best in her features. It was liking the same kind of *Pu-er* tea, and finishing each other's sentences at the dinner table.

Quentin wondered if elapsed time transcended the temporary, fleeting value of something so ephemeral as love. Shared history was concrete and enduring, even if it wasn't as solid as it may appear.

"You say nothing. You are not in love."

"No. I love her. I feel love for her...," he said, as if to convince himself.

"But, you love me as well."

Quentin couldn't get her out of his mind. Their naked bodies together, like puzzle pieces finding each other.

"Britka and I make love," he said.

"*Verdade?*" Marisa said, unconvinced.

"What does she wear when you make love?"

"Wear?"

"For example, does she wear ladies' underpants?"

"That's none of your business."

"I think she wears ladies's underpants to bed. She does not let you remove them. She ties them on her waist with a belt. She does not let you touch her body..."

"You are a very rude girl," he yelled.

"Do you wish that I am a virgin? I will pretend that I am a virgin. I am your virgin *puta*. Do you still want to fuck me?"

Quentin was silent. He was losing Marisa and he didn't know why.

Marisa looked with pity on Quentin and the evidence on his face of his predicament.

"What is the difference to you between making love and fucking?" he asked.

"Fucking is out of need. It is not always beautiful. So you fucked me out of need. What can I say? I am disappointed."

Marisa's words stabbed Quentin like a shiv. He wanted so much for Marisa to want him like he wanted her. He assumed that she felt an attraction to him; otherwise, why would she travel all this way? Now, he felt like a worn stoneware dining set at a garage sale: it caught the eye, but on closer inspection wasn't worth the asking price.

"I do make love to my wife," Quentin said, returning to her question.

"You are lying. If that is the case, why did you accept me?" she asked.

Quentin wasn't going to tell her now that he wanted her like the moon. That he longed to move his palms down the outlines of her silhouette hips.

"I thought you were in trouble," he said, grasping.

"What kind of trouble?"

"At the office. After what happened to Almeida. I thought you might be in trouble."

"How so?"

"Out to get you."

"Get me?"

"Hurt you."

Marisa started laughing. "What an imagination you have. So, you are saying that you did this for me? You know, I have a boyfriend. His name is Jorge. We do not sleep together, except sometimes. I was not a virgin before we fucked, here in this room."

"Does Jorge know you are with me?"

"I told him that I had to visit my aunt in Belo Horizonte."

"So, you lied?"

"As did you," she said.

"Do you plan to see your aunt?"

"Maybe. I may be pregnant."

Quentin's heart skipped a beat. Even taking every precaution didn't mean it was impossible.

"By Jorge?"

"By you."

"No. I used protection."

"Brazilian?"

"Yes."

"Unreliable. The Catholic Church does sabotage to them. The Pope likes more babies."

Quentin hadn't considered the possibility that the prophylactics were damaged intentionally. Of all places to be buying such a life-critical commodity -- a Catholic country, where contraception was wrong.

"There is a way to tell if you're pregnant," he said.

"I do not understand," she said, her face turning battleship gray.

Seeing this change, Quentin switched sides. "I want you to be pregnant."

"You are definitely sick," she said.

Quentin looked at her from across the room as she walked slowly back to him. "You're trying to get a rise out of me, aren't you? You're yanking my chain about being pregnant. You probably didn't think I want to have a baby."

Marisa looked at him with confusion. "What is chain?"

"You're trying to put one over on me."

"Sorry. I Don't understand."

"You're joking!"

Marisa smiled at this suggestion. "No. I don't know," she said, waving him away.

"We could name it 'Sergio,'" he said.

"Sergio?"

"Yes, that seems like a strong Latin name."

"What if it's a girl?" she asked, puffing on her cigarette again.

"A girl? Things are different if it is a girl. If you are really pregnant, how do I know that I'm the father? What if you showed up yesterday already pregnant by your boyfriend?"

"You mean, that I lie to you that you are the father?"

"Yes, you lied to your boyfriend about coming here."

"OK, it is possible that I am not pregnant," she said.

"You're not, are you," Quentin said, looking her squarely in the eyes.

"How do I know?" Marisa said, throwing her hands up in the air. "You will see tomorrow morning, or the next day, when I am sick."

The doorbell rang, and Britka went to the door and looked through the square peephole to see who it was. A short man in a hat and suit was standing outside. She opened the door.

"Good afternoon, ma'am," he said. "My name's Edward Phil. I'm a reporter for the Scripps Howard newspapers. I wanted to see if you wouldn't mind answering some questions about your husband?"

Britka did a quick evaluation of the man and determined he was non-threatening. "Yes, of course," she said.

"May I come inside?"

"Yes, certainly."

The man entered without removing his hat. "Can we talk in the living room?" he said, motioning beyond the foyer toward the couch.

Something in his way of inviting himself into her home made Britka feel apprehensive all the sudden.

"I would prefer that we talk here," she said.

"Have it your way," he said.

"What are your questions?" she asked.

"Yes, of course. Have you spoken to your husband since his arrest yesterday?"

"No."

"Were you surprised to see your husband's arrest in the front page news?"

"It wasn't front page news here," she said.

"It was in our papers."

"Of course I was surprised. Quentin hasn't done anything illegal."

"Well, ma'am, I'd say that being arrested by the FBI as a spy is serious business."

"I'm confident that he will be cleared."

"Can I quote you on that?"

"Quote me? What are you talking about?"

"For my article."

"What is your article about?"

"I'm writing about how your husband was part of a clandestine group of Communist spies in the State Department who helped cause the defeat of Generalissimo Chiang Kai-shek and the Nationalist government. Your husband had a Chinese lover and fathered a child out of wedlock with her. She was Mao Tse-tung's personal assistant. Your husband tried to use his position in the State Department to get his lover a visa so she could join him and live here in America."

Britka smirked. "My God, that's brilliant," she deadpanned.

The man kept a stern face.

"The only new part to that worn-out story," Britka continued, "is the bit about the Chinese lover being a personal assistant to Mao. If anything, she was an agent of the Nationalists. How else do you explain the fact that she escaped to Taiwan after the Communists took control of the mainland? Did you bother to find out where she's living now? Taipei. What agent of Mao's would be living in Taipei?"

"So you confirm that the rest of the story is true," the reporter said.

"It's hogwash. All of it," Britka said.

"From your denial, I can assume that you too were in on the plan. Why else would you deny it?"

"Why else, indeed. How about, because it's a story fabricated by the Pro-Nationalist lobby in Washington? Listen, I don't know what happened over there during the War, but it was ugly. It was confusing, too, but the PAX Mission had the approval of both the State Department and the U.S. Army."

"Did that include sleeping with the enemy?"

"What do you mean?'"

The reporter put down his coat and removed his hat. He took a step toward her. Britka sensed a change in his tone and took a step back.

"I think you know what I'm talking about, Mrs. Liege. Your husband had an affair. That much is known. The woman had his baby. Don't you feel at least a little resentment about that, given the fact that you have been unable to have a child yourself? Maybe you've just been with the wrong man, or, maybe you're attracted to the Orson Welles type."

He took another step forward. Britka followed with another step back.

"I don't think we have anything more to talk about. I think you should leave."

"You don't really want me to leave, do you?"

Britka held up her hand to stop his advance. "No, I want you to leave, Mr. Edward Phil from Scripps-Howard. Let me make myself very clear. I want you out of this house. Now. This very instant. Gather your stuff, open that door, and walk out, before you regret it."

After she had shut the door and gotten her hand to stop shaking uncontrollably, she noticed that his hat still lay on the bench next to the door. She walked over to the liquor cabinet, opened it, and she pulled down a bottle of Dewar's Gin. She poured herself two jiggers' worth in a large martini glass and downed it.

She put the glass down and walked upstairs to Quentin's study. She opened the door and went to his rollaway desk. She pulled open the lower left drawer, where he had a collection of Chinese keepsakes -- miniature flags, commemorative key rings, a fountain pen with U.S. Army insignia, and calling cards from various friends, alive and dead. Underneath all of that was his Taoyuan diary from his time with the PAX Mission.

She placed the diary on the desk and took a deep breath. As far as she knew, Quentin had told her everything. She hoped that she wouldn't find anything more.

Quentin recalled how Britka had become violently ill with morning sickness. She was bedridden with nausea and had trouble keeping food down. It was as if her body treated pregnancy like a virus and shut down to only vital functions to rid itself of the foreign object.

"I have bad luck with pregnancy," Quentin said to Marisa.

In rereading parts of his diary from Taoyuan, he was surprised at how little he had written about Ai-ling while he was there. No mention of their trysts.

Five years later, after being recalled to the States, news of the Ai-ling's baby made its way to him.

Were you aware that someone named Ai-ling Chang claims you are the father of her child, and that she has applied for citizenship?

That possibility faded over time. Years went by, and he hadn't heard from Ai-ling. He wasn't sure if she ever made her way to the States.

"Please don't leave," he said grabbing her hand.

"Now you want me to stay?" she scoffed.

"Yes, I changed my mind."

"Why?"

"I wasn't thinking clearly earlier. Maybe it was from the *cachaça.*"

"I told you to stop. You did not listen."

"No, I didn't."

"I know your problem. We call it '*saudade.*'"

To Quentin, it sounded like "sow-DA-jee."

"Your heart is longing for something that will never come back," Marisa said. You are feeling alone. Your heart is looking for comfort and turns to a fond memory from the past."

Quentin considered this for a moment and said, "You're right. I did seduce you. I want to get married and have kids with you."

"I think I do need to leave," she said. "You and your Chinese lover, whoever that is, can get married together."

A gloom fell over Quentin's face.

Quentin had emptied every ounce of gasoline in his tank to burn down the flimsy shack of a relationship he had built with Marisa. Now, he desperately wanted to save it.

Quentin realized that this might be the last time he ever felt love. It made his chest feel heavy. The death of passion. What followed was arthritis, heart disease, emphysema, tuberculosis, then physical death.

He longed to hold her, to feel her hair with his fingers.

Quentin walked to the open window. The warm December smelled like wet carpet drying in the sun. The clouds had blown north, and an offshore breeze blew the heavy curtains to the side. A large wasp flew in and buzzed Quentin's ear. Outside, an escaped monkey had climbed a palm tree and was shrieking at the top of its register.

He remembered what she had said when she appeared at his door the day before:

My sister left for São Paulo last night, and I thought how much I wanted to be with you.

Don't you live with your parents?

No.

So you won't be missed.

I told my aunt that I will take a vacation for a few days.

What about the office -- what did you tell them?

I said that I had a fever.

A fever?

Yes. A fever.

He reached around her waist and unclasped her wool skirt. His heart was pounding in his throat, and his hands were shaking. Underneath her wool skirt was a corset girdle with garters. He unclasped the straps that held up her stockings and rolled the stockings down her thighs. She lay down on the bed. She lifted each leg as he worked his way down to her ankles. As he came back up to her girdle, he sensed what lay beneath her laced undergarments. He wanted to kiss her there, but she stopped him by putting her hand over his mouth.

Only for penis, she said, pointing to his crotch.

He nodded in affirmation, sat up, stepped off of the bed and went to the bathroom. He emerged holding three foil-wrapped prophylactics.

Ah, isso é bom.

He walked back to the bed. She sat up and unzipped his trousers and undid his waist belt. She slid his trousers down to his knees, and he stepped out of them.

Bom dia! *She said, giggling as she slid her hand into his boxer shorts and grasped his penis.*

The four poster bed in his hotel room squeaked. The loose headboard rocked forward and back, bumping against the wall.

Each time he entered her became more urgent and more necessary.

Marisa had seemed increasingly passive, letting him do his thing and then falling asleep. Quentin sensed the inequality -- not in age, but in attraction.

He sensed from her that he was just a *gringo* novelty rapidly losing its shimmer.

Loma Prieta

October 1989

Ai-ling was yelling at me in Mandarin from the passenger seat of a rental van as we were speeding down College Avenue. I couldn't understand a word she was saying. It was past midnight, and I was trying to keep the van from veering into oncoming traffic.

In the back of the van was a wheeled gurney, with Mr. Liege strapped down in it. We were coming from a Chinese doctor in Oakland Chinatown and were heading back to St. Matthews at full bore, because Mr. Liege seemed to be suffering another stroke.

College Avenue instead of San Pablo. Freeway, closed. Traffic, a nightmare.

My frantic driving was going to get us pulled over, and that would be the end of it. Transporting a patient without a hospital release, a misdemeanor. Kidnapping, a felony. Exceeding the speed limit by more than double, also a felony. If Mr. Liege died, involuntary manslaughter -- a third felony. I was looking at minimum five to twenty in state prison.

"He's making those gurgling sounds again!" I yelled to Ai-ling over the sound of the van's engine and the air conditioner blowing at full blast.

"*Dou shi ni de*" she yelled back at me. This, I understood, because I heard it said in a Taiwanese soap opera by a woman angry at her husband for getting the neighbor pregnant: "It's all your fault!"

Insofar as I procured the van, she was right, and to the extent that I agreed that the physician at St. Matthews had given up on Mr. Liege, yes. However, the plan was hers. Dr. Lim was her doctor.

I felt my face flush as I realized that something was seriously wrong with Mr. Liege, and he was miles from proper medical treatment.

As I look back at the particular insanity I experienced then, I can only attribute it to the earthquake.

The day before, Tuesday, October 17, an earthquake centered forty miles away in Santa Cruz leveled a section of the upper deck on the Nimitz Freeway in Oakland during rush hour. I was finishing up work and looking forward to going home. My daily commute took me across the Nimitz Freeway. If the earthquake had struck a half hour later, I would probably have been sandwiched between the upper and lower decks of the Cypress Overpass.

I was in the linen closet when the earthquake began just after five p.m. I was restocking the sheets and pillow cases when the shelves started wobbling, and the light fixture in the room suddenly went dark. The shaking continued, and out of instinct, I lifted my hands to steady the shelves so they wouldn't topple over and crush me.

When the shaking stopped, I turned the knob on the door, and to my surprise it was locked. I felt around on the ground and began picking up fallen items: detergent bottles, sponges, small boxes of rags.

I knew that Mr. Liege was considered a lost cause. The doctors said his condition was not going to improve. They had removed his feeding tube.

He had no living relatives to make the case to keep him on life support. He had no advance directives. Not even a will.

I had done some reading about Mr. Liege's condition, and one account compared it to solitary confinement. I thought that wasn't a very good comparison, because it assumed that patients experiencing locked-in syndrome couldn't hear what people were saying, but, they could hear, whereas people in solitary were deprived of all sensory input, and, as a result, gradually lost touch with reality.

That locked door was keeping me from doing what I should have done months before. St. Matthews had failed Mr. Liege, and nobody was advocating for him. Professor Mathieson was busy with fall classes, and maybe he thought there wasn't much more that could be done. Ai-ling, on the other hand, was interested and engaged.

It had been Ai-ling's suggestion to have Dr. Lim, a doctor of Chinese medicine, evaluate him. I knew it would be impossible for Dr. Lim to visit Mr. Liege without the approval of Dr. Merkel, and Ai-ling said that Dr. Lim refused to practice outside his office.

The earthquake changed how I saw things. St. Matthews was no longer a care home. It was a collection of intravenous bags, soiled sheets, corroded bedpans, secondhand hospital beds with cranky motors, and heart monitors that needed a kick to keep working.

Then there was Tiananmen. The Central Government had arrested the movement's leaders. There wasn't any hope for them. My mother was right to never return to China. The Communists were barbaric. St. Matthews was barbaric.

The only solution I saw was to bring Mr. Liege to the Chinese doctor.

The next morning, I was late getting to work. I showed up to find Ai-ling standing next to Mr. Liege's bed. She was holding a small teacup in one hand. In the other was a small, red ceramic teapot.

"What is it?"

"Gingko biloba. Chinese herbal medicine."

"You're going to give it to him?" I asked. "He can't swallow."

She nodded yes. "It's the only thing that may be able to cure him," she said.

I saw her point. Chinese medicine was the only option left. His condition hadn't changed in four months. Dr. Merkel had once been so excited about using a computer to help Mr. Liege regain his speech. Now, the Commodore sat in the corner gathering dust. Mr. Liege was just taking up a bed.

"Dr. Lim's office is in Oakland Chinatown."

"How do we get him to Oakland Chinatown?" I asked.

Ai-ling didn't answer.

It was then I had the idea of getting a van from a rental agency. We needed a gurney. We needed the orderly's help to lift him out of his bed. We needed to wheel him down the hall, past the nurse's station, to the elevator, without anyone noticing. On the ground floor, we had to get past the receptionist's desk.

"Are you sure it's going to help?" I asked.

"I think so," she said.

"Okay," I said. "Give me a day."

"We don't have a day," she said.

Chinese believe that earthquakes are omens. They are signs that something is wrong in the heavens. In 1976, an earthquake in China leveled the city of Tangshan in twenty-three seconds, killing thousands of people. Six months later, Chairman Mao died.

Mr. Liege's time was evaporating.

You had to be twenty-five years old to rent a vehicle from Ryder, and I was only just past drinking age. I told Ai-ling about my plan and said we had to rent the van in her name.

At the Ryder counter, the agent asked who was going to be the driver.

"I am," Ai-ling said, and she stepped a weak foot forward in half-convincing determination.

"May I see your driver's license?"

Ai-ling opened up her purse and pulled out her wallet. "Here it is," she said, handing it over to the agent.

The agent held it up and compared the photograph on the license to Ai-ling's face.

"Is this your picture, Mrs. Wong?" he asked skeptically.

"Yes, it is. I had my hair done after they took my picture at the DMV."

"So, you were born in Trenton, New Jersey?"

"Yes."

"That's my hometown, too," he said. "Do you ever go to Delorenzo's on Hamilton Street?" he said, smiling expectantly.

Ai-ling made a stern face. "Young man, I am Chinese. I don't care for Italian food."

The clerk became serious. "Yes, I see." He reached over to a file folder near the computer terminal and slid it over to his area. "I highly recommend that you get collision coverage for the vehicle. That way, it's fully covered, be it a fender bender, or, God forbid, something more serious.

"We're not going to crash it," Ai-ling said. "Decline coverage."

"Okay. Do you have your own liability coverage?"

"Yes."

"May I ask which company?"

"Allstate."

"Can I have the policy number?"

Ai-ling shrugged and let out a breath of exasperation. "*Wei shenma ma fan wo ya!*," she belted out at the clerk.

The agent stared at her with a blank look.

This was my cue to intervene. "I'm sorry. Would you excuse us for a moment?" I said as I pulled Ai-ling over toward the foyer. "That's not your driver's license," I whispered.

"So?" she shot back at me. "It's my friend's. She let me borrow it."

"She let you borrow it?"

"She died last month. Kidney failure. Her time came too soon."

"Died? Where?"

"St. Matthews."

"Did you even know this woman?"

"In a way, yes. She was senile. I pretended to be an old friend. We talked in Mandarin quite often."

"Don't you have a driver's license of your own?"

"I do, but it expired."

"So, get a new one."

"It expired in 1959."

"You're joking."

"No. 1959. That was the last time I lived in the States."

"I thought you taught Mandarin at Berkeley?"

"I did. In 1959."

"Christ." I knew this wasn't going to work. "Were you lying about the insurance too?"

"I told you, we're not going to crash."

I knew we needed to start fresh. Ryder wasn't going to rent to Ai-ling with her fake driver's license and nonexistent insurance. I went back to the agent and apologized for Ai-ling's outburst. I told him we would return later with the proof of insurance.

I learned two things about Ai-ling during this experience. First, Ai-ling wasn't afraid to lie to get what she wanted, and, second, she had been living in Taiwan for the past thirty years. Still, something didn't sit right.

"If you've been living in Taiwan the whole time, then why did you give me that story about working in a Datong brick factory during the Cultural Revolution, where you were made to wear a dunce cap and were paraded through the streets?"

"I was there as well," she said, looking into my eyes through her bifocals. "I remember it clearly."

"How is that even possible? No one from Taiwan got to visit Mainland China during the Cultural Revolution."

"I did," she said. "Remember, I knew Mao. I knew Zhou Enlai. They let me in."

I didn't believe her. What she was suggesting was not only impossible, but also no Taiwanese in her right mind would voluntarily go to China back then for fear of being imprisoned and executed as an enemy of the state.

"You've never been to Trenton, either, have you?" I asked.

"What makes you say that?"

"A hunch."

"No. I haven't. I have been to Princeton, though."

We ended up at a "Rent-a-Wreck" sort of place that happened to have a Chevy 350 van with an area in the back large enough to fit a gurney. The floor was exposed metal, and it had metal things that stuck out so you could tie down a gurney with rope.

The man at the desk of the rental agency didn't bother with insurance, and he didn't care about the fact that it was my credit card and Ai-ling's driver's license that we used to complete the transaction.

Next, we had to find a ramp.

Ambulances that brought patients to St. Matthews didn't have ramps. The EMTs relied on brute force to lift patient and gurney into the patient compartment of the ambulance. There was no way that Ai-ling and I could lift Mr. Liege out of his hospital bed into a gurney, and then, him along with the gurney, into the van. Hence the need for a ramp. With a ramp, Ai-ling and I could just roll him up into the back of the van.

For the ramp, and for transferring Mr. Liege from his hospital bed into a gurney, I needed the orderly, José.

José's brother worked at an auto repair shop down the hill. I remembered tow trucks using ramps to get cars to drive up onto the beds of pickup trucks. They were fairly lightweight, too, made of aluminum. I asked José if I might be able to borrow two ramps from his brother so I could change the oil on my Honda.

"You? Change the oil?" José said, doubting me.

"My boyfriend is going to do it."

"You have a boyfriend?"

"Yes." I lied.

"I was gonna say, you can't even change a bed pan properly."

This was José's way of being friendly. Of course I knew how to change a bed pan properly.

"You know," he said, "my brother is a big Raiders fan."

I wasn't surprised, because José himself wore Raiders T-shirts to work every day, even though the Raiders had moved to Los Angeles back in 1982.

"What do the Raiders have to do with ramps?"

"Everything to do with ramps. First, ramps are for tires. Tires are black and white, like Raider colors. Second, no tickets, no ramps. See? I told you they were related."

"How many?"

"Let's see," he said, scratching his chin in mock thought. "Two. One for each ramp."

"Which game?"

"Redskins. October 29th."

José brought the ramps by at lunch. I told him to leave them next to the beige van in the visitor lot. I thanked him and told him I owed him two Raiders' tickets.

"Say, José," I said as I was washing out my plastic lunch container in the coffee room sink, "I need to take a hospital bed in for repair. Would you mind helping me move a patient?"

"Sure."

I didn't have to negotiate this one, because it was his job to do that sort of thing.

"Which one?" He asked.

"Room 221, near the elevator," I said.

"When?"

"Now."

"Hold on. Let me punch in first." José disappeared out the door and headed to the elevator. He returned a few minutes later at the entrance to Mr. Liege's room, where I told him to meet me.

Mr. Liege was asleep, as he often was now. His body was losing muscle and fat, as it had nothing else to metabolize since his feeding tube was removed.

"What's wrong with the bed?" José asked.

"The motor seems to be burned out."

José lifted up the remote console and pressed a button. The top third of the bed jolted up several inches. The sudden movement made me jump. Mr. Liege's eyes opened.

"Sorry, man," José said to Mr. Liege. José looked at me. "It seems to work fine."

"Really? It didn't work when I tried it this morning. Maybe it's an intermittent failure. I should probably still get it looked at," I said.

"Hmm. Okay. I could just swap out the motor right here," he offered. Apparently, José knew how to do this.

"I don't want to trouble you," I said, trying to maintain the ruse.

"No. No trouble at all. I can do it after three thirty."

"That's great. In the meantime, can we still move him to the gurney?" I pointed to the lightweight wheeled bed I had placed next to Mr. Liege's regular bed.

José looked at me for a moment with a questioning look before saying, "Sure."

Mr. Liege turned out to be much lighter than I had thought. Despite his six foot tall frame, he couldn't have weighed more than ninety, maybe ninety-five pounds.

After we transferred him to the gurney, José asked if I wanted him to roll the broken bed down to the basement. I said yes.

José rolled the bed out of the room, and I spoke to Mr. Liege, whose eyes were still open.

"I don't know how much longer you have to live, Mr. Liege. As you know, Dr. Merkel had your feeding tube removed. Ai-ling and I want to take you to a Chinese doctor tonight to see if he can do anything. I hope that's all right with you."

I stared into his eyes, but I couldn't tell if he registered what I had said. His breathing was quick and short, as usual.

I returned home shortly thereafter. It took me almost an hour and a half to go twelve miles because everyone heading southbound on Highway 80 had to exit before the Cypress Overpass and take surface streets. However, despite the backup, it was a rare showing of drivers behaving patiently and courteously.

Once in my apartment, I sat down at the kitchen table and went through the plan in my head. What was the expected outcome, I wondered? Would he miraculously regain his speech? Be able to move his limbs? Very unlikely. Would the few hours outside St. Matthews hurt him in any way? I vowed no. It was a last ditch effort to save a dying man. It was utterly insane.

My roommate came home and dropped her backpack at the entrance to the kitchen. She walked over to the freezer and pulled out a box of spring rolls. She pulled a tab on the corner of the box and opened it up.

"Want any?" she asked, glancing in my direction.

"Sure," I said.

"How'd your day go?" she asked.

I told her I had to find two tickets to the Raiders-Redskins game on the 29th.

"Did you try the student union? Sometimes, people post things like that for sale."

I thanked her for the suggestion. I asked if I she could throw in a second spring roll.

She popped open the plastic liner and dumped the contents out onto a hard, plastic plate. She opened the microwave oven door, placed the plate in the center, and pushed a preprogrammed setting on the console. The metal box began humming.

"Dwinelle Hall was closed today so they could inspect for earthquake damage," she said.

"Where did you have Anthropology?" I asked.

"Class was moved to Harmon Gym."

"Harmon? Where in Harmon?"

"We carried folding chairs upstairs and met in the wrestling room. One student fell asleep on the mat. He was snoring."

"Must've pulled an all-nighter," I said.

"Hey," I said, changing the subject, "have you ever tried traditional Chinese medicine?"

"My mother has had acupuncture," she said. "It cured her psoriasis."

"What about medicine? Have you taken any before?"

"Goldenseal. For insomnia."

It turned out that the best time to steal a patient from St. Matthews was late evening. The night shift nurses were less experienced. They got last dibs on shift assignments, and nobody liked the night shift. I didn't know anyone on the night shift, because I got off work at five.

Ai-ling and I agreed to meet in front of St. Matthews at half past ten, when most of the residents would be asleep. The van was still in the visitor's lot with the ramps leaning up against the passenger side.

The first hurdle was getting inside. I brought my employee badge, and was going with the excuse that I had forgotten my book bag in a patient's room. I didn't feel great about having to lie, but it was easier that I didn't know any of the staff.

I told Ai-ling to meet me around the back at the utility entrance, where I planned to let her in once I got inside. I walked through the automatic opening double doors fully expecting to present my case to the nurse at the front desk. Miraculously, the desk was unstaffed. I hurried back outside and called to Ai-ling to come back.

This was before the age of video cameras everywhere. If it were today, the YouTube clip would have shown a jittery, ponytailed, young Asian female with a gray-haired, Asian grandmother entering the reception area, looking left, then right, like burglars in a Keystone Cops movie, and running past the front desk to the elevator area.

I pressed the "up" button and hoped that the elevator would arrive before the front desk nurse returned to her post. I don't know why I didn't just take the stairs. It would have been the smarter thing to do. We only had to go up two flights. I guess I was being mindful of Ai-ling's advanced age.

The elevator bell dinged to announce its arrival, and the doors opened. Pressed up against the wall were José and a nurse engaged in some serious mouth-to-mouth. I let out a gasp, and they stopped and looked right at me. The nurse screamed. I guess she wasn't expecting to see people waiting for the elevator at this time of night. The residents were either asleep, or their doors were locked so they couldn't escape.

"Hi," I said in a calm voice. My heart was beating in my throat.

"Lisa," José said, surprised. "What're you doing here?"

"I forgot my book bag. Remember that patient we moved today? I think I left it in his room. Do you know if it's open?"

"I'm not sure. What was the number?"

"221."

"Yeah. It should be," he said. "Baby," he said, turning his attention back to the nurse, "is room 221 unlocked?"

"I'm not sure," she said as she straightened her hair. She walked past Ai-ling and me. José motioned for us to follow her.

Back at the front desk, the nurse sat down and pulled out a three ring binder. She paged through an alphabet of names.

"What's the patient's name?" she asked.

"Liege," I said.

"H, I, J, K, L. Lawson. Leffe. Here it is: Liege. Oh yes, that's unlocked. He's not going anywhere. No need to lock that one."

"Can I go up and see if my bag is there?"

216

The nurse seemed like she wasn't a day over eighteen, which meant she couldn't be a nurse, but just wore a nurse's uniform. She looked up at José for an answer.

"Yeah, no problem. We may not be here on your way out, though," he said with a grin. The "nurse" betrayed no reaction.

"Thanks, José," I said.

"Is this your grandmother?" he asked, looking at Ai-ling.

"I am her mother's stepsister," Ai-ling said. I was relieved that Ai-ling stepped in like that.

Ai-ling and I returned to the elevator and went to the second floor. I don't know what was running through her mind at the time, but I felt that we'd had a close call and may still be caught. At the same time, the run-in with José, along with the timing of his late night tryst, was serendipitous. We had a short window in which to get Mr. Liege down to the lobby and out the main doors without being seen.

I wondered if Chinese medicine could have saved my dad. He was a chain smoker, and in that sense he did damage to himself. My parents grew up in the Chinese countryside, and the few times I've been to rural China I've been flabbergasted by the casual use of petroleum-based cleaning solvents in public spaces -- chemicals known to be carcinogens and long since banned in the United States. My mother's miscarriage -- I still wonder about that to this day. I guess that's partly why I later went into pharmaceuticals: using chemistry to reverse the negative effects of our environment.

When the elevator doors opened on the second floor, the hallway was dark. I was used to having all the residents' doors open and daylight streaming in through their windows. Now, with the doors closed and only the Exit signs illuminated, it seemed spooky.

Room 221. The door was closed, like the others. I turned the handle, and it was unlocked, just as the nurse had said. As I pushed the door open, the room's darkness enveloped me. Ai-ling was right behind me, but I could have been alone, she was so quiet. The only visible thing in the room was a small, red light, which was where the emergency call button was located. If pressed, it signaled the nurse's station on the second floor, down at the end of the hall.

The night shift nurses were supposed to be doing the rounds, which meant that we were bound to run into one of them. At the same time, if the nurses on the second floor were anything like José's girlfriend, we had nothing to worry about.

"What do we do now?" Ai-ling whispered.

"Come over here," I said, guiding her by her hand to the head of the gurney. "You push, and I'll steer."

"I can't see," she said. "Can I turn on the lights?"

"I'd rather not. I don't want to wake him up."

Ai-ling let go of my hand, and I felt her brush past me. Suddenly, the room became bright. I saw Ai-ling standing next to the light switch next to the door.

"*Shenma dou kan bu dao*," she said.

I couldn't fault her for having poor night vision.

With the lights on, we could see Mr. Liege asleep on the gurney. His body hadn't moved from earlier in the day when José and I had transferred him from his hospital bed. His thin, bony limbs were outlined by the bed sheet and light, cotton cover sheet and gave his body a skeletal relief. He looked dead, save for his short, fast breathing.

We wheeled Mr. Liege to the door. I turned the handle and opened it just enough to peek my head out and see if any nurses were around. I opened the door wider and held it in place with my right foot while I pulled the gurney past me. Ai-ling didn't have to push very hard.

We got to the elevator, and I pressed the "Down" button. When the door opened, I pulled the gurney in, and I told Ai-ling to wait with when we got to the bottom while I checked the front desk. Just as José said, the nurse wasn't there. I figured that they must have gone into one of the empty resident rooms to use the bed. I wondered if they changed the sheets? Then, I thought that I had probably changed their sheets and not even realized it.

Ai-ling and I wheeled Mr. Liege out the double doors and into the cool evening air. A pillow of moisture overhead obscured the stars. A moth fluttered up against a street lamp.

I worried about Mr. Liege getting a chill, so I covered his body with my coat. St. Matthews didn't normally provide residents with many blankets, because the temperature in the rooms was kept stiflingly high. Many residents had poor blood circulation and got cold easily.

I opened the passenger door and scooted toward the back to open the double metal doors. I stepped out and went around to the passenger side to get the ramps. I lined them up, one at a time, between the bed of the van and the ground. I lined up the wheels of the gurney to match the two ramps and went around to the head of the gurney.

"Ai-ling, this time, you take the front and steer. I will push."

"OK," she said.

I pushed the gurney up as Ai-ling backed into the van. She hit the back of her head on the top part of the door frame.

"Ai-ling!" I said. "Are you all right?"

Ai-ling stopped for a moment and felt the back of her head. "No blood. I'm fine."

Once we had Mr. Liege inside the van, I locked the gurney's wheels and tied the gurney's frame down to metal eye loops welded into the van's bed using rope I had picked up at the hardware store.

With the gurney secured, I strapped down Mr. Liege with two belts that came attached to the gurney: one for his torso, and one for his thighs.

Through all of this, he remained asleep.

We got into the van, and I started the engine. I wondered if anyone would even notice that Mr. Liege was AWOL? We pulled out of the parking lot and headed down San Pablo Avenue.

Ai-ling was quiet. I don't know if she was being respectful in trying to not wake Mr. Liege or if she was worried stiff. I thought about a nightmare I'd had the day after the earthquake and I've had multiple times since then -- a well-worn, mini-movie from my library of bad dreams: I'm driving home from work across the Bay Bridge. I'm following cars in front of me. It's dark. I follow their red tail lights. Suddenly, a panel of the roadway ahead of me falls away. I slam on the brakes. My car skids to a stop. Half of the chassis hangs over the edge, and through the darkness, I can see the water a hundred feet down. The hood dips forward, and the whole car begins sliding through the opening and my body is thrown upward, into the back seat before I crash into the water.

It was at the Ashby stoplight that I was jolted back to the present. A Ford Winstar family van had cut in front of me. I honked, but the van sped off ahead -- but not without my catching a glimpse of the license plate frame that read, "World's Greatest Mom."

I caught up with the van at the next stop light and pulled up in the next lane. I looked over, and the driver indeed seemed to be of "mom" age. She did not make eye contact. Maybe she had seen me coming after she cut in front of me.

I wondered what drove someone to put "World's Greatest Mom" on her car. Was it under-appreciation? Was it extreme self confidence? Why the urge to boast, and, on top of that to claim the entire world in the process?

It was, and is, a tragic flaw of us in America. Overstating things. What was her hurry anyway, I wondered? We ended up at the same stoplight. If we didn't end at the same one this time, sure enough, we'd see each other at the next one. Didn't the World's Greatest Mom get that? We may like to think we're immune to the laws of physics, that we're immortal, but, spoiler alert, we all die in the end.

Even now, twenty-three years later, I see this self delusion at the airport. People push their way into lines, sometimes even cut places, but in the end they all find themselves stuffed into the same goddamn airplane, like marinated anchovies.

Dr. Lim's office was on the outskirts of Oakland Chinatown, off the 5th Street exit on I-880, though with the freeway closed, we had to cross over to 17th and Telegraph from San Pablo, and then to Broadway. The neighborhood was near Jack London Square. Jerry Brown hadn't yet become mayor, so the area was still run-down. I was worried about what might happen after I parked the van.

Ai-ling spotted the correct address--she had been there many times before, but only during daylight hours. Attached to the door with clear, plastic packing tape was a small placard that read, "*Lin Zhongyao.*"

"Is that his office? It looks like a house," I said.

"He lives here," Ai-ling said. "He has his office and clinic in the back of his house."

I waited in the van while Ai-ling got out and knocked on the door. I half-hoped that Dr. Lim wouldn't be there. That way, we could take Mr. Liege back to his room and be done with this escapade. I admit that I was getting cold feet now that we were here out in front of Dr. Lim's clinic. Part of me thought we wouldn't get this far.

A man shorter than Ai-ling answered the door. His eyeglasses seemed to be oversized for his small, balding head. It looked like he was wearing pajamas, which meant that he hadn't been expecting us. That meant Ai-ling hadn't alerted him to our coming.

A long discussion ensued with hand raising on both sides. It didn't look promising. I looked at my watch probably two dozen times while the van idled next to the curb.

When the animated dialogue ended, Ai-ling came stomping back to the van. She opened the passenger door and looked at me with disappointment.

"Dr. Lim refuses to see us."

221

"Why?"

"He claims I told him I would be bringing a patient who could walk on his own."

"Did you?"

"I never said that."

"Did he know we were coming?"

"Dr. Lim owes me a lot."

"Apparently, he doesn't see it that way."

"He's got a big ego now," she said. "He said he didn't want to get involved with a terminally ill patient."

"Is that how you described Mr. Liege?" I asked. If I were Dr. Lim, I would feel the same way.

"No," she said. "He read my mind. He is a mind reader."

"Are you serious?" I said, ready to turn off the ignition and walk away. "He's not a mind reader, right? You're saying that to humor me. Why didn't you call him in advance? Tell him we were coming? Was that so hard?"

"I was nervous."

"Well, so was I."

"I didn't think he would refuse. He says his insurance will not cover treating terminal patients. He also asked if there was a doctor's release allowing Lao Du to be transported here. Do you have one?"

"Are you kidding me? Of course not! Do you think his doctor would allow two untrained people to take someone in his condition in a rental van down to a sketchy part of Oakland to see a Chinese herbalist?"

"He does acupuncture as well."

"It doesn't matter. My point is, there's no way we could get a release."

"Did you try?"

"No, of course not."

"Maybe you should have."

At this point in the conversation, I considered walking away for the second time. "You know," I said. "I don't have to be here. This van is rented in your name. You're responsible for it."

"It's on your credit card."

She was right. Besides, she had used a dead person's driver's license for I.D., so she wasn't directly linked to any of this. I was.

"I'm not going to leave," she said.

"Neither am I," I said, resigned to the situation.

"Let me talk to him again," she said. She opened up the passenger door, stepped down onto the sidewalk, and walked back Dr. Lim's door. She knocked on it.

Dr. Lim reappeared at the doorway. Ai-ling spoke with him for another couple of minutes. Then, she turned around and walked back to the van. This time, she smiled and gave a thumbs-up sign.

"He has agreed to come outside and inspect Lao-Du."

"'Inspect?'"

"Diagnose his condition."

"Now?"

"Yes, he went back to change into different clothing."

"Oh, okay."

A few minutes later, Dr. Lim emerged from his office door wearing a white lab coat with his name written in cursive on the left breast pocket. I turned off the engine and went outside to join Ai-ling at the back of the van. I opened the double doors and turned on the overhead cabin light.

Dr. Lim stepped up into the back of the van and held Mr. Liege's right wrist.

"His pulse is very weak," he pronounced. He asked about Mr. Liege's lifestyle, emotional state, work habits, and diet. Unfortunately, neither Ai-ling nor I could answer those questions. Dr. Lim then went closer to Mr. Liege's face and opened up his mouth to look at his tongue. "His kidney function is very poor. So is his spleen. Yin energy is predominant."

Just at that moment, Mr. Liege began coughing. A gurgling sound came from his mouth. It sounded like he was choking on phlegm.

"I must leave," Dr. Lim said suddenly. He backed out of the van. I saw him walk quickly back to his house, and he disappeared.

"Ai-ling, what's happening?" I asked. "Why did Dr. Lim run off like that? Mr. Liege could be dying. Should we call an ambulance?"

Ai-ling sat there silently while Mr. Liege continued to make drowning sounds.

"What should we do?" I demanded.

"We should go back to St. Matthews," she said, finally.

"Is he going to make it? What if he's having a stroke?"

"I don't know. I don't know," she said, shaking her head.

I went closer to Mr. Liege's face, and I saw that his eyes were open. Clearly, he was suffering.

"Now, I want to ask you an unrelated question. It has recently come to our attention from a close advisor to the President that you fathered a child during your time there."

"That is false."

"Did you have a relationship with one of the translators there?"

"Yes."

"Was her name 'Ai-ling Chang?'"

"No. Her name was 'Sun.'"

"Ai-ling Sun?"

"Yes, that is correct."

"Do you have any reason to believe you are not the father of her child?"

The Gringo and his delicate wife decided to go for a stroll through the evening summer breeze. As they walked past the backs of fruit carts, there was the smell of monkey shit. They came upon a crowd gathered around the body of an old man lying dead in the middle of the street. The driver had sped off and was sure to be gone for good. The Gringo got a good look at the old man and shuddered at the sight of himself lying in a pool of blood on the warm asphalt. His delicate wife told him there was no resemblance whatsoever. The Gringo came to his senses and brushed it off as some sort of macumba, or, Brazilian black magic.

The Gringo and his delicate wife strolled on and came across a story poet reading from one of his works. "**Cordel** de Recife," read the sign over his book stall.

"This is the story of a young man," the poet began.

The Gringo and his delicate wife did not speak Portuguese, but they understood every word.

"This young man worked on a plantation," the poet began. "He owed his life, and that of his forebears, to the Colonel, the owner of the plantation. The young man heard about a place where the bricks of homes were made of crystal, the doors of silver, the floors of satin. Ponds were filled with port wine, and rivers flowed with milk.

"One night, the young man stole away from the plantation into the deep darkness of the jungle. He walked all night by the light of the moon until the next morning, when he bartered some vegetables and bottles of liquor for a seat on a coach bound for the coast. Once there, he boarded a skiff heading up river.

"The journey took several days. It took a month. Accounts vary. The fisherman, who piloted the skiff, told the man where to disembark, and he jumped out and swam ashore. He reached a small embankment that opened into a jungle clearing.

"The young man fought through serpentine vines with a Chinese long sword in one hand and a small machete in the other. He did not know where he was going, or for how long. Presently, he came to a clearing and saw before him something amazing.

"He saw men, children, and women -- all beautiful and happy. They offered him plates of cooked beef, stones of rock candy, and wells full of coffee. Rice from the ground came ready to eat.

"He felt a strong urge to sing out loud, so he did, whereupon everyone in the town began singing, 'Long Live the Chinese Revolution' and various Brazilian peasant tunes accompanied by Chinese **pipa**, **sheng**, **er-hu**, and Brazilian **berimbau**, **pandeiro**, and **cavaquinho**.

"Many days passed like this. The young man could not get enough. He felt alone. He realized that such an experience was wasted if he couldn't share it with someone else.

"Finally, one day, he decided to return home. Before he did, the townsfolk made him promise to not tell anyone about how to get there, because if he did, there was no saying how quickly the place would be overrun by smugglers and hooligans and military types. If he did say anything, he would no longer be able to find the secret location, or so they said.

"Upon his return to the plantation, the young man was very surprised to find that he hadn't been missed. Even the Colonel hadn't noticed his absence and simply said, 'Good morning,' as he did every day.

"One night, over glasses of rum, the man got very drunk, and he told his buddies about the amazing town. The next day, all the men could talk about was that special place, and how they were going to collectively flee their debts to the Colonel and steal away in the middle of the night, with the young man as their guide. As one would expect, word made its way back to the Colonel.

"The Colonel made an example of the young man. He brought in an evil doctor from the city, who made a potion out of poisonous frog venom and pregnant mountain lion's blood, which he mixed together and masked with the sweetness of sugar cane juice and rice wine.

"The Colonel had the young man placed in a small cage next to a running stream. The day's heat and the sound of water nearly drove the young man crazy as he was not given anything to drink for almost a full day. Finally, when a servant came by with a cool drink for the young man, he fed him the poisonous drink.

"The young man drank the potion like it was his first glass of water. Not long afterward, he began talking to himself and drooling like a maniac. The Colonel released the young man and brought him back to the fields, where the other men were working.

226

"'See?' the Colonel yelled to them, 'How can you trust someone who is stark-raving mad?' The other men stared in horror at the transformed figure who once was their hero. Some believed that he was crazy. Others feared what would befall them if they dared to try to escape.

"The young man wandered the plantation for a day or two, and then he wandered into a neighboring plantation. By then, everyone in the area knew about the crazy man who talked nonsense about a place that didn't exist."

"Eventually, the evil potion wore off, and the young man came back to his senses. When something so drastic like that happens, people remember. From that point on, the young man was unable to get a job at any of the plantations in the area. Left without a means to live, he eventually made his way to the city.

"Today, the young man is old, and all he has in the way of possessions is this sad story to tell about that fantastical place. He makes his living the only way he can: by telling his story to people like you."

The poet looked Quentin directly in the eyes, and he was looking in the mirror at his own face. "Fang Luo," he said to his reflection. "Yes, you are my son."

"I'll drive," I said to Ai-ling, "if you promise to keep an eye on him. We can't let him die. Do you hear me?"

"Yes," Ai-ling said, looking in fear at a convulsing Mr. Liege.

"Try to hold him still," I said. I started the van. My hands were sweating so much that the steering wheel was slipping under my fingers. My head was spinning. I understood what it meant to drive an ambulance: the urgency of life and death.

I pulled out onto Broadway and headed back the way we came, but the traffic light was red, so I stayed on Broadway instead and headed up to College Avenue. I knew at some point I would have to connect back to San Pablo -- either on Dwight, or a few blocks further on Bancroft. There were more stoplights and stop signs on that route, but it was better than the dead stop that had developed on San Pablo.

When I turned onto College Avenue, I started running red lights.

"It's all your fault!" Ai-ling yelled at me.

A wave of guilt came over me. I felt that I had let my mother die. I should have done more -- driven through traffic at an unsafe speed, even, to get her help -- but it never came to that. I wanted so bad to have had an opportunity to do something heroic for my mom. "Heroic" meant not giving up, not taking Dr. Merkel's word as gospel.

It was Ai-ling's idea to see Dr. Lim. Why couldn't Dr. Lim do something heroic? What did he have to lose?

"Ai-ling, tell me something. Now, be honest," I said, trying to maintain my focus on the road. "Did you ever live in Datong and work at a brick factory?"

I glanced over at her, and I could see tears welling up in her eyes.

"I don't know what we should do now."

"Ai-ling!" I yelled. "Focus. Tell me the truth. Did you ever go back to China after you moved to Taiwan?"

"No."

"Okay then," I said, relieved to clear that up, finally. "Now, tell me truthfully, were you ever in Taoyuan? Did you really meet Mr. Liege there?"

"I still love him," she said.

"You didn't answer my question."

Mr. Liege stopped making that gurgling sound, and his coughing subsided. I asked Ai-ling to check on his breathing, and she said he was breathing normally again.

I turned down Dwight and flew past Bongo Burger and Shakespeare Books on Telegraph Avenue. A block down, I remember seeing a Berkeley Police cruiser parked next to Barrington Hall, the most famous co-op for drug overdoses and

Kool-aid parties. To my surprise, the traffic lights were green all the way down to Shattuck.

Rather than wait for the light, I turned right and headed to University Avenue, where I turned left. The rest of the drive was fast and smooth at that hour of the night. We were far enough north on San Pablo at that point that there was no traffic at all.

"How do you know this man?" I continued, desperately trying to get to the bottom of this mystery. At this point, for all I knew, she had lied about everything. She didn't know Mr. Liege from the mailman. Mr. Liege may have had no idea who she was.

We pulled up to the loading area in front of St. Matthews, and I turned off the ignition, opened the driver's door and went around back to open the van's double doors. I stepped up and crawled into the back to untie the rope. The knots had tightened since when I initially tied them. My hands were shaking, and fingers were failing me.

"Ai-ling, do you have a knitting needle or tweezers?" I asked, hoping to get something to pry the knot apart.

Ai-ling opened her door and came around. "Here," she said. I looked up and was stunned to see her holding a large Bowie knife.

"Where did you get that?"

"I carry it in my purse for protection."

"What am I supposed to do with it?"

"Cut the rope."

"With that?"

"Yes."

I took the knife from her and placed the edge of the blade next to the knot and started sawing at it back and forth. In a matter of seconds, the knife sliced through the knot. I crawled over to the next piece of rope, whose knot seemed equally tight. I sawed through it as well.

Ai-ling was on the other side of the gurney. I passed the knife back to her. "Here, you do those knots."

I heard a car approaching. I backed my way out of the van and saw a squad car pulling up with its lights flashing. It stopped several parking spots away. "Put your hands up against the car," a voice bellowed out of a loudspeaker.

"Ai-ling!" I yelled. "Ai-ling! It's the police!"

Ai-ling came out of the back of the van as well.

"Both of you! Put your hands on the side of the van, where we can see you."

Ai-ling and I put our hands up and placed them palms down against the van. I heard two doors open.

"Now, lie face down on the ground!"

"*Wo bu dong*," Ai-ling said, unsure what the officer had said.

"Do what I do," I said as I backed up from the van with my hands up and kneeled down to the ground. I placed my hands down in front of me and slowly lowered myself to where I felt asphalt pebbles pressing into my cheeks and lips.

"*Bu xing! Wo bu gan*," Ai-ling said in defiance.

"Ai-ling! Listen to me!"

"Ma'am, I need you to get down on the ground right now," said the officer.

From my vantage point, all I could see were Ai-ling's beige shoes. I was unable to see what she was doing, but I heard one of the officers say, "She's got a knife!" Then, "Drop the weapon, or we will shoot!" I could imagine both police officers standing, legs spread, guns drawn behind the squad car doors, pointing their guns at this old Chinese woman in a hand-sewn padded coat, wool slacks, and Rockports.

Ai-ling was standing against the van, frozen.

"*Xiao lu*," she pleaded.

"Drop the knife, Ai-ling. Let go of it," I yelled.

I heard the knife hit the ground. It bounced under the van.

"Now, come down to the ground," I said as calmly as I could.

The police handcuffed both Ai-ling and me while we were on the ground. We listened to the recitation of our Miranda Rights.

"What in the hell is going on here? Enrique, look at this," one of them said.

The officer who had handcuffed us went over to see.

"Is this a patient from St. Matthews?" Officer Enrique yelled out from inside the van.

"Yes," I said from the ground.

"We need an ambulance," Officer Enrique said as he emerged from the back of the van. He spoke into his walkie talkie for dispatch to send one immediately.

"I don't know what you were trying to do, but you are in some serious trouble. That man in the back of the van seems to be dead."

Officer Enrique stood over me while his partner helped Ai-ling get up. He escorted her over to the squad car and helped her climb in the back.

"OK, your turn," Officer Enrique said. "Get up."

With my hands bound behind my back, I tried to roll over to my side to stand up. I struggled on the ground like a beached whale. Officer Enrique lifted my right arm and managed to get me on my feet. He was kind enough to let me walk on my own to the waiting door where Ai-ling had climbed in.

"Nope. Other side," he said.

I went around the back of the car and climbed in the passenger door on the other side.

Ai-ling and I sat in the back of the car for what seemed like an hour. First, we had to wait for the ambulance to arrive from the fire department. When they pulled up, they sprang into action -- checked Mr. Liege's vital signs and spent some time trying to untie the other two knots. They finally gave up on the rope and simply transferred Mr. Liege's limp body from the gurney in the van to their own gurney. At that point, they had his body sealed up in a dark bag.

Officer Enrique called for dispatch to try to reach Mr. Hom, the owner of St. Matthews, by telephone. They were unable to get through to him, but they did go inside St. Matthews and notify the nurse at the front desk, who, by that time, was a different nurse than the one José had been with. A group of nurses, none of whom I knew, eventually came outside and stood on the front steps and stared at us handcuffed in the back of the squad car. I didn't see any nurses there I knew. If I had, I wondered how they would react.

My thoughts were first on Mr. Liege and the fact he was dead. I had killed him. That heavy feeling was compounded by feelings of trepidation about living the rest of my life behind bars. The worst that could happen to Ai-ling would be deportation. I was going to be a lifer in prison.

The autopsy on Mr. Liege determined that he had died around 9:00 the night before. The cause was pulmonary failure. I found this out from the public defender who was assigned to my case. I didn't believe it, because Mr. Liege was definitely still breathing when we took him from St. Matthews. Then, there was the whole coughing and gurgling fit on the drive back to St. Matthews: dead people didn't do that. Regardless, the autopsy ruled out any criminal case against Ai-ling and me.

Then, there was the civil case. Mr. Hom was asked if he wanted to press charges. He declined.

Ai-ling and I were released the following afternoon. On one hand, I was overjoyed. On the other, I knew that they had gotten the autopsy wrong: I killed Mr. Liege. He had a stroke in the back of the van out in front of Dr. Lim's clinic in Oakland.

Tak

He repeated my last name, "Furukawa," after I introduced myself.

"Are you *Sansei*?" he asked.

"No," I said. "I'm Chinese American, but my husband is *Sansei*," meaning third generation Japanese American.

I was at the home of Fred Takahara. He was a retired Army officer who had served with Mr. Liege in Taoyuan. The telephone number I had didn't work, so I looked up his name on the Japanese American Citizen's Association web site for Sacramento. He was the Chapter President, and I contacted him through E-mail. We agreed to meet on a Sunday, so I left in the morning from Piedmont and made the hour and a half drive east.

"Where were your husband's parents interned?" he asked.

"Tule Lake."

"That's where they sent the troublemakers."

I knew that the famous "No-No Boys" had been sent to **Tule Lake**. They got that name for answering "No" to two questions -- the first asking if they would serve in the armed forces on combat duty, and the second asking if they would foreswear allegiance to the Japanese Emperor and vow allegiance to the United States. They were American-born, so the question about the Emperor was insulting.

Mr. Takahara was wearing khaki shorts, flip-flops and a T-shirt that had a drawing of a Harley Davidson on it that read, "Have You Hugged Your Hog?"

"Those were dark times," he said. "After the ***Korematsu*** decision, things seemed bleak," he said. "Thanks to Reagan, though, we finally got some compensation."

"Didn't it take a few years, though, before any compensation was paid?" I asked.

"Yes, thanks to George Bush. H.W., that is. Come on back, I'll show you the garden," he said. He led me through the house to a pair of sliding glass doors. On the ground sat hedge trimmers and several branches from a camellia tree.

"Some buddies and I went to Cuba two weeks ago. This cigar shop was selling "Have You Hugged Your Hog?" T-shirts. You'll be hard pressed to find many Harleys in Havana, unless their vintage, from the 1950s. We wanted to go before Cuba opens up and becomes too popular."

I asked him how an American could legally go to Cuba.

"It's a little tricky. First, you fly to Mexico City. There, you board a nonstop to Havana. When you arrive, you tell the immigration guys to not stamp your passport. My Spanish is rusty. Besides, they speak a different kind of Spanish in Cuba. It's faster, and they use different words. The immigration guys understood what I wanted."

Mr. Takahara's wife came out to the backyard with a tray of iced barley tea and two *mochi* rice balls.

"Thanks, honey," he said. "These *mochi* came from a shop a few blocks away. They supply all the Japanese restaurants in Sacramento. Try one."

I picked up a pink glob of pounded rice wrapped in a leaf. "Do I eat the leaf?" I asked.

"Yeah, sure, if you like," he said. "I don't eat it, but it can't hurt. It's slightly bitter."

I bit into the soft mass and tasted a mix of grass and perfume followed by a stab of sweetness from the red bean paste.

Mr. Takahara's wife waited to see my reaction. "Do you like it?" she asked.

"I'm not sure," I said.

Mr. Takahara chuckled. "These are the real deal," he said.

"Real Japanese mochi," His wife said.

"I met Haruko when I was stationed in Tokyo during the Korean War," Mr. Takahara said. "Being second generation

234

Japanese American, I spoke kid Japanese with my parents. Later, I studied formal Japanese at Fort Ord, but until that time, I had never lived in Japan."

"Tak spoke very strange Japanese," Haruko said, grinning at him. "It made me laugh when he ordered *ramen.*"

"Living there taught me a lot," Mr. Takahara said. "Then, of course, my wife." He glanced at Haruko and winked. "Haruko is ten years younger. She's from a different generation. I'm still head over heels."

Haruko waved him away and looked at me. "He's always saying that," she said, "but he never shows it."

"Of course I do, honey," he said grinning. "That's why I got a Harley, so we could ride together."

"That's your toy," she said. "I told you before, I'm not interested."

"Now, when Haruko and I go back to Japan, it's kinda of strange," he said. "It's like time travel. Haruko's Japanese is dated. They stare at her when she talks, like she's a ghost from the past. It's like they have to process her ancient Japanese."

"My Japanese is not ancient," Haruko said, putting her hands on her hips.

I thanked Mr. Takahara for meeting with me, and I explained that Professor Mathieson from U.C. Berkeley had contacted me recently to say that he was retiring. He had been going through some old files and came across Mr. Takahara's name from an interview he did with Mr. Liege as part of an oral history of the PAX Mission to Taoyuan. I said that as a favor to Professor Mathieson I would try to meet with some of the people mentioned in the interview to see if there was anything to add to the record.

"Did you keep in touch with Mr. Liege after the War?" I asked.

"You know, not really," he said. "I retired from the U.S. Army, and we came back to the States. I returned to Stanford to finish my bachelor's degree. I was a Sophomore when the Japanese bombed Pearl Harbor, so I didn't get to finish college at the time. The G.I. Bill helped me get my bachelor's degree. Then, I went to Berkeley for my Ph.D in history. I finished my dissertation in 'Fifty-nine, the year before Quentin returned from Brazil. So we just missed each other."

"So, you knew he went to Brazil?"

"I knew through Professor Mathieson. Mathieson was my thesis advisor."

"What about after Mr. Liege came back to the States?"

"Not really," he said. "I rejoined the Army and went overseas again. We were traveling in different circles. I was in Army Intelligence. It's not the sort of job where you want to be corresponding with someone fired by the State Department for being a Communist."

He took a bite of his mochi. "Aren't these good?" he said. "After the Vietnam War, we moved to Sacramento, and I got a teaching position in the History Department at Sac Sate. Haruko got a job at Department of Finance. Now, she's at the State Board of Equalization. Going on nineteen years, isn't it, Haruko?"

"It was hard with kids," Haruko said.

"How many do you have?"

"Two. Jim and Albert. Jim is married and lives in Santa Clara. He works for Intel. Albert is a painter and lives in New York City," she said. "Jim has two girls."

"Haruko has one more year before she retires. We haven't decided what we're going to do after that, but I want to take her to China."

"Do you plan to visit Taoyuan?"

"I hadn't thought of it," Mr. Takahara said as he looked in Haruko's direction. I'm more interested in seeing the usual tourist things. The Great Wall and the Forbidden City."

I told them that I had been going to China for work.

"It has changed so much in the past ten years," I said. "I was in Beijing in May on the night we accidentally bombed the Chinese embassy in Belgrade. The next day, crowds of protesters gathered in front of the American embassy and were throwing rocks."

"It's okay to protest there when it's against a foreign country," Mr. Takahara said, chuckling to himself.

"They do the same thing to the Japanese Embassy," Haruko said.

I agreed that it was strange, given how things had changed so much since Tiananmen.

"You know, I don't think much about my time there during the War," Mr. Takahara said. "The living conditions in Taoyuan were awful. It was like camping in the Andean high desert without the right gear. There was improvisation."

"What do you mean?"

"Well, take the radio equipment, for example. We were sending and receiving messages from Army headquarters on rusty, old gear salvaged from the Embassy basement in Chunking. Our radio guy, his name was Burly, had a way with electronics. He could make a radio out of a K-ration."

I asked him about Ai-ling.

Mr. Takahara scoffed and said, "Where do I begin? She was brilliant. One of the smartest people there."

Haruko interrupted, "Why don't we go inside and sit down. I'll make some snacks."

Mr. Takahara motioned for me to follow Haruko, and we went inside. We sat down at a dark teak wood dining table.

"So, tell me what you know already."

I said that I met Ai-ling after Mr. Liege was brought to St. Matthews. We met again for tea at her place.

"She tried to persuade me to visit Taiwan," I said.

"What else?" Mr. Takahara asked.

"I know that she and Mr. Liege knew each other fairly well. She showed me several pictures of them in Taoyuan."

"Is that it?"

"Yes," I said. I told him that not long after Mr. Liege died, I was fired from my job and went back to school to get my Master's degree. I never found out where Ai-ling went.

"I see," Mr. Takahara said. "Why were you fired?"

"It's a long story," I said. I didn't want to get into Mr. Liege's stroke and the arrest. "It was interesting that she didn't come to his service," I said.

"His memorial service?" Mr. Takahara said. "Yes, I'm sorry I couldn't make it either. Did you go?"

I told him I had. I didn't tell him how guilty and ashamed I still felt about having caused the second stroke that killed him.

"As I said earlier, we weren't that close," he said.

"There was quite a turnout," I said, trying to move the conversation away from his death. Many people who said they knew him. I mean, we're talking kids younger than me with pony tails, and dreadlocks, and bongo drums."

"I take it Professor Mathieson was there?" He asked, looking up at me.

"Oh, yeah. He got a little angry with the bongo drummers, because their banging was drowning out the minister's eulogy."

"What were they doing there?"

"They were protesting the U.S. invasion of Panama."

Mr. Takahara looked confused. "What did that have to do with
Quentin?"

"Don't ask me," I said. "I guess they felt kinship with his plight."

"It's interesting to see which events people latch onto to promote their cause," he said. "Take Tiananmen. We were quick to call the protesters 'pro-Democracy,' and in turn the protesters

238

were media savvy enough to build a statue called the 'Goddess of Democracy.' It was brilliant!"

He finished his *mochi* and took a sip of tea. "We study this in my modern China course. If you look at the conditions on the university campuses, it provides some context. Students had no privacy. Add to that the restricted interactions between the sexes, limited number of school dances, twenty-something libidos, and the result was sex-driven mayhem."

"Sorry, but getting back to Ai-ling," I said.

"Oh, yes. She followed him to Berkeley."

"They were there at the same time?"

"Either they were, or she arrived a year before he returned from Brazil."

I said that Professor Mathieson told me Ai-ling taught beginning Mandarin at Berkeley for a few years, but that she left before Mr. Liege returned.

"Oh, then I must be mistaken," Mr. Takahara said. "When you get to be eighty, it's the details that go first."

Mr. Takahara looked nowhere near eighty, and I said so.

"I don't believe it myself. I'm from just south of here. From the time I could walk I was picking strawberries. Now, it's all houses put up by a developer named Heliopolis."

I mentioned that there had been a rumor about Mr. Liege fathering a child with Ai-ling.

"Yes," he said, and he scratched the top of his nose. "After he was recalled from Taoyuan to Washington, she ran away. They say she was pregnant again."

"Again?"

"Apparently, it wasn't the first time."

"Do you believe the story about the baby?"

"Yes, unfortunately, I do." Mr. Takahara's face became tense. "Quentin had a falling out with his wife before coming to Taoyuan. They had tried to have children but were unsuccessful. I don't think birth control even entered his mind."

239

"Why do you think he was recalled?"

"At the time, Quentin was working in areas beyond my clearance level. I do know there was a shipment of radio equipment. He was under pressure," Mr. Takahara said. "Especially from this special ops guy named 'Flannigan.'"

"What happened?"

"That's a topic of debate. I honestly can't tell you what happened. All I know is that one morning I came outside to find ten pallets of gear next to the caves. A week later, it was gone. There was an official investigation. The State Department started something called the 'Loyalty Research Board.' They wrote a report on it."

"Were you a witness in the investigation?"

"Yes, but my name was withheld for privacy reasons."

"Who was in charge?"

"It was Colonel McKesson's baby. He pinned the blame on Quentin. Quentin was the fall guy. Flannigan and McKesson got off without a scratch. Look, I don't know if Quentin was a Communist or not. I do believe, though, that someone in the PAX Mission was giving the Communists information, helping them out in various ways. Maybe including giving them radio equipment."

"Who were the radios intended for?"

"I don't know. I'm not the best person to ask. I heard that they were going to be used in a trade at some point. There was an attempt to get the Communists and Nationalists to reconcile, and the radios may have been part of it. Regardless, it was way above my pay grade."

"How long did you stay on in Taoyuan after Mr. Liege was recalled?"

"The PAX Mission ended soon after the Japanese surrendered. All the stuff that happened afterward is one big blur. I don't have fond memories of that time. I would just as well forget about it. Give Joe McCarthy credit, though. He wasn't totally off his rocker."

"What makes you say that?"

"Look at the **Rosenbergs**. They were Soviet spies."

"I'm still curious about the baby. Do you know anyone else who might be able to help me out?" I asked.

"There's Matsuda," Mr. Takahara said. "He lives in Japan..."

I told him that the company I worked for was a Japanese-German joint venture, and that I got to visit Japan a few times a year.

"I don't know if he's even alive. I got to know him well. He was considered a 'model prisoner,' which meant he got to leave the prisoner camp a few hours a day. I know that he and Ai-ling were close."

"Do you think he could have gotten her pregnant?"

"You mean, instead of Quentin?" He chuckled. "I doubt it. Matsuda played for the other team, if you get my drift."

"How do you know?"

"Believe me, I know. Taoyuan was a small village. Word got around quickly."

"Did you know anyone on the PAX Mission who was gay?"

"Yeah," Mr. Takahara said, suddenly looking serious. "Flannigan."

Matsuda

It wasn't until ten years after Mr. Liege's death that I saw the name "Saburo Matsuda" in print. My company, Santomi-Bremen, was based in Osaka, Japan. I worked out of a satellite office in Fremont, California. I traveled overseas a lot, although mostly to our R&D facility in Tianjin, China.

Santomi-Bremen had received approval from the Food and Drug Administration to market a non-Thimerosal based Hepatitis B vaccine. Thimerosal was a mercury-containing preservative added to vaccines to prevent fungus and bacteria from forming in multi-dose containers. There were claims that Thimerosal was causing autism, so the FDA phased it out for childhood vaccines like Hepatitis B.

As part of a cost cutting effort, the company decided to move the new Hepatitis B vaccine production from Osaka to Tianjin. It was going to put several thousand Japanese out of work.

News about the move was covered by all the major Japanese dailies -- Nikkei, Sankei, Asahi, Yomiuri. I received an E-mail alert from our public relations office that a well-known Japanese labor leader, Saburo Matsuda, was planning to lead a strike at the plant. I did a quick web search and discovered that Saburo Matsuda had been a fixture in the Japanese labor movement since the late 1950s, and that his signature tactic was to storm shareholder meetings with several club-wielding thugs and demand labor concessions.

A further search revealed an article in the Herald Tribune from a decade earlier, where he said that he had been a prisoner of war during WWII, and that he spent most of his captivity at the Communist base camp in Taoyuan. It was there that he began reading Karl Marx.

As it happened, I had a series of meetings planned in Osaka in September, so I tried to see if I could find out how to contact Matsuda and talk to him about his time in Taoyuan. This seemed to be the same Matsuda that Mr. Takahara had mentioned.

My meetings were scheduled over a two-week period, so the best time for me to meet Matsuda was over the weekend. My flight from San Francisco landed in Osaka in the middle of a Category 5 "super typhoon." When I got to baggage claim, the rain was so heavy that the carpet at the baggage carousels was soaked through.

I arrived at the office in Namba around six in the evening, and everyone was still working. I asked the receptionist if I could get a desk and a computer. She said that the typhoon had knocked out the internet connection to the building, so I had to wait. The desk assignments could only be done online.

That evening, from my hotel room at the New Otani, I sent an E-mail to an address I had found on a web site for the Japanese Labor Community Foundation. Saburo Matsuda was listed as one of the board directors.

I was surprised to find the next morning a reply from him in my Inbox. We agreed to meet at his home in Saitama Prefecture, just north of Tokyo, on Saturday afternoon.

Saturday morning, I boarded a bullet train at 6:45 at New Osaka Station. Even though the typhoon had passed through the area, the rain was still coming down in occasional, heavy bursts.

When I arrived in Tokyo, I transferred to the Yamanote Line and got off in Shibuya. I checked into a small business hotel on Dogenzaka Street. It was a one-room affair with a bed and desk, washer & dryer combination, and a small bathroom capsule where the bath and sink were moulded together out of fiberglass.

I dropped off my suitcase and went back to Shibuya Station and boarded the Shonan-Shinjuku Line heading north.

Matsuda lived in a rain-stained, concrete, three-story apartment building in Toda.

His apartment was on the second floor. When he answered the door, I saw a man in his eighties with a slight stoop and closely cropped, white hair. He looked up at me through dark lenses held together by wire rims. His face was gaunt.

Matsuda was wearing a brown cardigan sweater and wrinkled, olive green trousers. He invited me inside and introduced me to his interpreter, a woman in her mid-thirties with large, round glasses and a pageboy haircut.

I removed my shoes and walked into his one-bedroom flat. The walls were devoid of any decoration. The kitchenette, which I passed by on my way to the sitting area, had a single burner and was covered with cobwebs and dust.

Matsuda invited me to sit down. The room was roughly seven feet wide with six tatami mats in a two by three pattern. In the center sat a small, square table surrounded on each side with a flat pillow for sitting. I sat down with my legs off to one side since I was wearing a skirt. Matsuda sat opposite me. The interpreter sat between the two of us.

I said I was surprised he didn't have more stuff.

"I went through my things several years ago and gave it all away," he said. "A clean house is a clean mind."

I asked if he cooked for himself.

"This apartment building was abandoned several years back," he said in Japanese through his interpreter. "Eventually, the City of Saitama gained possession of it. They put it up for auction, and our community made a bid. Before all of us moved in, we knocked out the dividing wall between two units on the ground floor and built a commercial kitchen and communal dining area. Each resident is assigned to a cook team, so naturally, that is where I take my meals."

I told him that I had never heard of such an arrangement, but it was probably very convenient for someone his age.

"So," he said, "I understand that you want to ask me some questions about my time in China. First, though, please tell me about yourself. Where do you work?"

I began by saying that I worked for Santomi-Bremen.

He smiled and said, "Oh really?"

I told him about how I recognized his name from speaking with Fred Takahara, who had been an interpreter in the U.S. Army. I said that I had taken care of Mr. Liege a decade ago after he suffered a stroke and was unable to move or talk. I said that he had died four months later. I also mentioned that someone named "Ai-ling" had visited him several times before he died, but she disappeared soon afterward.

Matsuda nodded as his interpreter conveyed my words to him in Japanese.

"Let me ask you," he said. "It is very interesting that you work for Santomi-Bremen. What do you do?"

I told him I was in product marketing.

"Yes, I see," he said. "Do you know that I am an AIDS advocate?"

I told him I didn't.

"Yes," he continued, "we have been pressuring Santomi-Bremen to put more money into AIDS research."

"We are definitely putting money into HIV," I said, "but it's very expensive. There haven't been any major breakthroughs. The virus constantly mutates..."

"*Mutate* -- what does *mutate* mean?" the interpreter asked me.

"Changes," I said --

"I understand," Matsuda said, interrupting his interpreter.

"You should do more," he said in Japanese. "Some Japanese have AIDS because of blood transfusions. Others got it from sex tourism, like in Thailand. Finally, there are those who inject drugs. I am not one of them."

I asked him if he had corresponded at all with Mr. Liege after the War.

He shook his head slightly. "I don't know how much you know about Liege-san," he said. "I did not maintain contact with him, but I did write to Ai-ling."

I asked if she was a friend.

Matsuda chuckled to himself. "Yes, she was a friend."

"Was she with you in Taoyuan?"

"Yes."

I asked when was the last time he'd heard from her.

"The year that Emperor Hirohito died. Miwa-chan, when was that?"

The interpreter said something to Matsuda.

I looked at her, waiting for a translation. She was counting her fingers.

"1989," she said, looking at me.

"Do you remember what she said?

"I will have to look," he said. "I do have a letter from before then."

He uncrossed his legs, stood up with a hunched back and walked slowly over to the closet door. He slid it open to reveal a large futon folded neatly on the top shelf. Below that was a small, plastic filing cabinet. He opened the top drawer and pulled out a thin airmail envelope.

"Here it is," he said, holding it up to show me. He walked slowly back to the table and handed it to me. I opened the unsealed envelope. The stationery felt like rice paper. The writing was in Chinese.

"You can read this?" I asked.

"Oh yes," he said, "can you?"

I told him I could.

The letter was postmarked April 9, 1967. Taipei, Taiwan. Here is my recollection of what it said:

My Dear Saburo,

You are the only one I know who could truly appreciate my predicament. I know that I told you in the past that my husband was a pilot. What I didn't tell you was he was a pilot for the U-2. The past two years, he has been flying missions over Mainland China.

Six months ago, his plane was shot down over Hainan. U-2 pilots are trained to eject at high altitude and deploy their parachutes. In my husband's case, that didn't happen. The Mainland Chinese recovered the fuselage, but no body. At least, that is what I am being told.

The truth is, it would be embarrassing for the Taiwan government to admit that one of their pilots had been shot down by the Communists, much less been captured and interrogated.

Because of the secret nature of the U-2 missions, I have no evidence that any of this happened. The newspapers didn't report anything. Officially, nothing happened. The hypocrisy is driving me crazy.

I have no way of knowing if he is dead or alive. I may never know. My life is in limbo, and the Air Force doesn't know what to do. They refuse to give me widow's benefits, because he's not officially missing or dead. No military funeral. No medal. No recognition for his service to his country.

I am leaving this place once and for all. Twenty years is a lifetime. Taoyuan seems like several lifetimes ago.

Incidentally, I was listening again to "The Lark Ascending" by Vaughn-Williams. It's so Chinese. It makes me long for an earlier time, but then it makes me sad.

Please give my best to your family.

Ai-ling

———————————————————————

The letter didn't say anything about Mr. Liege, so I folded it up and placed it back in the envelope and handed it back to Matsuda. As I was doing that, I paused.

I opened the envelope again and looked at the date. I remembered Ai-ling telling me she was working in Datong, China in a brick factory when she got the news of her brother being shot down over Hainan.

I asked if Ai-ling had a brother.

"She never mentioned it," Matsuda said.

"Do you know if she ever worked in a brick factory in Datong?"

"Datong?" Matsuda said. "No, I don't think so. She never did manual labor, as far as I know."

"When did she move to Taiwan?"

"I'm not sure the exact date, but it was soon after 1949."

"Did she marry someone in the Air Force?"

"Yes, and, according to her letter, he flew the U-2 spy plane."

"Did she ever move to Berkeley?"

"Yes," Matsuda said. "She told me that she was teaching Mandarin at the University."

I asked if he had any more letters.

"No," he said. "After we gave away my things, my letters ended up in the garbage."

The interpreter looked at him and nodded her head in affirmation.

I asked him about his time in Taoyuan.

He said something in Japanese and made eye contact with the interpreter.

"Baby?" the interpreter said in English as she gave a questioning look back to Matsuda.

"Baby?" I asked.

"His baby," Matsuda said. "Liege-san's baby."

"Mr. Liege had a baby?"

"Yes," he said. "It's my fault. I told Ai-ling I would say I was the father."

"So Mr. Liege fathered a child with her?"

Matsuda didn't respond. He unfolded his legs, leaned on the small table to stand up. His right arm was shaking and barely able to support his weight. The interpreter hurried over and encouraged him to stay seated.

"I am gay," he finally said, looking directly at me. "I did not sleep with her."

"Did Mr. Liege know that?"

"No," Matsuda said. "I doubt it." He began to cough in a deep, throaty way that smokers cough. "Liege-san was in a difficult way," he said, recovering. "He spent most of his time with the Chinese. When the rumor got out that Ai-ling was pregnant, the Chinese didn't want him. I am not sure the Americans knew. You see, there were two."

"Two babies?"

"No. Two pregnancies. The first, she had an abortion."

"Where?"

"In the hospital."

"Was this widely known?"

"Among the Chinese leadership, yes. I don't know about the American side."

"What happened?"

"General Chu Teh pressured Liege-san to marry her, but he was already married, so Ai-ling had an abortion."

"What about the second time?"

"Liege-san got notified that he had to move back to Washington. This time, Ai-ling said she wanted to keep the baby. Liege-san was smoking opium to deal with pain in his teeth. I think he had an abscess."

"Did Mr. Liege know that Ai-ling was pregnant the second time?"

"She told him before he left. Ai-ling met him in Shanghai. That was my suggestion. Unfortunately, she fled to Taiwan after that."

I knew from talking to Professor Mathieson that after Mr. Liege was recalled to Washington, his life went downhill. He had been investigated by the Loyalty Research Board and fired from the State Department. He had moved with his wife to Brazil because he couldn't find a job in the States.

"My own story is similar," Matsuda said. "I was returned to Japan under an agreement with the Americans to exchange prisoners of war. Back in Tokyo, there was disease and starvation. American jeeps would drive by and occasionally toss chocolates to the children, but former soldiers like me, especially prisoners of war, were treated badly. I wandered the streets for several years eating scraps from garbage cans. Being homosexual, I had to be very careful. One time, I ran into Yukio Mishima outside a gay bar. My shirt had holes in it, and my shoes were bound with twine, and I hadn't showered in several weeks. He said I looked disgusting.

Matsuda stopped to cough again. "Miwa-chan, would you please get me some tea?"

The interpreter got up and went over to the kitchenette.

"Were you able to eventually find work?" I asked. Miwa translated from the kitchenette.

"Work. If you could call it that, yes. I was a labor organizer. I led protests against companies that were opposing unionization. I was arrested twice."

"I understand you have a reputation for storming company board meetings."

Matsuda smiled coyly. "I may have done something of that sort," he said. "It gets attention, but I am too old for that now."

"So, what happened to the baby?" I asked.

"Ai-ling didn't know what to do. We spent much time talking before she left."

"Weren't you a prisoner of war?" I asked.

"I was a model prisoner. That meant I had freedom to leave the guarded compound on Mondays and Thursdays for two hours at a time. I got to know Ai-ling through our love of Western music. We liked Satie and Vaughn-Williams. She owned a Victrola, as well as several records."

The interpreter returned to the table and placed cups of tea in front of me and Matsuda. I thanked her.

"*Doumo*," Matsuda said to her. He picked up the cup and took a sip. "*Umai*," he said. He tilted his head back, and the muscles under his eyes relaxed. He smiled in satisfaction.

Matsuda continued, "When word came that Liege-san was being recalled, Ai-ling had known for several weeks that she was pregnant. She came to me in tears. I told her that she had two choices: tell him, which would have certain repercussions, or say I was the father, which, if you knew me, was highly unlikely."
"Why didn't she tell him?"

"I don't know," Matsuda said. "In any case, Liege-san believed her when she said I was the father."

"Was it possible to get an abortion?"

"She had done that once before. She didn't want to do it again. Also, she didn't want the Communist Party leadership to know. That is why she left and went to Shanghai."

"To have an abortion?"

"Maybe, but after she met Liege-san in Shanghai and told him the baby wasn't his, which it was, she changed her mind."

"When did she write to you?"

"Not until after the War. I was back in Japan by then, and she was living in Taiwan."

"So that means that she escaped to Taiwan when the Communists took control of the mainland?"

"It would seem so," Matsuda said, nodding his head. "but before that, she gave up her son for adoption."

"What?" I said in exasperation. "Why?"

"I don't know" Matsuda said.

"She met her husband in Taiwan?"

"Possibly."

252

"Considering the letter you showed me, he was a pilot."

"Yes, he started as a pilot with the Flying Tigers during the War."

I asked Matsuda if he had ever smoked opium.

"Oh, yes, of course. I traded black coal with Liege-san for American magazines."

"Black coal?"

"That is what it was called."

"How did you get it?"

"Traders came to Taoyuan by camel. They came down the valley in the dark of night. The only way you knew they were coming was by the gentle clinking of bells around the camels' necks."

"So Mr. Liege smoked opium?"

"Liege-san spoke beautiful Chinese. Much better than mine. When he first arrived, he was respected by the Americans and the Chinese equally. That changed when Colonel McKesson arrived. The Colonel didn't trust Liege-san. Maybe because Liege-san could communicate with the Communists in Chinese. Liege-san spent more time with the Chinese, especially Ai-ling, than he did with the Americans."

"What was Ai-ling's job?"

"She was an interpreter. Just like Miwa-chan," he said. He looked over at Miwa and grinned. "Communist Party officials knew that Liege-san was having relations with Ai-ling."

"Did the Communists have anything to do with Liege's recall to Washington?"

"I don't know, however, it is unlikely. The Communists needed Liege-san. Liege-san was their only friend."

Epilogue

After I returned to Oakland, I was busy with the China relocation project. On top of that, there had been a class-action lawsuit filed against Santomi-Bremen for adverse side effects relating to a blood thinning drug we manufactured in Mexico. Between trips to Tianjin, I was meeting with our corporate counsel to prepare a defense.

It was about nine months after my visit with Matsuda that I received a large padded envelope from Miwa-chan, Matsuda's interpreter. Inside it was a letter written in awkward English explaining that Matsuda had been suffering from Alzheimer's and was now in an assisted living facility in Saitama City. The letter said that the burden of caring for Matsuda had become too heavy for the community, and they had decided by consensus to move him to a home where he could get more attention.

Also enclosed was a photocopy of a letter from Ai-ling to Matsuda, dated May 4, 1990. It was postmarked Berkeley, California. Like the previous letter, it was written in Chinese.

My Dearest Saburo,

I hope that the spring season brings with it warmth and beauty to the cherry blossoms in Toda.

My teaching position at Taiwan National Defense University had come to an end, and I have earned enough years to retire finally. The university's pension, combined with my husband's (yes, the Air Force finally did decide to give me survivor's benefits) should be more than enough to keep me happy. Incidentally, the Ministry of National Defense erected a small memorial here on campus to the Taiwan U-2 pilots killed in action. My husband's name is proudly etched in stone now for his service. So many years have passed since he was killed, yet I still think I hear him in the kitchen every morning before I get out of bed.

As you know, I moved back to Berkeley to care for Quentin. He suffered a stroke after Britka passed, and I'm afraid to say it eventually killed him, but not before I was able to tell him about our son, Fang Luo. You may have seen him on television. He was the one who stood in front of the long line of tanks the day after the Tiananmen massacre by the People's Liberation Army.

I received word the other day that, the day after he stopped those tanks, Fang Luo was arrested and put in prison camp. It's not clear if he is in Inner Mongolia or Heilongjiang province. It's possible, too, that he was sent to a labor camp in North Korea.

I do not know where to begin. I gave him up for adoption when he was only four. I wanted to kill myself so many times.

I am not going to give him up this time. I am going back to China to try to find him.

Ever yours,

Zhang (Sun) Ai-ling

The last item I found in the envelope was a photocopy of a passport from Taiwan. The name in the passport was 松田三郎, Saburo Matsuda's name. His picture must have been taken twenty years earlier. It was a black and white photograph with his thick hair combed over to the right and a severe, accusing look in his eyes. It was an unnerving look. I wondered where the photograph had been taken. The passport had expired in 1980. It said that his birthplace was Kaohsiung, Taiwan, 1910.

The Japanese had occupied Taiwan for fifty years until the end of World War II, so it was possible that Matsuda had been born to Japanese parents stationed there. When I inquired at the Japanese Consulate in San Francisco, they directed me to follow up with the Taiwan Expatriate's Friendship Association in Tokyo. Apparently, this group was formed by Japanese nationals born in

Taiwan. This group was the most likely to be the best source of information.

I contacted the Taiwan Expatriate's Association by E-mail. Later, I called them on the telephone. Unfortunately, there was no answering machine, and I never received a response to my E-mail message. So, one of two scenarios seemed possible: either Matsuda's mother and father had been Japanese, or his mother had been Chinese and his father Japanese, hence his Japanese surname.

I contacted Professor Mathieson, who was retired now and living in Ashland, Oregon. He suggested a third possibility -- that Matsuda could have been ethnically Chinese, and that he had emigrated to Japan after the War and taken a Japanese surname.

If that were the case, I asked Professor Mathieson, what was he doing in a Japanese prisoner of war camp in Taoyuan?

"Who knows," he said, "for all we know, Matsuda could have been put there by the Nationalists as a spy."

I never followed up on Ai-ling and Mr. Liege's son, Fang Luo. I did a quick calculation and concluded that when Ai-ling wrote her final letter to Matsuda, just before she left for China, Fang Luo would have been around forty-five. Tank Man could have been that age, but I have watched the video clip hundreds of times, and it is impossible to guess how old he is.

It's a testament to the thoroughness of the Chinese Communist State bureaucracy that nobody knows the whereabouts of Tank Man, or if he ever survived prison camp.

In the years since Tiananmen, Taiwan and Mainland China have remained officially at war, but the economic and cultural ties grow deeper. Direct flights between the mainland and Taiwan began in 2008, and today about forty percent of Taiwan's exports go to Mainland China. Taiwan-based companies have invested billions of dollars in the Mainland.

Finally, the Nationalists and the Communists seem to be willing to let go of the past, but some things, like Tiananmen, should never be forgotten.

- Oakland, April 2015

Glossary

8th Route Army

Originally a branch of the Nationalist army, led by Mao Tse-tung and Chu Teh. Later renamed the People's Liberation Army after the Japanese surrender in 1945, when the Nationalists and Communists renewed their focus on fighting each other.

Beijing

Capital of the People's Republic of China. Before 1949, it was called "Peking."

Berimbau

Single-string musical percussion instrument played with a bow.

C-47

Two-engine propeller aircraft developed by the Douglas Aircraft Company from the DC-3 for military transport. Also known as the "Douglas C-47 Skytrain."

C-54

Four-engine propeller aircraft, larger than the C-47, developed by the Douglas Aircraft Company from the DC-4 for military transport. Also known as the "Douglas C-54 Skymaster."

C-rations

"Combat individual ration," a packaged meal distributed to U.S. military personnel during World War II.

Cachaça

Clear Brazilian alcohol derived from sugar cane.

Cavaquinho

Small, four string guitar.

Ch'i p'ao

Pinyin: Qi pao. Tight-fitting one-piece Chinese dress for women, also called a "Mandarin gown."

Chennault

Lieutenant general in the U.S. Army during World War II. Led the Flying Tigers, a volunteer force of American pilots stationed in Kunming, China. In 1943, he proposed a limited air offensive against the Japanese in China, but General Joseph Stilwell opposed it, because Stilwell wanted to focus on building up the Chinese infantry. Chennault received Chiang Kai-shek's blessing, but Stilwell continued to oppose the idea.

Chiang Kai-shek

Leader of the Kuomintang (referred to interchangeably as the "Nationalists"), and President of the Republic of China. Leader from 1928 until his death in 1975, in Taiwan. Married to Soong Mei-ling, sister of Madame Sun Yat-sen (Soong Ching-ling).

Chinese Communists

Chinese Communist Party (C.C.P) was formed in 1921. The Party grew out of the leftist faction of the Kuomintang. After the death of Sun Yat-sen in 1925, they gradually split from Chiang Kai-shek. Chiang's troops attacked the Communists, and drove them to retreat on the Long March. Led by Mao Tse-tung, the Communists prevailed over the Nationalists in the civil war that ended in 1949. The U.S. did not officially recognize the People's Republic of China until President Carter and Chinese leader Deng Xiaoping established diplomatic ties in 1979.

Chou En-lai

Pinyin: Zhou Enlai. Like Mao Tse-tung, a key leader in the Chinese Communist Party. After 1949, served as Foreign Minister in the Communist government. Considered more moderate than Mao.

Chu Teh

Pinyin: Zhu De. Commander-in-Chief of the Communist 8th Route Army during the Second Sino-Japanese War and World War II.

Chungking

Pinyin: Chongqing. Provisional capital of the Republic of China from 1937 following the Japanese invasion of Nanking (Pinyin: Nanjing), which had been the capital after the creation of the Republic of China in 1912. Located on the Yangtze River, Chunking is called one of the "three furnaces" for its hot summer temperatures. The city was heavily bombed by the Japanese during the Second Sino-Japanese War, which overlapped with World War II.

Chungshan

Known more commonly as a "Mao suit," made of a plain front with two breast pockets, two lower front pockets and five buttons down the center. It traditionally comes in blue or olive green.

Cordel

Literally "string." Cheaply printed booklets containing popular folk stories sold in market stalls in northern Brazil. Vendors display the books by strings.

De Gaulle

Charles de Gaulle was leader of Free France (in exile in London) from 1940–44, and headed the Provisional Government from 1944–46. He was President of France from 1959 to 1969.

Deng Xiaoping

Wade-Giles: Teng Hsiao-ping. Reestablished diplomatic ties with the U.S. in 1979. Introduced major economic reforms in the early to mid-1980s while keeping a lid on political reform. Blamed for ordering the People's Liberation Army to fire upon protesters in Tiananmen Square in 1989. Died in 1997 at age 92.

Er-hu

Two-stringed musical instrument played with a bow.

F.D.R.

Franklin Delano Roosevelt. President of the United States from 1933 to 1945. Died before the end of World War II and succeeded by Vice President Harry Truman.

Flying Tigers

All-volunteer force of American pilots led by Claire Lee Chennault, Lieutenant general in the U.S. Army Air Corps. Official pilots for the Chinese Air Force during World War II and used Kunming as a base of operations to fly in supplies over the "Hump" (Himalayas) from bases in India after the Japanese closed off the Burma Road.

G.I. Bill

Provided cash to war veterans to pay for university tuition and living expenses.

G.I.s
"General infantry." Generic term U.S. Army soldiers during World War II.

Good Housekeeping
Women's magazine begun in 1885 featuring articles about women's interests. Products featured in the magazine had the famous "Good Housekeeping Seal," which meant they were tested by the magazine.

Great Leap Forward (1958-1961)
Disastrous policy championed by Mao to rapidly transform China from an agrarian economy to an industrial one. Called for agricultural collectivization, and private farming was prohibited. To meet production quotas, villages and collectives lied about crop production volume and melted down their only cookware to create pig iron. This resulted in millions of deaths from starvation.

Guavasteen
Also known as a "pineapple guava."

Hai Rui
"Hai Rui Is Dismissed From Office" was a play written in 1959. Interpreted by Mao to be a criticism of his dismissal of a key leader in the Chinese Communist Party.

Hangchow
Pinyin: Hangzhou. Large city southwest of Shanghai. The Japanese flew bombing missions out of Hangchow during World War II.

Herbert Walker Bush

George Herbert Walker Bush, forty-first President of the United States. Served as U.S. Envoy to China from 1974-1975. As Ronald Reagan's vice president, opposed the Justice Department by supporting reparations for Japanese Americans interned during World War II.

Hsi-shuang Ba-na

Pinyin: Xishuangbanna. Located in Yunnan province in southern China and straddles the Mekong River.

Hu Yaobang

General Secretary of the Communist Party from 1982 to 1987. One of two potential successors to Deng Xiaoping. His death in 1989 led to protests that ballooned into massive demonstrations in Tiananmen Square.

Hump

Eastern section of the Himalayas. During World War II U.S. military flew transport aircraft from India, over the Hump, to China, loaded with supplies for the war effort. Conditions were unpredictable, and aircraft were known to crash.

India-Burma Theater

Also known as the China-Burma-India, or "C.B.I." Theater. Described war operations comprising those countries. The CBI Theater came up primarily in the context of U.S. and British supply logistics supporting the war effort in the region. General Joseph Stilwell had operational oversight over the CBI Theater.

Jeep girls

World War II slang for "prostitute."

J.F.K.

John Fitzgerald Kennedy. Thirty-fifth president of the United States. Assassinated in 1963.

K'ang

Platform made of bricks upon which Chinese families traditionally slept. Underneath the brick platform is an area for placing burning coal or burning a fire. Ventilation is provided through a flue that directs exhaust to the outside.

Korematsu

Landmark case brought by Fred Korematsu and heard by the Supreme Court in 1944. The court decided the exclusion order sending Japanese Americans to internment camps during World War II was constitutional. The decision was overturned in 1983.

Kunming

Capital city of Yunnan province. End of the Burma Road, which connected Burma to China and served as a primary supply line in China's battle against the Japanese. During World War II, Kunming was a joint military command center which housed Chinese, American, British and French troops in support of the China-Burma-India Theater. After the Japanese occupied Burma and cut off access to the Burma Road, the Flying Tigers flew supplies over the Himalayas ("the Hump") from India.

Kuomintang

Also"K.M.T." The Nationalists' political party. Formed the basis of the Republic of China after the overthrow of the Qing Dynasty in 1911. Led by Sun Yat-sen until his death in 1925. Chiang Kai-shek took over leadership and stayed in power from 1928 through World War II, the fleeing of the Nationalists to Taiwan in 1949, and up to his death in 1975.

Le-shan

Pinyin: Leshan. The Leshan Giant Buddha is a 200-plus foot stone statue built into the side of a cliff facing the confluence of three rivers in the southern part of Sichuan province, China.

Long Bar

L-shaped bar located in the Shanghai Club, exclusive to men, during the 1920s and 1930s. Popular hangout for foreigners.

Long March

1934 to 1935. Following the split with Chiang Kai-shek and the Nationalists, and faced with overwhelming military force, the Communists embarked on a 6000-mile retreat over a one-year period. They ended up in Shensi (Pinyin: Shaanxi) province. Only ten percent of the people who began the Long March survived.

Ma-po tofu

Pinyin: Mapo doufu. Popular spicy Chinese dish from Sichuan province consisting of cubes of tofu with spicy chili, bean sauce, and minced pork.

Madame Sun Yat-sen

Soong Ching-ling was the wife of Sun Yat-sen. Lived from 1893 to 1981. Her sister, Soong Mei-ling, was the wife of Chiang Kai-shek.

Mao Tse-Tung

Pinyin: Mao Zedong. Leader of the Chinese Communist Party from 1949 until his death in 1976. He emerged as the leader of the Communists after the Long March in 1934. Had four wives during his lifetime, the last of whom was Jiang Qing.

Mao Zedong.

See: "Mao Tse-tung"

Maotai

Brand of distilled grain alcohol. Made in Guizhou province, China. Has distinct flavor and smell, unlike more potent distilled spirits like vodka.

Marco Polo Bridge Incident

Marco Polo Bridge is located in Beijing. Trigger point for war with Japan (July 7, 1937) where troops from the Chinese Nationalist government and the Japanese Imperial Army exchanged fire and artillery. Prior to the incident, Japan had taken over Manchuria and installed Pu-yi, the last emperor of the Qing Dynasty, as head of a puppet state.

Mei Lan-fang

Pinyin: Mei Lanfang. Famous Peking opera singer.

Mochi

Sugared rice cake made out of pounded rice.

Nationalists

Kuomintang government, led by Chiang Kai-shek, in contrast to the Communists, led by Mao Tse-tung. The Nationalists split from their alliance with the Communists in 1934 when Chiang Kai-shek's troops turned on them and forced the Communists into the Long March. Following the end of World War II, the Nationalists continued fighting the Communists, and eventually fled mainland China for Taiwan in 1949. There, they established the government of the Republic of China, in contrast to the People's Republic of China on the mainland, which is Communist.

O-Chem

Organic Chemistry, one of the requirements for many pre-med undergraduate programs.

O.S.S.

Office of Strategic Services. Formed during World War II as an intelligence gathering agency and led by William Donovan. Precursor to the Central Intelligence Agency. Conducted intelligence operations in China, as well as Europe, during World War II.

P-chem

Physical Chemistry, one of the requirements for many premed undergraduate programs.

P.O.W.

Prisoner of War.

Pai-chiu

Pinyin: Bai jiu. Literally "white alcohol." Distilled spirit still popular in China today.

Pandeiro

Brazilian hand frame drum. The drumhead is tunable, and the rim holds metal jingles.

Peking

Pre-1949 name of Beijing and former imperial capital under the Qing Dynasty, which ended in 1911. China's capital moved between Peking and Nanking over the course of successive dynasties, leading up to the Qing. Following the overthrow of the Qing Dynasty, and with the establishment of the Republic of China in 1912, the capital moved back to Nanking (now: Nanjing), and later to Chungking. After 1949, the capital was reestablished in Beijing.

People's Liberation Army
Chinese Communist army. Formerly the 8th Route Army.

Pidgin
Simplified version of English that was used in Hong Kong and parts of occupied China, where communicating with English speakers was necessary to conduct business and daily affairs. Phrases include, "No can do," (unable or unwilling to do something), and "Chop chop" (hurry).

Pinyin
Form of romanization for Mandarin Chinese that was developed by the Chinese Communists after the Communist Revolution in 1949. In this book, Wade-Giles is generally used for pre-1949 period, and Pinyin post-1949. Example: Mao Zedong (Pinyin), Mao Tse-tung (Wade-Giles).

Pipa
Four-stringed Chinese musical instrument. Sometimes called a "Chinese lute."

Pointee-talkee board
Nonverbal communication tool employing pictures and used by Americans to communicate with Chinese who were unable to speak either English or Chinese Pidgin English. The name itself comes from Chinese Pidgin English.

Pro-kit
"Prophylactic kit." Issued to U.S. military servicemen to help prevent the spread of venereal disease. Contained ointment (see "sulfanilamide"), soap-impregnated cloth, cleaning tissue, and directions for use.

Ramgarh
Located 200 miles west of Calcutta. Training center for Chinese troops during the Second Sino-Japanese War and World War II.

Rosenbergs
Julius and Ethel Rosenberg were American citizens executed in 1953 for passing information about the atomic bomb to the Soviet Union.

Sheng
Mouth-blown instrument with a number of vertical pipes.

Shensi
Pinyin: Shaanxi. Province located in northwest China. Known for its plateau of silty, erosion-prone sediment deposited by wind storms. Capital city is Sian (Pinyin: Xi'an).

Sian
Pinyin: Xi'an. Capital city of Shensi (Pinyin: Shaanxi) province.

SSR-5, SST-5, SSTR-5
Radio equipment used during World War II included the SSTR-5, which was composed of an SSR-5 receiver and a SST-5 transmitter. The set was designed to operate on battery power.

Stilwell
General Joseph Stilwell. Military liaison between Chiang Kai-shek and American military for most of Second Sino-Japanese War and World War II. Top American commander in the China-Burma-India Theater from an operations standpoint. Spent several years before the War building roads in China. Conversant in Mandarin Chinese. Called "Vinegar Joe" for his less-than-diplomatic personality.

Sulfanilamide

Included in first aid kits issued to American soldiers during World War II. Used to prevent venereal disease.

Sun Yat-sen

Father of modern China. First president of the Republic of China, which he helped establish following the overthrow of the Qing Dynasty in 1911. At age 13, went to school in Hawaii. As an adult, spent time in exile in Japan. Died in Peking in 1925. His widow, Madame Sun Yat-sen (née Soong Ching-ling), was the sister of Chiang Kai-shek's wife, Soong Mei-ling.

Tai Li's Secret Police

Tai Li was head of the Nationalist government's military intelligence under Chiang Kai-shek. In the 1930s and 1940s, Tai Li had agents within both the Chinese Communist Party and some Japanese quasi-official organizations based in China. Considered one of the most powerful men in China. Tai Li's base of operations during World War II was Chungking.

Taiwan/Republic of China

In 1949, Chiang Kai-shek and the Nationalists fled to Taiwan after ceding mainland China to the Communists. Taiwan became home of the Republic of China, while the mainland became the home of the People's Republic of China.

Teng Hsiao-ping

See: Deng Xiaoping

Toisan

Chinese dialect spoken by residents of the Taishan area of southern China. Many Chinese immigrants who arrived in the United States in the early twentieth century spoke Toisan. Until recently, the most commonly spoken dialect in San Francisco's Chinatown.

Tule Lake
One of many Japanese American internment camps during World War II. Located in northern California, near the Oregon border.

U-2
High altitude, jet engine spy plane with sophisticated imaging equipment. Built by Lockheed. The U.S. flew U-2 missions over the Soviet Union, China, Vietnam, and Cuba. The Republic of China also flew the U-2 out of Taiwan, and in 1965, Mainland China shot one down.

Victrola
An early record player.

Voice of America
U.S. government-sponsored radio broadcast delivered over shortwave radio frequencies during the Cold War. It is still broadcast today in many different languages over FM, AM, shortwave radio. Nowadays streamed over the internet.

W.P.A.
The Works Progress Administration came into being by order of President Franklin Roosevelt in 1935 as way to provide employment to millions of people affected by the Great Depression. Many public works projects from that period still stand today.

Wade-Giles
Form of romanization for Mandarin Chinese developed in the nineteenth century. Still in limited use today, primarily for historical purposes. Replaced largely by Pinyin. In this book,

Wade-Giles is used for the pre-1949 period, and Pinyin for post-1949. Example: Mao Tse-tung (Wade-Giles), Mao Zedong (Pinyin).

Y.M.C.A.
Young Men's Christian Association. Large American missionary organization in China responsible for building schools and teaching English.

Yangtze
Longest river in Asia. Runs through the city of Chungking (Pinyin: Chongqing). Called, "Changjiang" in Mandarin Chinese.

Yunnan
Southern Chinese province bordering Burma (now Myanmar). Capital city is Kunming.

Zé Carioca
Equivalent to "Joe Rio." Cartoon parrot created by the Walt Disney Company in the 1940s.

Acknowledgments

I would like to thank:

Readers of my first draft;

My language teachers -- Hu Changping, Yvonne Swun, Cecilia Chu, Wang Qun Jamieson, John Jamieson, Cindy Shih, and Yashi Tohsaku;

Gordon Mennenga at the Iowa Summer Writing Festival;

Chalmers Johnson, who inspired me to keep learning about the interwar period;

The Group in Asian Studies at U.C. Berkeley, and the School of Global Policy and Strategy at U.C. San Diego;

Beers Books in Sacramento for their wonderful collection of delightful discoveries;

The music of Céu and the music of Pat Metheny;

Gerry Ward at the Sacramento Public Library's I Street Press;

My family.

Reading Group Guide

The idea for this book originated from studying microfiche of police records from the Shanghai Municipal Government. I stumbled upon the collection in college while I was taking a break from studying for finals in the now defunct Government Documents Library at U.C. Berkeley.

As an exchange student at Beijing University in 1988, I saw student protests on campus, but they were nothing like the protests a year later. Back at Berkeley by then, I watched events in Tiananmen unfold from a safe distance. Newspapers and television coverage characterized the protests as "pro-democracy," but there were more pressing issues at stake: corruption, nepotism, and the bleak future for college graduates.

Barbara Tuchman's "Stilwell and the American Experience in China, 1911-1945," provided my introduction to the famous China specialist and foreign service officer, John Stewart Service (upon whom part of Quentin's character is based). Many China specialists like Service were fired during the 1950s for their dealings with the Chinese Communists during the War. Not all were reinstated with full pensions.

Not much has changed between 1950 and today. We still view China through a distorted lens.

Questions for Discussion:
1. Was the State Department justified in firing Quentin?
2. Why didn't Ai-ling tell Quentin about their son earlier?
3. Tak has mixed feelings about Quentin. Why?
4. Does Lisa have a reason to doubt Matsuda's version of events?
5. One prevalent theme is the struggle between the Nationalists and the Communists. What did the U.S. learn from the PAX Mission?

Suggested reading:

"Honorable Survivor: Mao's China, McCarthy's America, and the Persecution of John S. Service," by Lynne Joiner

"The China Hands," by E.J. Kahn, Jr.

"Beyond Loyalty: The Story of a Kibei," by Minoru Kiyota

"The Man Who Stayed Behind," by Sidney Rittenberg and Amanda Bennett

"Prisoners of Liberation: Four Years in a Chinese Communist Prison," by Allyn and Adele Rickett

"Lost Chance in China: The World War II Dispatches of John S. Service," by John Service, edited by Joseph Esherick

"Radio Warfare: O.S.S. and CIA Subversive Propaganda," by Lawrence C. Soley

"The American Black Chamber," by Herbert O. Yardley

"OSS in China: Prelude to Cold War," by Maochun Yu

About the Author

Robert Blair Osborn graduated from U.C. Berkeley with a B.A. in Asian Studies. He studied intensive Chinese at Beijing University the year before the Tiananmen Square protests and later taught on the JET Program in Japan. He received his Master's of Pacific and International Affairs from U.C. San Diego's School of Global Policy and Strategy. He lives in Sacramento with his wife and three children.

For inquiries, write to sordello7@gmail.com

Made in the USA
Charleston, SC
12 June 2016